Sea Lovers

*S*EA LOVERS

Selected Stories

VALERIE MARTIN

NAN A. TALESE
Doubleday
New York   London   Toronto   Sydney   Auckland

Copyright © 2015 by Valerie Martin

All rights reserved. Published in the United States by Nan A. Talese/Doubleday, a division of Penguin Random House LLC, New York, and distributed by Random House of Canada, a division of Penguin Random House Ltd., Toronto. Originally published in Great Britain by Chatto & Windus, an imprint of Penguin Random House Ltd., London, in 2012.

www.nanatalese.com

DOUBLEDAY is a registered trademark of Penguin Random House LLC. Nan A. Talese and the colophon are trademarks of Penguin Random House LLC.

The following stories first appeared in these publications: *Black Warrior Review:* "Sea Lovers" (volume II, number 2, Spring 1985); *Conjunctions:* "His Blue Period" (Spring 2001); *The Consolation of Nature and Other Stories:* "The Cat in the Attic," "The Freeze," and "Spats" (Vintage Contemporaries, 1989); *The Massachusetts Review:* "The Incident at Villedeau" (volume 55, number 1, 2014) and "The Open Door" (Summer 2002); *New Orleans Review:* "The Consolation of Nature" (volume 9, number 2, Fall 1982); *Ploughshares:* "The Change" (Spring 1998); *The Unfinished Novel and Other Stories:* "Beethoven" and "The Unfinished Novel" (Vintage Contemporaries, 2006); *Web Conjunctions:* "Et in Acadiana Ego" (July 2011).

Book design by Maria Carella
Jacket design by Emily Mahon
Jacket illustration by Eleftheria Alexandri

Library of Congress Cataloging-in-Publication Data
Martin, Valerie, 1948–
   [Short stories. Selections]
   Sea lovers : selected stories / Valerie Martin. — First edition.
      pages ; cm
   ISBN 978-0-385-53352-2 (hardcover)   ISBN 978-0-385-53353-9 (eBook)
   I. Title.
   PS3563.A7295A6 2015
   813'.54—dc23   2015003401

MANUFACTURED IN THE UNITED STATES OF AMERICA

10 9 8 7 6 5 4 3 2 1

First Edition

For Dr. Kenneth Holditch, who got me started
And for my students, who keep me going

Contents

Introduction

The stories in this volume are selected from work published over a period of thirty years. As I read them chronologically, I had the sensation of falling through my life in writing. Though I was never consciously trying to change the way I write, on looking back I note a distinct evolution.

My early stories have a young writer's excitement about formal innovation, as well as a young woman's preoccupation with personal relationships. They appear unsophisticated to me now, innocent, unguarded, and sometimes uncouth. My lifelong preoccupation with nature and with death as the debt we owe to nature makes these stories severe and lyrical. Many of the characters are animals going about their animal lives while the human characters, vexed and tormented by their personal dramas, turn their backs on the natural world. I've gathered four of these stories here, under the title "Among the Animals."

Sometime in the '90s, after living in Rome for a few years

and reading Chekhov's stories avidly and for the first time, I consciously raised the ante of the conversation I'd been having with myself about the short story. First by accident and then with intent, I undertook a series of stories about the lives of artists. My mental description of these excursions into the daily ordeals of painters, novelists, dancers, poets, and actors was "Art saves your life, art ruins your life." The four stories included here under the title "Among the Artists" are enlivened by an element somewhat dampened in the earlier work, namely humor. There's still plenty of darkness, death is hanging over the scene, animals are getting the worst of it, the humans are competitive, mean-spirited, and engaged in a struggle that should be ennobling but is often degrading, yet the distant eye upon the dismal doings is lighthearted and amused.

The final grouping, "Metamorphoses," includes stories that hark back to my childhood fascination with a magical world in which animals and humans changed forms or merged. The last two stories, the only ones previously uncollected, are set in an imagined past that is both mythical and historical.

Acadia is the name given to the eighteenth-century French settlement in Nova Scotia by the residents thereof. It is a variant of the word *Arcadia*: the paradise of Greek myth inhabited by fantastic creatures, the playground of the gods. When the French were driven out of Acadia by the British, they made a long and difficult journey to Louisiana. The bayous and swamps where they settled, surviving by fishing and trapping, became known as Acadiana. This is the world, fantastical, atmospheric, and tragic, of the two final stories in this collection. The question "Are we animals, or are we something else?" has engaged my imagination throughout my writing career, and I have addressed it most particularly in short stories. These Acadiana stories offer an answer at once whimsical and disturbing: We are neither, and we are both.

AMONG THE ANIMALS

SPATS

The dogs are scratching at the kitchen door. How long, Lydia thinks, has she been lost in the thought of her rival dead? She passes her hand over her eyes, an unconscious effort to push the hot red edge off everything she sees, and goes to the door to let them in.

When Ivan confessed that he was in love with another woman, Lydia thought she could ride it out. She told him what she had so often told him in the turbulent course of their marriage, that he was a fool, that he would be sorry. Even as she watched his friends loading his possessions into the truck, even when she stood alone in the silent half-empty house contemplating a pale patch on the wall where one of his pictures had been, even then she didn't believe he was gone. Now she has only one hope to hold on to: He has left the dogs with her, and this must mean he will be coming back.

At the door Gretta hangs back, as she always does, but Spats pushes his way in as soon as she has turned the knob, knocking the door back against her shins and barreling past her, his heavy tail slapping the wood repeatedly. No sooner is he inside than he turns to block the door so that Gretta can't get past him. He lowers his big head and nips at her forelegs; it's play, it's all in fun, but Gretta only edges past him, pressing close to Lydia, who pushes at the bigger dog with her foot. "Spats," she says, "leave her alone." Spats backs away, but he is only waiting until she is gone; then he will try again. Lydia is struck with the inevitability of this scene. It happens every day, several times a day, and it is always the same. The dogs gambol into the kitchen, knocking against the table legs, turning about in ever-narrowing circles, until they throw themselves down a few feet apart and settle for their naps. Gretta always sleeps curled tightly in a semicircle, her only defense against attacks from her mate, who sleeps on his side, his long legs extended, his neck stretched out, the open, deep sleep of the innocent or the oppressor.

Lydia stands at the door looking back at the dogs. Sometimes Ivan got right down on the floor with Spats, lay beside him holding his big black head against his chest and talking to him. "Did you have a good time at the park today?" he'd croon. "Did you swim? Are you really tired now? Are you happy?" This memory causes Lydia's upper lip to pull back from her teeth. How often had she wanted to kick him right in his handsome face when he did that, crooning over the dog as if it were his child or his mistress? What about me? she thought. What about my day? But she never said that; instead she turned away, biting back her anger and confusion, for she couldn't admit even to herself that she was jealous of a dog.

Spats is asleep immediately, his jaw slack and his tongue lolling out over his black lips. As Lydia looks at him she has an unexpected thought: She could kill him. It is certainly in her power. No one would do anything about it, and it would hurt Ivan as nothing else could. She could poison him, or shoot him, or she could take him to a vet and say he was vicious and have him put down.

She lights a match against the grout in the countertop and turns the stove burner on. It is too cold, and she is so numb with the loss of her husband that she watches the flame wearily, hopelessly; it can do so little for her. She could plunge her hand into it and burn it, or she could stand close to it and still be cold. Then she puts the kettle over the flame and turns away.

She had argued with Ivan about everything for years, so often and so intensely that it seemed natural to her. She held him responsible for the hot flush that rose to her cheeks, the bitter taste that flooded her mouth at the very thought of him. She believed that she was ill; sometimes she believed her life was nearly over and she hated Ivan for this too, that he was killing her with these arguments and that he didn't care.

When the water is boiling she pours it over the coffee in the filter and takes her mug to the table. She sits quietly in the still house; the only sound is the clink of the ceramic mug against the bare wood as she sets it down. She goes through a cycle of resolutions. The first is a simple one: She will make her husband come back. It is inconceivable that she will fail. They always had these arguments, they even separated a few times, but he always came back and so he always would. He would tire of this other woman in a few weeks and then he would be back. After all, she asked herself, what did this woman have that she didn't have? An education? And what good was that? If Ivan loved this woman for her education, it wasn't really as if he loved her for herself. He loved her for something she had acquired. And Lydia was certain that Ivan had loved *her*, had married her, and must still love her, only for herself, because she was so apparent, so undisguised; there wasn't anything else to love her for.

She takes a swallow of the bitter coffee. This first resolution is a calm one: She will wait for her husband and he will return and she will take him back.

She sets the mug down roughly on the table, for the inevitable question is upon her: How long can she wait? This has been going on for two months, and she is sick of waiting. There must be something she can do. The thought of action stiffens her spine, and her jaw clenches involuntarily. Now comes the terrible vision of her revenge, which never fails to take her so by surprise that she sighs as she lays herself open to it; revenge is her only lover now. She will see a lawyer, sue Ivan for adultery, and get every cent she can out of him, everything, for the rest of his life. But this is unsatisfactory, promising, as it does, nothing better than a long life without him, a life in which he continues to love someone else. She would do better to buy a gun and shoot him. She could call him late at night, when the other woman is asleep, and beg him to come over. He will come; she can scare him into it. And then when he lets himself in with his key, she will shoot him in the living room. He left her, she will tell the court. She bought the gun to protect herself because she was alone. How was she to know he would let himself in so late at night? He told her he was never coming back and she had assumed the footsteps in the living room came from the man every lonely woman lies in bed at night listening for, the man who has found out her secret, who knows she is alone, whose mission, which is sanctioned by the male world, is to break the spirit if not the bones of those rebellious women who have the temerity to sleep at night without a man. So she shot him. She wasn't going to ask any questions and live to see him get off in court. How could she have known the intruder was her husband, who had abandoned her?

Yes, yes, that would work. It would be easily accomplished, but wouldn't she only end up as she was now? Better to murder the other woman, who was, after all, the cause of all this intolerable pain. She knew her name, knew where she lived, where she worked. She had called her several times just to hear her voice, her cheerful hello, in which Lydia always heard Ivan's presence, as if he were standing right next to the woman and she had turned away from kissing him to answer the insistent phone. Lydia had heard of a man who killed people for money. She could pay this man, and then the woman would be gone.

The kettle is screaming; she has forgotten to turn off the flame. She could drink another cup of coffee, then take a bath. But that would take only an hour or so and she has to get through the whole day. The silence in the house is intense, though she knows it is no more quiet than usual. Ivan was never home much in the daytime. What did she do before? It seems to her that that life was another life, one she will never know again, the life in which each day ended with the appearance of her husband. Sometimes, she admits, she had not been happy to see him, but her certainty that she would see him made the question of whether she was happy or sad a matter of indifference to her. Often she didn't see him until late at night, when he appeared at one of the clubs where she was singing. He took a place in the audience, and when she saw him she always sang for him. Then they were both happy. He knew she was admired, and that pleased him, as if she was his reflection and what others saw when they looked at her was more of him. Sometimes he gave her that same affectionate look he gave himself in mirrors, and when he did it made her lightheaded, and she would sing, holding her hands out a little before her, one index finger stretched out as if she were pointing at something, and she would wait until the inevitable line about how it was "you" she loved, wanted, hated, couldn't get free of, couldn't live without, and at that "you" she would make her moving hands be still and with her eyes as well as her hands she would point to her husband in the crowd. Those were the happiest moments they had, though neither of them was really conscious of them, nor did they ever speak of this happiness. When, during the break, they did speak, it was usually to argue about something.

She thinks of this as she stares dully at the dogs, Ivan's dogs. Later she will drive through the cold afternoon light to Larry's cold garage, where they will rehearse. They will have dinner together; Larry and Simon will try to cheer her up, and Kenneth, the drummer, will sit looking on in his usual daze. They will take drugs if anyone has any, cocaine or marijuana, and Simon will drink a six-pack of beer.

Then they will go to the club and she will sing as best she can. She will sing and sing, into the drunken faces of the audience, over the bobbing heads of the frenzied dancers; she will sing like some blinded bird lost in a dark forest trying to find her way out by listening to the echo of her own voice. The truth is that she sings better than she ever has. Everyone tells her so. Her voice is so full of suffering that hearing it would move a stone, though it will not move her husband, because he won't be there. Yet she can't stop looking for him in the audience, as she always has. And as she sings and looks for him she will remember exactly what it was like to find herself in his eyes. That was how she had first seen him, sitting at a table on the edge of the floor, watching her closely. He was carrying on a conversation with a tired-looking woman across from him, but he watched Lydia so closely that she could feel his eyes on her. She smiled. She was aware of herself as the surprising creation she really was, a woman who was beautiful to look at and beautiful to hear. She was, at that moment, so self-conscious and so contented that she didn't notice what an oddity he was, a man who was both beautiful and masculine. Her attachment to his appearance, to his gestures, the suddenness of his smile, the coldness of his eyes, came later. At that moment it was herself in his eyes that she loved—as fatal a love match as she would ever know.

The phone rings. She hesitates, then gets up and crosses to the counter. She picks up the receiver and holds it to her ear.

"Hello," Ivan says. "Lydia?"

She says nothing.

"Talk to me!" he exclaims.

"Why should I?"

"Are you all right?"

"No."

"What are you doing?"

"Why are you calling me?"

"About the dogs."

"What about them?"

"Are they OK?"

She sighs. "Yes." Then, patiently, "When are you coming to get them?"

"I can't," he says. "I can't take them. I can't keep them here."

"Why?"

"There's no fenced yard. Vivian's landlord doesn't allow dogs."

At the mention of her rival's name, Lydia feels a sudden rush of blood to her face. "You bastard," she hisses.

"Baby, please," he says, "try to understand."

She slams the receiver down into the cradle. "Bastard," she says again. Her fingers tighten on the edge of the counter until the knuckles are white. He doesn't want the dogs. He doesn't want her. He isn't coming back. "I really can't stand it," she says into the empty kitchen. "I don't think I will be able to stand it."

○

She is feeding the dogs. They have to eat at either end of the kitchen because Spats will eat Gretta's dinner if he can. Gretta has to be fed first; then Spats is lured away from her bowl with his own. Gretta eats quickly, swallowing one big bite after another, for she knows she has only the time it takes Spats to finish his meal before he will push her away from hers. Tonight Spats is in a bad humor. He growls at Gretta when Lydia sets her bowl down. Gretta hangs her head and backs away. "Spats!" Lydia says. "Leave her alone." She pushes him away with one hand, holding out his bowl before him with the other.

But he growls again, turning his face toward her, and she sees that his teeth are bared and his threat is serious. "Spats," she says firmly, but she backs away. His eyes glaze over with something deep and vicious, and she knows that he no longer hears her. She drops the bowl. The sound of the bowl hitting the linoleum and the sight of his food scattered before him brings Spats back to himself. He falls to eating off the floor. Gretta lifts her head to watch him, then returns to her hurried eating.

Lydia leans against the stove. Her legs are weak and her heart beats absurdly in her ears. In the midst of all this weakness a habitual ambivalence goes hard as stone. Gretta, she thinks, certainly deserves to eat in peace. She looks down at Spats. Now he is the big, awkward, playful, good fellow again.

"You just killed yourself," Lydia says. Spats looks back at her, his expression friendly, affable. He no longer remembers his fit of bad temper.

Lydia smiles at him. "You just killed yourself and you don't even have the sense to know it," she says.

○

It is nearly dawn. Lydia lies in her bed alone. She used to sleep on her back when Ivan was with her. Now she sleeps on her side, her legs drawn up to her chest. Or rather, she reminds herself, she lies awake in this position and waits for the sleep that doesn't come.

As far as she is concerned she is still married. Her husband is gone, but marriage, in her view, is not a condition that can be dissolved by external circumstances. She has always believed this; she told Ivan this when she married him, and he agreed or said he agreed. They were bound together for life. He said he wanted nothing more.

She still believes it. It is all she understands marriage to be. They must cling to each other and let the great nightmarish flood of time wash over them as it will; at the end they would be found wherever they were left, washed onto whatever alien shore, dead or alive, still together, their lives entwined as surely as their bodies, inseparably, eternally. How many times in that last year, in the midst of the interminable quarrels that constituted their life together, had she seen pass across his face an expression that filled her with rage, for she saw that he knew she was drowning and he feared she would pull him down with her. So even as she raged at him, she clung to him more tightly, and the lovemaking that followed their arguments was so intense, so filled with her need of him that, she told herself, he must know, wherever she was going, he was going with her.

Now, she confesses to herself, she is drowning. Alone, at night, in the moonless sea of her bed, where she is tossed from nightmare to nightmare so that she wakes gasping for air, throwing her arms out before her, she is drowning alone in the dark and there is nothing to hold on to.

○

Lydia sits on the floor in the veterinarian's office. Spats lies next to her; his head rests in her lap. He is unconscious but his heart is still beating feebly. Lydia can feel it beneath her palm, which she has pressed against his side. His mouth has gone dry and his dry tongue lolls out to one side. His black lips are slack and there is no sign of the sharp canine teeth that he used to bare so viciously at the slightest provocation. Lydia sits watching his closed eyes and she is afflicted with the horror of what she has done.

He is four years old; she has known him all his life. When

Ivan brought him home he was barely weaned and he cried all that first night, a helpless baby whimpering for his lost mother. But he was a sturdy, healthy animal, greedy for life, and he transferred his affections to Ivan and to his food bowl in a matter of days. Before he was half her size he had terrorized Gretta into the role he and Ivan had worked out for her: dog-wife, mother to his children. She would never have a moment's freedom as long as he lived, no sleep that could not be destroyed by his sudden desire for play, no meal that he did not oversee and covet. She was more intelligent than he, and his brutishness wore her down. She became a nervous, quiet animal who would rather be patted than fed, who barricaded herself under desks, behind chairs, wherever she could find a space Spats couldn't occupy at the same time.

Spats was well trained; Ivan saw to that. He always came when he was called and he followed just at his master's heel when they went out for their walks every day. But it ran against his grain; every muscle in his body was tensed for that moment when Ivan would say "Go ahead," and then he would spring forward and run as hard as he could for as long as he was allowed. He was a fine swimmer and loved to fetch sticks thrown into the water.

When he was a year old, his naturally territorial disposition began to show signs of something amiss. He attacked a neighbor who made the mistake of walking into his yard, and bit him twice, on the arm and on the hand. Lydia stood in the doorway screaming at him, and Ivan was there instantly, shouting at Spats and pulling him away from the startled neighbor, who kept muttering that it was his own fault; he shouldn't have come into the yard. Lydia had seen the attack from the start;

she had, she realized, seen it coming and not known it. What disturbed her was that Spats had tried to bite the man's face or his throat, and that he had given his victim almost no notice of his intention. One moment he was wagging his tail and barking, she told Ivan; then, with a snarl, he was on the man.

Ivan made excuses for the animal, and Lydia admitted that it was freakish behavior. But in the years that followed, it happened again and again. Lydia had used this evidence against him, had convicted him on the grounds of it; in the last two years he had bitten five people. Between these attacks he was normal, friendly, playful, and he grew into such a beautiful animal, his big head was so noble, his carriage so powerful and impressive, that people were drawn to him and often stopped to ask about him. He enjoyed everything in his life; he did everything—eating, running, swimming—with such gusto that it was a pleasure to watch him. He was so full of energy, of such inexhaustible force, it was as if he embodied life, and death must stand back a little in awe at the sight of him.

Now Lydia strokes his head, which seems to be getting heavier every moment, and she says his name softly. It's odd, she thinks, that I would like to die but I have to live, and he would like to live but he has to die.

In the last weeks she has wept for herself, for her lost love, for her husband, for her empty life, but the tears that fill her eyes now are for the dying animal she holds in her arms. She is looking straight into the natural beauty that was his life and she sees resting over it, like a relentless cloud of doom, the empty lovelessness that is her own. His big heart has stopped; he is gone.

THE CAT IN THE ATTIC

Why, on the eve of his sixtieth birthday, was Mr. William Bucks, owner and president of Bucks International, rushing down his own staircase on the arm of his employee Chester Melville? And why was Mrs. Bucks, the entrepreneur's young and beautiful wife, perched above them on the landing, screaming her contempt at the spectacle of her husband and her lover in full retreat? And why, especially why, did Mr. Chester Melville turn to his mistress and, in a voice trembling with rage, cry out, "You killed that cat yourself, Sylvia, as surely as if you had strangled him with your own hands."

This story is difficult to tell; it has so little of what one might call "sensibility" in it. But it is possible to experience a certain morbid epiphany by the prolonged contemplation of the inadequate gestures others make at love, and in fact such an epiphany has of late been proved a fit subject for a tale. Chester Melville's failure to love was matched, was eclipsed, was finally rendered inconsequential by the calculated coldness of the woman he failed to love, though at the moment we see them here this observation would have been small comfort to Chester. He understood, at last, that there was something in Sylvia Bucks that no man could love, something not right; I hesitate to say evil, but perverse, organically amiss. He had felt something for her, nonetheless. Pity, at first, and a devilish curiosity. She had inspired in him a spirit of fierce possession, and he was touched to the heart by the smoothness of her skin and the soft anxious cries she uttered in her search for the orgasm she could never find, no, not, she had confided, since the day of her marriage.

Her husband, Mr. William Bucks, or Billy to his intimates, was an unprepossessing man, tall, balding, his large features crowded anxiously in the center of his face as if they intended to make a break for freedom. He had an eager, friendly, almost doglike manner that made you forget, when you spoke to him, that he was worth a fortune. His software company was one of the quiet superpowers of the computer industry. He had created it himself, by the power of his formidable will. His natural business acumen was extraordinary and no doubt accounted for some of his success, but it was this indomitable will that impressed Chester in their first interview. Billy Bucks liked Chester on sight and wanted him as an employee. He had persuaded him to leave his secure, uninteresting niche at IBM to join the Billy Bucks personal adventure.

Before Chester attended his first dinner party at the Buckses' home, he made subtle inquiries among his fellow workers as to what he might expect. He was told that the food would be bad, the drinks first-rate and plentiful, that his employer would be gracious and his wife unpleasant. She was twenty years younger than her husband, and their marriage, which had survived the pitiful storms of only one short year, was not a pleasure to watch. Mr. Bucks, he was told, adored his wife and would neither say nor hear a word against her. Mrs. Bucks was flamboyantly rude to her husband, and (this last was confided to him by a nervous young man who appeared miserable at finding himself in the possession of such damaging information) she was hopelessly addicted to cocaine.

Chester went to the party with only mild trepidation. He did not expect to have his own fate altered by passing an evening in the same room with Sylvia Bucks. He considered himself invulnerable to attacks of lust, for he had recently recovered from a long love affair in which he had been driven to the limits of his resources by a selfish, obstinate woman who had made him swear more than once that he would not love her. She had destroyed some small desperate part of his natural self-consciousness, so that he thought he deserved a better fate than loving her would ever bring him. There are disasters in love that serve finally to increase one's own self-esteem; this failure was of that order. But Chester was bitter, overconfident, and unaware that his senses were wide open. Mrs. Bucks seemed to look directly into this odd mixture of indifference and vulnerability in the first moment they met. Superficially she was gay, charming; her voice was a little husky. She was, perhaps, too solicitous, but her eyes couldn't keep up the pretense. Like her husband, she was tall; her skin and eyes were as pale as her hair, so that she gave an impression of fading into the very light she seemed to emanate. Chester saw that she was sad, and a glance at his employer, who stood effusing cheerfully at her side, told him why. Though it had been very high, she had had her price, and it was her peculiar tragedy to be, while not sufficiently intelligent to follow the simple and honest dictates of her conscience, not stupid enough to be unaware of the moral implications of her choice. It was not until much later that he understood this and realized that the eloquent and pleading looks she directed at him several times on that first evening were not, as he thought, intended to evoke some response, but were meant to express her awareness of the acute ironies that constituted her situation.

The servants operated as slightly inferior guests in the Bucks household, and by the time they bothered themselves to get dinner on the table, the party was too raucous to care. It was just as well, for the hostess, who had disappeared into the bedroom at several points and whose teeth were chattering audibly from cocaine, could not decide where everyone should sit, though she was unshakable in her conviction that this choice was hers to make. The food, when at last the guests seated themselves before it, was cold and tasteless. The chef, Chester observed, specialized in a sauce created from ground chalk and cheddar cheese that congealed upon meat and vegetable alike. Mrs. Bucks paddled her fork contentedly in this mess. He watched her closely and observed that she never actually brought a bite to her lips. When dinner was over, the party adjourned to the living room for more alcohol. Mrs. Bucks disappeared again into her bedroom.

Why did Chester follow her?

He didn't actually follow her. The bathroom door was near her bedroom door, and after he had availed himself of the former, he found himself pausing outside the latter. How long did he pause? It was not a very long time, but as it was unnecessary to pause at all, it was clearly longer than he should have. After a moment the door opened and Mrs. Bucks stood facing him.

"Mrs. Bucks," he said.

She sank against the doorframe. "You scared me to death, Mr. Melville."

"I wish you'd call me Chet," he replied.

She looked up at him, but her eyes hardly focused. She was wearing a strapless top, and from the smooth skin of her shoulders the scent of the perfume she wore rose and overpowered the air. It was a wonder to him that a woman of such wealth would choose such an oppressive scent; it didn't smell expensive. Perhaps it was some unwanted memory of another woman, a woman one would expect to wear too much cheap perfume, that caused Chester to move a little closer. Mrs. Bucks continued her unsuccessful effort to see him. He leaned over her, brought his lips to her shoulder, and left there several soft impressions. She didn't resist, or even speak, and for a moment he was terrified that she would push him away, screaming for her husband, his employer. Instead she sighed and said his name, "Mr. Melville," very softly, nor did he correct her again.

"May I call you?" he asked as she turned away from him and took a few wobbly steps toward the dining room.

"Yes," she replied, without looking back. "I wish you would."

So because of a momentary lapse in his usually sound judgment, Chester Melville entered into a clandestine affair with his employer's wife. He knew she would be a difficult woman, and that he would not be able to trust her for a moment. He knew as well that she would never be content with him, for she was committed to her need, not for love, but for some distraction from what must have been a dreadfully empty and insensitive consciousness. But it was partly this insensitivity that attracted Chester, for it made him want to give her a good shaking. He was also, after that first awkward kiss in the hall, mesmerized by her physical presence. She had a feline quality about her, especially in the way she moved, that made him feel as one does when watching a cat, that the cool saunter strings the beast together somehow, that it is the sister to the spring.

Chester was gratified to find that Sylvia had no desire to speak ill of her husband. In fact, she rarely mentioned him. There was, however, someone who competed with Chester for his mistress's affections. Though Sylvia had not been wealthy long, she had adopted the absurd custom many wealthy people have of making a great fuss about small matters. The smaller they were, the more they might appear as vital cogs in the great machine of her life. One of these manias was her cat, Gino, who was a constant consideration in all her plans. It was as if, should she disappear in the next moment, there wouldn't be enough servants left behind to care for his needs or understand his temperament. In her imagination Gino was always longing for her company, always disappointed, even disapproving, when he got it.

One evening, while Billy Bucks was inspecting a new plant in Colorado, Chester Melville sat on an uncomfortable bar stool at the Bucks establishment, drinking a glass of white wine and talking affably with his cantankerous mistress. Gino appeared suddenly in the doorway, as if to present himself for inspection. Sylvia squealed at the sight of him, pushed roughly past Chester, and scooped the cat up into her arms, repeating his name in a sensuous voice she reserved for him alone. Chester noticed that he was very large for a cat, and that his shoulders had the meatiness of an athlete's. He allowed himself to be squeezed and fussed over, turning his strong body slowly, sinuously, against his mistress's straining, perfumed bosom, but he kept his cold green eyes on Chester.

He seemed to size up the competition. "So you're here too," his eyes informed Chester. He had a wonderful deep frown, as if nothing could be more distasteful than what he contemplated. When he was released and set upon the counter, he walked quickly to Chester and, standing before him, considered his face, feature by feature.

"Oh, he's looking at you," Sylvia cried.

Chester was not moved to respond, and Gino, for his part, did not so much as turn an ear in her direction. After a few moments he strode away, not toward his anxious mistress, who stretched out her arms invitingly, but to the end of the counter, where he stopped, looked over his shoulder, and cast Chester one more penetrating, almost friendly look before he leaped soundlessly to the floor.

"That's an interesting cat you have," Chester observed.

"Oh, Gino," Sylvia replied. "Gino is wonderful. Gino is my love."

Chester was to see Gino many times. Each time he was so impressed with the animal, with his cool manner and athletic beauty, that he found himself looking at other cats only to see how poorly they compared with Gino. But he was to remember him always as he was that last afternoon, a few months after their first encounter, stretched out on Sylvia's bed, one heavy paw resting on a silken negligee, his long tail moving listlessly back and forth across the arm of a sweater. The bed was strewn with Sylvia's clothes; a suitcase lay open, half packed, at the foot; and Sylvia herself stood, half clad, nearby. She was fumbling helplessly with a silver cocaine vial, a gift from her husband, but she could scarcely see it through her tears. Chester stood leaning against the dresser. "It's not going to do you any good to run away if you take two bags of cocaine with you," he was saying. "You need to think things through, you need to be alone, and you need to leave the coke behind."

"I need to get away from you," she said. "Not cocaine."

"Sylvia." He sighed.

The vial gave way and she tapped a thin line of the white powder across her forearm.

"Sylvia," he said again. "I love you."

At this moment Gino stood up and began to stretch his back legs. Sylvia gathered him up. "No one loves me but Gino," she crooned to the indifferent animal. "Gino's going with me. I promised him a yard, I always promised him a yard, and now he'll have one."

The "yard" was, in fact, one thousand acres of Virginia pine forest. Sylvia was running away, but her destination was her husband's summer place, a building designed to house nine or ten male aristocrats intent on a return to nature. It looked rough, but it wasn't. There were servants, a wine cellar, a kitchen created to serve banquets. Here Sylvia proposed to spend a week alone, because, as she told her sympathetic spouse, the chatter and confusion of city life were wearing her down. She told Chester Melville that on her return she would give him the answer to his proposal that she leave her husband. At that moment in the bedroom, she determined to take Gino with her, nor could she be dissuaded from this resolution by any appeal, not about the impracticality of the plan or the unnecessary strain to the animal's health. No, Gino must go, and so he went. He was tranquilized, shoved into a box, and loaded into the airplane with Mrs. Bucks's suitcases. One can only imagine the horrors of the three hours spent in the howling blackness of the airplane, the strange ride along the conveyor belts to his impatient mistress, who pulled him out of the box at once and, cooing and chattering, carried him to the car. When they arrived at the estate, Gino was given an enormous meal, which he could scarcely eat, and then Sylvia carried him to the back terrace, overlooking a wilderness of breathtaking beauty, and set him free. "Here's your yard," she said.

In the week that followed, Gino took advantage of the outdoors, but Sylvia did not. She moved about restlessly from room to room, annoying whomever she encountered. She made a particular enemy of Tom Mann, the caretaker of the estate. Most of the year he lived alone on the property; he had a small cottage a hundred yards from the house, and he exhibited the silent humorlessness that comes of too much solitude. He loved the property and probably knew it better than its owner ever would. Sylvia's unexpected presence was an annoyance to him, and he couldn't disguise his personal distaste for her. She made the great mistake of offering him some cocaine, and the expression on his face as he declined to join her told her clearly what he thought of her.

She was miserable, but she tried to amuse herself. She made desperate late-night phone calls. She forced the cook to prepare elaborate meals she didn't eat. She played rock records loud enough to be heard on the terrace, where she danced by herself, or with Gino in her arms, until she collapsed in tears of frustration. She took three or four baths a day, watched whatever was on television, and tried, without success, to read a book about a woman who, like herself, was torn between her rich husband and her lover. At the end of a week, she had decided only that she must have a change. She packed her bags and inspected Gino's traveling box. An hour before she was to leave, she went to the back door and called her beloved pet.

But he didn't respond. She called and called, and she made the cook call. Then she enlisted Tom Mann in the search, and together they scoured the house and the grounds, but the cat was not to be found. At last she was forced to go without him. He would show up for dinner, they all agreed, and he could be sent on alone the next day. So she went to the airport, anxious but not hysterical. The hysteria started that night, when Tom Mann called to say Gino had not shown up for supper.

Sylvia's first response was to inform Tom Mann that he was fired, an action that brought down on her for the first time in their marriage the clear disapproval of her husband. "The man has worked for me for twenty years," he told her petulantly. "He's completely trustworthy and he can't be replaced."

"He finds Gino, he goes, or I go," she responded. "It's that simple."

But it wasn't that simple. Billy Bucks was forced to call his employee and apologize for his wife's behavior. "She's not herself," he explained, though he had begun to suspect the unhappy truth, which was that Sylvia was, at last, entirely herself. "She's so fond of that cat," he concluded limply. Tom Mann, who knew his own worth, told his employer that he would continue in his post on the condition that he be spared any future communication with Mrs. Bucks. Billy, humiliated and chagrined, agreed.

The staff at the estate was instructed to make the search for Gino their first priority. Two days after Sylvia's departure, the big house was searched, but since Gino was not found and no one was staying in it, Tom Mann closed it up, as was his custom, and retired to his own cottage. He was of the opinion that Gino had taken to the woods, and the only consolation he could offer his employer was the probability that, as the animal had not turned up dead, he might yet be alive.

Sylvia spent the next three weeks in a constant state of panic, and she poured out her bitterness upon the two men who, in her myopic view, were the authors of her woe. Chester Melville knew what Billy Bucks suffered, and though he could not openly sympathize with him, he found himself curiously drawn to his employer. The two men worked closely, like men under fire, bound together by the camaraderie of terror. Every evening Billy called Tom Mann and received his monosyllabic report while his wife stood nearby, her eyes filled with bitter tears, her cocaine vial clenched in her angry fist.

Then Gino was found. Tom Mann was bothered by a leak in his roof, and a cursory inspection revealed that a large section needed to be reshingled. He remembered that there were a number of shingles in the attic of the house, though how they had arrived there he didn't know. He walked hurriedly through the cold empty rooms, hardly looking about him, for there was nothing indoors that he really cared for. Up the stairs he climbed, his heavy steps echoing hollowly in the still, cool air. When he opened the attic door, the sick, sweet smell of death rushed over him, chilling him like a blast of cold air, and he remembered, all at once and clearly, that just three weeks ago he had come up here to store an awning he'd taken down for the winter, that he'd left the door open for a while, and now he knew that Gino, whose emaciated corpse lay before him, the death-frozen jaws coated with the plaster he'd chewed out of the wall in his futile struggle for life, must have come in without his knowledge. Tom Mann was not a man easily moved, but the pitiful condition of the once powerful animal brought a low moan to his lips.

Gino was buried within the hour. The caretaker chose a spot near his own house, at the foot of a weeping willow tree he himself had planted twenty years earlier. He marked the grave with a flat stone to keep the body from being disinterred by passing animals. When this was done, he phoned his employer and told him of Gino's fate.

Chester Melville was sitting in Billy Bucks's office when the call came through. He knew the substance of the message at once, simply by observing the sudden pallor of Bucks's complexion and the feebleness with which he concluded the call. "I'll tell Mrs. Bucks at once," he said. "I appreciate your call, Tom." He placed the receiver carefully into its cradle and rubbed his eyes with the heels of his hands.

"Gino's dead," Chester said.

Billy lowered his hands slowly and stared at his employee. He had heard everything in those two words, and he knew, though he had never suspected it for a moment, that he was addressing his wife's lover. The two men looked at each other disconsolately. "I can't tell her over the phone," Billy said at last. "I'll have to go home. Will you come with me?"

"Sure," Chester said, "if you think it will help."

"I think it will help me," Billy replied.

So the two men left the safety of their office building and trudged wearily through the snowy streets to Bucks's palatial flat. Sylvia was drinking coffee and perusing a magazine when they came in, and the sight of their grim faces so unnerved her that she let the magazine slip to the floor.

"Tom Mann called," Billy said. "I'm afraid it's bad news."

The scene that followed went on for a long time. Gino, who had been in reality a hearty, handsome, greedy, and independent beast, who had probably not spent one moment of his intensely feline life longing for anything that might come to him in human form, who had tolerated his mistress as cats do, was now resurrected as the only real love Sylvia had ever known. In the midst of her furious accusations, Chester realized that he had been willing to put his happiness, his job, and his entire future on the line for a woman who, because she knew herself so well, could only scorn any man who was mad enough to love her. He also observed that Billy Bucks knew this as well, but had married her anyway. As the two men beat their retreat down the stairway, Chester, overcome by his sense of his own foolishness, shouted back to her, "You killed that cat yourself, Sylvia, as surely as if you had strangled him with your own hands."

When they were gone, Sylvia smashed her husband's heirloom crystal, but that, she thought, could be replaced. She took a large knife from the kitchen and slashed a small Corot landscape, a particular favorite of her husband's, until it hung from the frame in strips. Then she went to the bedroom and ripped his down pillow until the feathers rose about her like a snowstorm. All she could hear was her lover's parting remark. She began to stab and stab her marriage bed itself, calling out to Gino as she drove the knife deeper and deeper, but nothing she could do would bring poor Gino back to her, nothing she could ever do.

THE CONSOLATION OF NATURE

Lily's hair was her mother's pride. In the afternoons, when she came home from school, she sat at the kitchen table, her head resting on the back of her chair, while her mother dragged the wooden brush through the long strands. Lily told her mother what had happened at school that day, or she talked of her many ambitions. Her mother, preoccupied with her work, holding up a thick lock and pulling out with her fingers a particularly tenacious knot, responded laconically. She looked upon this ritual of her daughter's hair as a solemn duty, like the duties of feeding and clothing.

One afternoon they sat so engaged, conversing softly while outside the rain beat against the house. Lily's mother observed that she couldn't take much more rain, that it would surely rot her small, carefully tended vegetable garden, that it seemed to be rotting her own imagination. Lily agreed. It had rained steadily for three days. Her head rose and fell, like a flower on its stalk, with each stroke of her mother's care, and each time it did she lifted her eyes a bit, taking in a larger section of the tiled floor before her.

Her mother shouted and threw the brush at the stove.

Lily sat up and looked after the brush. She was quick enough to see the disappearing tail and hindquarters of a rat as he scurried beneath the refrigerator. These parts, Lily thought, were unusually large, and this notion was quickly confirmed by her mother's cry as she clung momentarily to the edge of the table. "Good Christ," her mother said. "That's the biggest rat I've ever seen."

Lily drew her legs up under her and watched the spot where the rat had been. Her mother was already on the telephone to her father's secretary. "No," she said, "don't bother him. Just tell him there's a rat as big as a cat in the kitchen and he needs to stop at the K&B on the way home for a trap. Tell him to get the biggest trap they make." When she got off the phone, she suggested that they move to the dining room to finish Lily's hair. "It's the rain," her mother said as she closed the kitchen door carefully behind them. "The river is so high it's driving them out."

Lily sat at the dining table and pulled her long hair up over the back of her chair. Her mother resumed her vigorous brushing. It was strange, Lily thought, to sit at the big dining table in the dull afternoon light. The steady beating of the rain against the windows made her drowsy, and her mind wandered. She thought of how the river must look, swollen with brown water, swirling along hurriedly toward the Gulf of Mexico. She had never been to the mouth of the river, though she had gone down as far as Barataria once with her father. It had not been, as she had imagined, a neat little breaking-up of water fingers, the way it looked on the map. Instead, it was a great marsh with a road through it. There were fishing shacks on piers, wood, and other odd debris scattered in the shallow areas. She remembered that trip clearly, though two years had passed and she had been, she thought, only nine at the time. They had stopped to buy shrimp and her father had laughed at her impatience to have hers peeled. That was when she had learned to peel shrimp, and she did it so well that the job now regularly fell to her.

Her mother had not stopped thinking of the rat. "I can't get over his coming out in broad daylight like that," she remarked as she pulled the loose hairs from the brush.

"Who?" Lily asked.

"That rat," her mother replied. "I don't even want to cook dinner with that thing in there."

Lily could think of no response, so she stood up, turning to her mother and fluffing her hair out past her shoulders.

"That looks lovely," her mother said, touching Lily's hair at the temple. Then, as if she were shy of her daughter's beauty, she drew her hand away. "Do you have a lot of homework?" she asked.

"Plenty," Lily said. "I guess I'd better get to it."

When her father arrived that evening at his usual time, it was with chagrin that his wife and daughter learned he hadn't gotten their message and had come home trapless to his family.

"Well, go out and get one now," her mother complained. "I don't want to spend a night in the house with that thing alive."

"It's pouring down rain," Lily's father protested. "I'll get one tomorrow. He's probably moved on already anyway."

"Give me the keys," she said. "I'll get it myself."

Lily stood in the kitchen doorway during this argument,

and she stepped aside as her mother came storming past her, the keys clutched in her angry fist. Her father sat down at the kitchen table and smiled after his affronted mate.

"Did you see this giant rat?" he asked Lily.

"Sort of," she said.

"Are you sure he wasn't a mouse?"

"I think it was a rat," Lily speculated. "His back was kind of high, not flat like a mouse."

"When have you ever seen a rat?" her father asked impatiently.

Lily looked away. She had, she realized, never seen a rat, except in pictures, and she knew that if she said, "In pictures," her father would consider her to have less authority than she had already. "He was big, Dad," she said at last, turning away.

When her mother pulled the trap from its purple bag, Lily felt a twinge of sympathy for the rat. The board was large; the bar, which snapped closed when it was set, was wide enough to accommodate Lily's hand; the spring was devilishly strong and so tight that her father forced the bar back with difficulty. He tested it with a wooden spoon, and the bar snapped closed, lifting the board well off the floor. Her father baited it with a slice of potato, and the family turned out the lights and settled in their beds. Lily lay with her eyes open, listening for the snap of the bar, but she didn't hear it, and while she was listening she fell asleep.

The next morning the trap was discovered just as it had been left. Lily's father gave her mother a cold, skeptical look and sprang the trap again with a spoon. Her mother concentrated on cooking the breakfast, allowing the matter to drop. When he was gone to work, she turned to Lily as if to a conspirator and said, "I'll get some poison today and we can try again tonight."

Lily didn't think of the rat again during the day. Her school-work was oppressive, but at lunch break, for the first time that week, the students were turned out of doors. The clouds had cleared off, leaving a sky of hectic blue, a sun that beat down on the wet ground with the thoroughness of a shower. Lily and her best friend sat on the breezeway, watching the braver students, who sloshed through the puddles in search of exercise. They discussed their summer plans and confided in each other their mutual fear that they would be separated the following fall.

"If I get that grouch Miss Bambula," Lily's friend said, "I think I'll die. She looks just like a horse."

Lily wondered which would be worse, to be with her friend and have Miss Bambula or to be without her friend and Miss Bambula. One of the boys in the yard hailed the two girls, holding up for their long-distance inspection the squirming green body of an anole. Lily stood up and went out to him. She liked anoles and this one, she saw at once, was of a good size.

That afternoon, when her mother brushed her hair, the rat didn't appear. "Maybe your father's right," her mother said hopefully. Later, after she had practiced piano, Lily rejoined her mother in the kitchen to help with dinner. She sat at the table with a large bowl of green beans, which she proceeded to snap, throwing the ends into a small bowl, the fat centers into another. Her mother stood at the counter, peeling pota-toes. They worked without speaking, and it was so quiet in the room that they heard the scratching of the rat's claws against the floor before they saw him. They both turned, looking in shocked silence at the refrigerator. His ugly face appeared first; then he took a few timid steps forward and stood before them. Lily saw that his black lips were drawn back over his teeth and his cheeks pulsated with his nervous breathing. She sucked in her own breath and dropped the bean she was holding.

The rat made a sudden dash for the stove, moving so quickly that Lily's mother let out a little cry as she jumped out of his path. "Mama," Lily said softly as they both bolted for the kitchen door. Her mother held the swinging door open and wrapped her arm protectively around her daughter's shoulder as she passed through. In the dining room they stood together and Lily allowed herself, for a moment, the luxury of closing her eyes against her mother's shoulder. "Don't worry, baby," her mother said. "I got the poison this morning; we'll get him tonight."

Lily's father was incredulous when they told him of the intruder's boldness, and he smiled in disbelief when Lily, holding up her hands, estimated the creature's true dimensions. "She's not kidding," her mother said angrily. "He's really big. We got a good look at him this time."

"All right," her father said. "We'll put out the trap again. I just wish he'd show his face when I'm here."

"Christ," her mother replied. "That's not my fault. If he's still here tomorrow I'll take his picture. Would you believe that?"

"That's not a bad idea," her father said.

That night, before they went to bed, the family gathered in the kitchen and laid out their arsenal. The trap was baited and placed near the wall; the poison, which was inside a plastic box with a hole at one end, was placed near the stove with the hole turned toward the wall.

"Can he get in that little hole?" Lily asked.

"I hope so," her mother replied.

Alone in her bed, Lily slept, then woke, then slept again. Toward morning she opened her eyes abruptly, with the sensation that she had cause to do so. She raised herself on one elbow and looked out into the darkness of her room. She could see nothing, but she heard distinctly a scratching sound, the sound, she knew at once, of claws against wood. She fell back and put her hands over her mouth, as if to hold in a scream, though she made no sound. Her heart pounded so furiously that she could hear it, and she felt in her legs, which were drawn up now beneath the sheet, the sudden ebbing of strength that usually follows a nightmare. The sound continued, and it seemed to her that it became louder, closer, as the moments passed. She consoled herself with the thought that the rat would doubtless find little to interest him in her room and would soon opt for the swift or slow death that awaited him in the kitchen. If only she'd put a trap in her room, she thought.

The scratching was very close and then, when it sounded as though the creature was under the bed, abruptly it stopped. Lily breathed uneasily, afraid and unable to move. Then she heard a sound she was never to forget, the metallic protest of the bedsprings as they received the weight of the animal's body. Lily's eyes burned into the humid dark air and she opened her mouth, but still no sound came. She had begun to perspire; her gown clung wetly to her narrow chest. Again she heard the squeaking springs, and this time she knew exactly where the sound came from. The rat was just behind her head. Though she couldn't see him and didn't have the strength even to turn her head so that she might see him, she felt the nervous twitching of his snout, the horrible inhalation of his breath, as he pulled himself up over the headboard of the bed and looked down upon the paralyzed young girl before him.

For a moment the animal contemplated her, and then, as if they were one, both moved. The rat sprang forward, his front legs stretching out before him as his back feet propelled him out into the air. Lily, finding her strength and her voice at once, sat up, throwing her hands over her head and screaming "No!" But it was too late. Her left hand encountered the rat's side and inadvertently she slapped him toward her own back. He landed squarely on the top of her head, and as she swung her legs over the side of the bed and rose to her feet, he slid down her back. His body was enormously heavy. In his panic he clawed at her hair, tangling himself and enraging Lily so that she threw herself against the wall, thinking to crush him. This gave him the leverage he needed to pull free of her hair. He slipped down over her buttocks and dropped to the floor. He was running when he hit the wood, scrambling back toward the bed. Lily was already in the hall. Now, she thought, she could run until she dropped. But she only ran to her parents' door, throwing it open before her with a scream. Her mother was raised up on her elbow looking at her; her father sat on the edge of the bed fumbling for his slippers. It was to her father that she ran, but not for comfort. She caught him by his shoulders, forcing him to fall back across the sheets, and she held him down there, her hair falling wildly about her as she screamed into his astonished face, "You kill him, you kill him now! Go and kill him now!"

Her mother sat up, pulling back Lily's hair, feeling her neck and shoulders frantically. "Did he bite you?" she asked. "Are you cut?" Then Lily turned on her mother, thinking that she would strike her, but when she was folded into the eager, smothering embrace, she gave in and clung to her mother's neck, hugging her close. Her mother glared over the girl's shoulders at the still prostrate form of her husband and repeated to him the injunction his daughter had just given him. "Go and kill him now," she said. "Don't leave this house until that animal is dead."

Lily's father sat up and resumed fumbling for his slippers. Lily and her mother lay locked together and neither watched him as he shuffled off toward the bathroom. They clung to each other, pulling the sheets up and adjusting the pillows so that they could sleep as they had when Lily was a baby, with their arms around each other. Outside, the rain began, softly at first, punctuated with the low rumble of thunder and flashes of lightning that radiated like nerves across the sky. Lily's father had turned on the light in the hall and she could hear him in the kitchen, opening the refrigerator, running water in the sink. The rain grew more intense; it beat insistently against the window in her parents' room, and she thought of how it must be outdoors, beating the flowers down into the already water-logged soil, beating the leaves back on the trees. She thought especially of the big plantain tree in the side yard, of how it bent down in the rain, its great leaves shiny and smooth, like sheets of brilliantly painted plastic. The rain washed over the house and seemed to carry great waves of sleep with it, impossible to resist.

In the morning Lily and her mother found her father asleep at the kitchen table, his arms spread out before him, his cheek pressed against the wood, his mouth slack from weariness. He had prepared himself a cup of coffee, which sat on the table near his left hand, but he had not drunk half of it.

Lily's mother woke him impatiently. He lifted his head, rubbed his eyes, and looked sleepily at his wife, then at his daughter. He put out his hand to Lily and drew her toward him. "Are you OK now, baby?" he said. "Are you sure it wasn't a dream?" Then, as she was about to protest, his face changed. He looked across her shoulder and Lily knew, without turning, what he saw. Her mother followed his gaze and her expression changed from aggravation to horror. Lily turned and saw him. He had come out silently and stood, calm, though, as always, poised for flight. He moved his ugly head back and forth, watching, sniffing, and Lily could hear again the horrible sound of his breathing. He confronted them and they couldn't look away, for his boldness was as wonderful as his size. Lily's mother reached back suddenly, took the half-full coffee cup, and threw it with all her strength at the animal. He was gone before the cup hit the ground.

For two days and nights the rat was under siege. The animal sensed the change in his situation and responded with the obsessive wiles of the hunted. Traps and poison failed to entice him, though he made frequent appearances in the vicinity of both. The family spent the weekend in an ecstasy of determination, baiting all possible hiding places with poison. Lily's parents moved the stove and refrigerator out from the wall. Lily helped to seal off any holes they discovered, along the baseboards, in the window casings, holes Lily thought much too small to be of use to the large creature that had glared at them so balefully. Her father assured her that it was in the power of rats to make themselves fit into small places, that they were like yogis who know the secret of folding themselves down into suitcases. Lily plugged the holes with spoons of wet plaster. Now that her father believed in the creature's existence, he seemed unable to give it enough credence, and she had been elevated from the position of hysterical visionary to that of reliable reporter on the natural scene.

On Monday morning her father called his office to say he wasn't coming in. The sky was black with clouds, and flood predictions were ubiquitous; he used this as his excuse. Lily's mother called the school and said that she was ill and needed Lily at home. This easy lie shocked Lily, though she was glad of it. Then the three sat at the kitchen table and discussed their plans. They had sealed the rat in the kitchen; they were sure of this. And when next he appeared, he wouldn't find it easy to escape. The pots and pans sat out on the floor in little groups; all the food was in boxes in the dining room. The cabinets stood open and empty. If he showed his face again there would be no place left to conceal it.

But though they sat at the table scanning the room for the better part of the morning, he took them by surprise. He appeared inside the cabinet beneath the sink, and none could say where he came from. Lily's father, who had armed himself with a hammer and a small ax, leaped to his feet and raced to the animal. By the time he had crossed the room the rat was gone. He fell on his knees and inspected every inch of the cabinet with his hands. "How the hell does he do it?" he said, and then, "Oh, this is it." Lily and her mother joined him and they all looked with wonder at the hole, which was really a broken flap in the plasterboard at the back of the cabinet. Behind it was another hole, smaller, ragged, and deep. It opened into darkness, and the outside edge of it was lined with half an inch of wood.

"Do you know what it is?" Lily's father asked.

"Why is it so dark?" she said, for it seemed to Lily that such a hole should open into daylight.

"Because it's inside a drawer," her father replied. He seemed immensely pleased with this pronouncement, like a detective who has discovered the long-sought final clue.

"The old dresser?" her mother said.

Her father stood up, gripping his gleaming ax, and started out the back door for the porch. Then Lily understood. On the porch there was a dresser in which, as a baby, she had kept her toys. It backed up against the house, against, she realized, this very cabinet. The rat had disappeared into the dark hole, but the dark hole was the inside of that dresser. Lily and her mother exchanged looks of mild surprise; then they too rushed out onto the porch. Her father stood poised before the dresser. "He's in there," he said. "I can hear him."

"Which drawer?" her mother asked.

"The middle, I think."

"What are you going to do?" Lily cried. She was suddenly desperately frightened.

"I'm going to open the drawer just a little and try to catch him in it." As he said this he squatted down, laying his ax near his feet, and pulled the middle drawer open an inch. Lily could hear the scratching of the animal's claws against the wood. Another inch, she thought, and they would see his dreadful face. Her father pulled the drawer out carefully, leaning back a little so that his face wouldn't be near the opening. Now he could see into the drawer. Then, abruptly, he pulled the drawer all the way out and threw it down on the porch. Lily saw her old metal tea set scattered across the bottom, and a plastic strainer she had once used for sand flew out of the drawer and rolled in a dizzy circle toward the screen. Except for that, the drawer was empty, and the space in the dresser where the drawer had been was empty as well.

"Did he go back in the kitchen?" her mother asked. The hole that had allowed the creature's easy entrance into their lives was now visible, and they stood looking into it as their greatest oversight. They heard a scratching, then a thudding sound that came distinctly from the top drawer. The rat was trapped at last and he was frantic. Lily's father turned toward them. "Get back," he warned. Then he pulled the drawer out slowly, carefully, an inch, then another. Inside the drawer the rat was still, crouched, silent, as light flooded his last dark refuge.

Lily grasped her mother's hand and found it cold but willing to hold her own. Her father leaned over the dresser, placing one hand against the front of the drawer while with the other he began to pound on the top. Still there was no sound, no movement from inside the drawer.

"Is he in there?" Lily's mother asked. Her father turned his head to answer his wife, and in that moment the rat made his move. He hit the front of the drawer with such force that her father's hand fell away, leaving the crack open and unprotected. In the next instant the creature flew up before them, straight up; his legs battled the air like wings, his teeth were bared. He leaped straight at Lily's father, who staggered backward and put out his hands to stop this attack. But the rat caught him at the base of his throat, sinking his sharp teeth into the flesh and clinging to the shirt cloth with his sharp claws.

Her father made a gasping sound and whirled around, clutching the animal at his throat. Lily saw his face—his eyes opened wide in shock, his teeth bared too now, in such fury as she had never imagined possible. The rat clung to him as he fell to his knees, dropping one hand for the ax while the other closed over the animal's face. His fingers went inside the rat's mouth, prying the teeth from his flesh, and when he had pulled them free he raised the gray body over his head and dashed it to the floor. Then the rat screamed. It was the only sound he had made in the struggle, and his voice was high, clear, terror-stricken. Lily saw the oily edge of the ax blade as it came down through the air. She remembered how her father had sharpened and oiled it that morning in preparation for this blow.

The edge came down and Lily turned to her mother, who was too stunned by what she saw to look away. There was the soft sound of flesh giving way, of small bones cracking, and it was quiet. When Lily looked back, the rat was in two pieces, his head and forequarters on one side of the ax, his back legs and long tail severed completely and thrown a foot away by the force of the blade. Lily's father stood looking down at the sight, clutching his throat with one hand. He knew he had won the contest, but his rage, Lily saw, was not yet under control. Her mother rushed to him, throwing her arms about him with a passion she had never shown him before, and he held her against him tightly. Lily looked away, allowing her eyes their fill of the curiously rewarding sight of the rat's bisected body. His blood oozed out upon the boards from his wounds and from his open mouth, which was already stiffening with death. The wonder of his death afflicted her. A moment before he had threatened everything; now his harmless body lay before her, bereft of horror, only dull, large, gray, mysteriously still. She turned away from them all and went back into the kitchen. Her hands were sticky from fear and she washed them at the sink.

That night Lily slept fitfully. When she woke she could think of nothing but the rat, of how she had lain and listened to him as he came closer and closer. She sat up and looked about the room. Didn't she hear the scratching of his claws against the floor; wasn't that hushing sound his rapid breathing? She lay back and turned to face the wall.

Her mother had kissed her when she went to bed, and her father had held her for a moment with warm confidence. She had touched the bandage on his neck tentatively. The doctor had suggested that the wound would become more painful before it began to heal. A rat bite, he told the family, was no joke, but there was no reason to expect complications. Her father had astounded the doctor with the story, keeping, as he talked, one hand resting protectively on his daughter's shoulder. He had, he was convinced, done what was necessary to set her fears at rest.

But now she was as full of fear as ever, and she knew she wouldn't sleep. She got up and turned on the light in her bedroom; then she looked under the bed and in the closet. But not seeing anything didn't give her the rest she sought. At length she decided to go out, to take the plastic bag out of the garbage can and look again on the remains of her enemy. She slipped on her robe, turned off her light, and went stealthily down the hall, passing her parents' bedroom door without a pause.

She opened the kitchen door, unlatched and opened the

screen, and stepped out on the porch. The rain had stopped, and through the swiftly moving clouds the moon cast its desultory beams. Lily accustomed her eyes to the light and to the unexpected beauty of the scene before her. She focused her eyes on the moonflowers, like pools of milk among the dark leaves that covered the fence. The roses nearby raised their thorny branches, holding out papery leaves and flowers, gray and black, toward the sky. Her mother's vegetable garden fairly hummed with life, and, as she stood there, Lily thought of her mother and of how they had worked together one day, preparing the soil for the seeds.

Her mother had turned the soil with a shovel, and Lily, crouched barefoot in the dirt, came behind her with a garden spade, breaking the big clods down with childish energy. She stopped, then stood up and stepped forward into the rough dirt her mother had just turned. As her foot came down she noticed that the soil was warm; it invited her to press her toes into it. Lily looked at her feet and smiled, overcome with a delicious sensation. "What's funny?" her mother asked, and when Lily looked up she saw that her mother was smiling on her in the same way she smiled sometimes on her roses, with undisguised admiration.

"It's warm," Lily said. "Underneath. You should take off your shoes."

Her mother's smile deepened and she indicated her shod foot, which rested on the wing of the shovel, with a look that explained her dilemma: She couldn't dig barefoot. Then she bent down and pressed her hand into the dirt near Lily's feet. She dug her fingers down and came up with a handful of the dark soil. She studied it intently for a moment, sifting it through her fingers. She had lectured Lily that morning on this chore and made it clear that the preparation of the soil was the most important work they would do that day. Everything, by which Lily understood her to mean the future of the garden, depended on its being done right. Now it was Lily's turn to smile, for she saw that her mother couldn't take her mind off the importance she attached to doing this work correctly. It was true, her fingers told her, the soil was warm, but her fingers asked a more penetrating question: Would it yield?

Examining this memory as she stood on the porch in the warm night air, Lily paused and shook her head affectionately at the thought of her mother's passionate gardening. The fruit of that passion stood before her: tomatoes and eggplants heavy on their vines; lettuce like great balls of pearl, luminous in the darkness; the airy greens of the carrots, rustling continuously with the movement of the air; the black tangle of the green peas, climbing skyward on their tall tubes of screen. The scent of the mint and parsley bed rose to Lily, and the sweetness of the air drew her out toward the steps. She looked down at the drawers of the old dresser, which lay scattered on the porch. Her mother had washed them furiously, as if to wash away the evidence of a desecration.

Then Lily thought of the rat, and she looked toward the garbage can with a sensation of dismay. It would be, she thought, foolish and unnecessary trouble to pull out his corpse now. She could consult her memory for a fresh, distinct, and detailed picture of his death; she could see, in her mind's eye, the blood darkening around his mouth, the dullness of his dead eyeballs. She wasn't certain that he wouldn't seek her out again, but she thought he would never again seek her in that particular form.

His menace had quite gone out of that form; she had seen it with her own eyes. Her father had discarded the pieces of the rat's body without anger; he had even commented on the creature's remarkable size, taking, Lily had observed, some comfort in having defeated so formidable an enemy. Now that he was a danger to no one, the rat possessed the power to be marvelous.

Lily turned away, pushing her hair back from her face. She had told her mother she wanted her hair cut off and, to her surprise, had received no objection. But now this seemed an unnecessary precaution. She returned to her bed, possessed of a strange fearlessness; it was as insistent as her own heartbeat, and as she drifted off to sleep it swelled and billowed within her and she understood, for the first time, that she was safe.

THE FREEZE

That night, as Anne was dressing in the bathroom, she took a long dreamy look at herself in the mirror. She had finished her makeup. This was the look she always gave herself, critical yet sympathetic; it was intended as a look at the makeup. She was forty years old, twice divorced, a woman who, half a century ago, would have been a statistical failure. But she didn't feel, really, as if she had failed at anything. She looked as good as she ever had. She was strong and healthy and she supported herself and her daughter all alone. She liked being alone, for the most part; she especially liked waking up alone, and she had no intention of changing this, yet she was so pleased by her own reflection in the mirror, it was as if she thought someone else saw her, as if someone were in love with her. And yes, she told herself, pulling the blue silk dress carefully over her head, perhaps someone was in love with her and perhaps she would find out about it tonight.

These were not the vague fancies of middle age. She had a lover in mind, and there was a good chance that he would be at this party. But it was absurd, she told herself, joking with herself, because it would have been absurd to anyone else. He was nearly twenty years younger than she. Aaron, she thought, invoking his presence with his name. A rich, charming college student who could certainly find better things to do with his time than make love to a woman twice his age.

She had seen him five times. First at a friend's; the same friend who was giving this party. He had come in with Jack, the son of the house, a bright, ugly boy who reminded Anne of her high school students. They passed through the kitchen; they were going to play tennis, but Jack paused long enough to introduce his new friend, Aaron Fischer. Anne's first impression of him was indifferent. He was clearly Jewish, his curly hair was blond, his complexion was clear and a little flushed. He looked intelligent. Anne was accustomed to searching for signs of intelligence in the young; it was her profession. He met her eyes as he shook her hand, a firm, self-assured handshake, with a look to match it. She didn't think he really saw her. Jack exchanged a few words with his mother and they went out, but as he turned away from her, Aaron nodded curtly and said, "Peace." They were gone.

"He's an interesting boy," her friend observed.

"I haven't heard anyone say 'Peace' since 1962," Anne replied.

"I hear he has principles too." The two women raised their eyebrows at each other.

"He must be some kind of throwback," Anne concluded.

A week later, as she was coming out of the university library, she saw him again. To her surprise he recognized her. "Anne," he said. "What are you doing here?"

She stammered. She had learned that Yukio Mishima had

written a play about the wife of the Marquis de Sade, and not finding it at the local bookstore, she had come to the library on purpose to read it. It had proved amusing and entirely unshocking, but the title alone was not something she thought this young man would appreciate. "I was just doing a little research," she said. "I'm a teacher, you know."

"You teach here?" He looked surprised, impressed.

"No. I teach at the arts high school."

"Oh," he said, "I've heard of that." Now, she thought, they would part. But he was interested and appeared to have nothing more important to do than stand on the library stairs chatting with a stranger. After a few more exchanges he suggested coffee, which, he said, was what he was out for, and she agreed.

They went to the bright, noisy university cafeteria, had three cups of coffee each, then proceeded to the dark cavernous university tavern, where they shared a pitcher of beer. Aaron talked with such ease and his range of interests was so wide that Anne, who had expected nervous chatter about his classes, found herself completely charmed. He was idealistic, almost militant in his adherence to a code, though precisely what code Anne couldn't make out. He was a chemistry major, this was his last year, and then he was applying to medical school. By the time they parted, when Anne explained that she must pick up her daughter, who was visiting a friend, Aaron had her phone number scribbled in his small leather notebook. He promised to call. The med school applications were voluminous; he had not, in his expensive education, been taught to use a typewriter, and Anne had offered, had insisted on helping him.

Then followed two long evenings in her living room. The applications were more tedious and time-consuming than she had imagined. Aaron exclaimed over the stupidity of the personal questions. Anne moaned every time she saw the printed grid that meant she had to retype his entire undergraduate transcript. The first night they finished off a bottle of red wine and, when they were done, sat talking comfortably for another hour before Aaron noted the time and hurried off, apologizing for having stayed so late and for having drunk all her wine.

The next night he arrived with a bottle of champagne. They shared it sparingly as they worked over his applications, and at the end of a few pleasant hours half of them were ready to be mailed. Aaron was thorough; he was applying to thirty schools.

She was charmed by him, by his youth, by his confidences, by his manner, which was so preternaturally social that she couldn't be sure how much of the pleasure he appeared to take in her company was simply the pleasure he took in any company. He lounged on her couch and looked about her apartment with an appreciative eye, and when he observed that it was time to go (he had a chemistry test at eight in the morning and he hadn't opened a book yet), he added that he did not want to go.

Was he asking to stay?

Anne was cautious. She discussed the matter with her friend, who assured her that it did sound as if the boy was more than superficially interested. And he was a delightful boy; in only a few years he would be, they agreed, a remarkable man. He might be shy; he might fear, as she did, that the attraction he felt for her was something he should not explore. He might think she thought of him as a child and be uncertain or unable to make the first move. Anne might have to make this move, whatever it was, herself. She should be careful. The timing in such matters was extremely delicate; on this the two women were in complete agreement. Anne would see him one more time, to finish the applications, but she might have to wait longer.

Their last meeting was a short one. He had everything completed; it was a matter of a few minutes' typing. He was in a hurry and he complained bitterly of the cause for it. "I have a date," he said. "This ugly girl called me and now I have to go to this stupid party. Why can't I say no? Why didn't I say no?"

"Perhaps she'll be intelligent," Anne suggested.

"No, she won't. She isn't. She's in my bio class and she's failing."

"Do girls call you a lot?" she inquired, pulling the last page out of the typewriter to indicate that the question didn't really interest her.

"Only ugly girls." He gave her a perplexed frown, designed to make her smile.

In a few minutes he was gone.

For two weeks Anne agitated herself with various fantasies. She lay in her bed at night, clutching her pillow, telling herself how it would be, how it would surely be. Their lovemaking would be dizzying; in fact, the first time would be such a relief for them both that they would collapse into each other's arms with the breathless passion of some long-frustrated, star-crossed Victorians. Then afterward she would laugh and tell him how hard it had been, because of their age difference and because they were so many worlds apart, to admit to herself that she was in love with him. For she was in love, she thought with a growing sense of wonder. Was it possible? She was in love as she had not been since she was a girl, only this was harder to bear and more intense, because she knew exactly what it was she wanted. And it wasn't a home, a family, his money, a ride in his Porsche. She would be content if they never left her apartment and she knew none of his friends. She only wanted him to make love to her; that was all.

And now she stood, dressed, perfumed, her eyelids darkened, her lips glistening, before her bathroom mirror, and she assured herself that it would be tonight. He would be there as he had promised her friend, and he would be there just for her. She would look different, so elegant that he would be taken by surprise. The dress was perfect; her dark hair, swept back and up in a fashion he had not seen, gleamed with health and life. He would see at a glance that she was perfect for him.

She stepped into her shoes, threw her reflection a last affectionate look, turned out the overhead light, and went into the hall. Hannah stood in the doorway of her daughter's room. "Anne," she said, "you look so nice. What a beautiful dress."

Anne blushed at the admiration she saw in the girl's eyes. "Do you like it?" she said, turning before her.

"It's lovely," the girl said.

Anne's heart swelled with pleasure. As they walked together to the living room, it struck her that she was extraordinarily lucky. She wrote her friend's number on the phone pad and promised Hannah that she would call if she went anywhere else.

"Don't worry about it," Hannah replied. "Nell's already asleep."

As she walked to the car, Anne looked back and saw Hannah standing on the porch. She was waving with one hand as she pulled the screen in tightly with the other. "Goodnight," Anne called out impetuously, but the girl didn't hear her. She got into her car, fishing in her purse for the keys.

The party was halfway across town. Anne concentrated on driving and on sitting a little stiffly so that she wouldn't wrinkle her dress. When she arrived her friend greeted her at the door. "He's here," she said. "You look terrific."

"Is he alone?" Anne asked.

"Yes. He's in the back, by the bar. I'll take you there."

"That's a good sign, don't you think?" Anne asked. They passed through the bright rooms filled with glittering crystal, hothouse flowers, silver trays of food, and chatting groups of people. "Your house looks great," she added.

"That he's by the bar?" her friend inquired.

"No, that he's alone," Anne replied.

"Of course it's a good sign." They had come to the last room, and as Anne stepped inside she saw Aaron leaning against the far wall. He was talking to an elderly man and he didn't see her. "It's a very good sign," her friend agreed. "Get yourself a drink."

Yes, Anne thought. A drink would help. Her knees were decidedly weak. She felt like some wolf waiting for a choice lamb to separate from the fold, and the idea of herself as hungry, as looking hungry to others in the room, struck her with enough force to make her lower her eyes. She told the bartender what she wanted in a voice she scarcely recognized, it was so oily, so sly, the voice of the inveterate predator. When she took the drink, he caught her eye and smiled. "This is a party," he said.

"I beg your pardon?" she asked.

"It's a party," he repeated. "You're supposed to be having a good time."

Then she understood him and was annoyed by him. "I just got here," she said, turning away. "Give me a minute."

Aaron was looking at her, had been looking at her, she understood, for some moments, and now he detached himself from the elderly man and made his way toward her. She thought he would say something about her appearance, in which she still had some confidence, and she drew herself up a little to receive a compliment, but when he was near enough to speak, he said, "Christ, that's my chemistry teacher. I didn't expect to find *him* here."

"Did you think he spent his evenings over a hot test tube?" she asked lightly.

He smiled, and his smile was so ingenuous, so charming, that she moved closer to him as if to move into the warm influence of that smile. "I did," he said. "And he might as well, for all he's got to say."

So their conversation began and continued for some time. Anne introduced him to some of the people she knew, and several times he went to the bar to refresh their drinks. He seemed content to be near her, to be with her, in fact, and she felt all her nervousness and foreboding melt away. The rooms filled with more and more people, until one had fairly to raise one's voice to be heard. A few couples drifted out onto the patio; it was unseasonably warm and the night air was inviting. Anne and Aaron stood in the doorway, looking out for a few minutes. "Let's go out," Aaron said. "The smoke in here is getting to me."

Anne followed him down the steps of the house and out into the darkness. As she did, she watched him and endured such a seizure of desire that her vision clouded. She was not, she realized, drunk; though she could scarcely see, her head was clear. She passed one hand before her eyes and gripped the stair rail tightly with the other, not to steady herself but to hold down a surge of ardor. I feel like dynamite, she thought; that was her secret thought behind her hand, and then she looked out. What a sweet thing it was to be alive at that moment, with all the eager force of life throbbing through her, the sensation of being stunning with the force of it so that if anyone looked at her they must stop and admire her beauty, which was only the fleeting influx of pure energy that sometimes comes to us, without any effort of our own.

But no one saw her and the moment passed. The patio was deep; one side was a high vine-covered wall, along which ran a ledge. People sat in little groups along the ledge and on the scattered iron chairs, and they stood about in groups among the plantains and the palmetto palms, talking, Anne discovered as she passed among them, about the weather. The weatherman had predicted a cold front, a drop in temperature of 30 degrees, with rain and wind by midnight. And here it was, eleven-thirty and 65 degrees. The sky was clear, black, and fathomless over-head.

She followed Aaron, who didn't look back until he had reached the far end of the patio. When he turned she came up to him slowly. "Is this far enough, do you think?" she asked, teasing.

"No," he said. "But there's a wall here."

She stood near him and they looked back at the house. It was so brightly lit that it seemed to be ablaze, and the noise of voices and music poured out the windows and doors like a liquid. Anne detected a melody she knew. "Oh, I like that record," she said.

"Who is that?" Aaron listened, then smiled. "Oh, that's Gato Barbieri. Do you like him?"

"I like that record," she said dreamily, for the music, even at this distance, was languorous and exotic. "It's pretty romantic though."

She met his eyes but he looked away. He had his hand on a branch of a crape myrtle tree, and his arm was so raised that Anne stood in the shadow of it. "I'm going to have to leave soon," he said, shaking the ice in his glass. "As soon as I finish this drink."

"I'm a little tired too," Anne lied.

Then he didn't move, nor did he speak. She stood looking down into her drink. She could feel his eyes on her hair and on her shoulders and she thought that he would touch her, but he didn't. She looked back toward the house, taking in the whole patio of people, none of whom, she saw, was looking in their direction. Say something, she told herself, but she couldn't think of anything. Aaron lifted his drink and sipped it; she heard the clinking sound of the ice, but she didn't look at him. The music was growing more emotional; it exacerbated her desire. She put her drink down at her feet and turned so that she faced the young man, so that she was very close to him, but she didn't meet his eyes because, she thought later, she didn't think it was necessary. Instead she placed her hands lightly on his shoulders and raised up on her toes, for he was several inches taller than she. She had barely touched his lips with her own when he pulled away. "No," he said. "No, thank you."

She dropped back on her heels.

"I'm really flattered," he said. "I really am."

She shook her head, hoping that this moment would pass quickly, that she could shake it away, but time seemed to seep out slowly in all directions like blood from a wound.

"Now I've hurt your feelings," he said.

She looked at the wall past his shoulder, at the bricks between her own feet. She could not look at him, but she moved out of his path. "Please go," she said, and he agreed. Yes, he would go. He apologized again; he had no wish to hurt her feelings; he was really so flattered . . . She cast him a quick look, enough to be sure that he was as uncomfortable as she. "It's all right," she said. "I'm all right. But please leave now."

"Yes," he replied. "I'll go." And he walked away. She didn't watch him cross the patio. She waited for what seemed a long time, without looking at anything or thinking of anything, as if she were stone. Then she was aware of being cold. The temperature had plummeted in a few minutes, and the other people on the patio were moving indoors, looking about, as they went in, at the trees and the empty air, as if they could see the difference they felt. Anne followed them, but no one spoke to her. Inside, her friend caught her by the arm and pulled her into the kitchen. "What happened?" she asked. "Aaron just left in a hurry. Are you meeting him somewhere?"

Anne smiled; she could feel the bitter tension of her own smile. "I made a pass at him and he turned me down."

"He did what?" Her friend was outraged.

"He said, 'No, thank you.'"

"That little prick!"

"I've never made a mistake like this." Anne paused, then added, "I was so sure of myself."

"God, what a jerk. Don't think about it."

Anne was suddenly very tired. "No," she said, "I won't."

"Stay a while," her friend urged. "Stay till everyone is gone. Then we can talk."

"I want to go home," Anne replied. "I want to drink some hot milk and wear my flannel pajamas and socks to bed."

"It's so cold," her friend agreed.

By the time she got to her car the temperature had dropped another five degrees. The wind whipped the treetops and riffled the foliage. Overhead the sky took on sheen, as if it had received a coat of wax. Anne was oblivious of everything save her own humiliation, which she did not ponder. Rather, she held it close to her and wrapped her senses around it. It was a trick she knew for postponing tears, a kind of physical brooding that kept the consciousness of pain at bay. She steered the car mindlessly around corners, waited at lights, turned up the long entrance to the expressway. There was hardly any traffic; she could drive as rapidly as she liked; but she only accelerated to forty-five. She looked down upon the quiet, sleepy city as she passed over it, and it seemed to her mysterious, like a sleeping animal breathing quietly beneath her. This must be what death is like, she thought. Coming into some place alien yet familiar.

That was stupid; that was the way people hoped it would be. But what would it be like? She asked herself this question as personally as she could, speaking to herself, who, after all, would miss her more than anyone. What, she asked, will your death be like?

Death was perhaps far away, but at that moment, because of her solitude, it seemed that he drew incautiously near, and she imagined his arms closing about her like a lover's. She shrugged. He was so promiscuous. Who could be flattered when sooner or later he would open his arms to all? Yet, she thought, it must be quite thrilling, really, to know oneself at last held in his cold, hollow eyes. Who else can love as death loves; who craves as death craves?

At home she found Hannah awake, surprised at being relieved so early.

"It's getting ugly out there," Anne told her. "You'd better go while you still can." She stood on the porch and watched the girl safely to her car. Now, she thought. Now, let's see how I am.

She closed the porch door and sat down on the couch, flicking off the lamp and plunging the room into welcome darkness. Tears rose to her eyes, but didn't overflow. Only her vision was blurred and a pleasant numbness welled up, so that she didn't care even to rub the tears away.

Surely this was not important, she thought. It was not an important event. Not worth considering. He was too young; that was all. She had misread him. It wasn't serious. He was flattered, he had said, and that word pricked her. If only he had not said that.

She covered her face with her hands and moaned. Never had she felt such shame; never had she been so thoroughly humiliated. The clear, distinct, precise memory of the failed kiss developed like a strip of film in her memory—his stiffening and drawing away, her own inability to comprehend it so that she had left her hands on his shoulders for many moments when it should have been clear to her that she should release him. He had so immediately withdrawn his lips from her own that she had found her mouth pressed briefly against the corner of his mouth, then his cheek, then thin air. She had staggered away, she knew now, though she had not known it then, staggered to the tree, which had the courtesy to remain solid and hold her up. There she had remained, devoid of feeling, while he beat his retreat, but now the bitterness came flooding in, and it was so pure and thick that she could scarcely swallow.

Ah, she hated him. He had known all along; he had teased her and smiled at her, confided his sophomoric fears and absurd ambitions to her, laughed at her weak jokes, observed her growing affection for him, encouraged her at every turn, all so that he might say, "No, thank you," and leave her standing alone, blinded by the shame of having wanted him.

"Well, I wouldn't have him now," she said aloud, "if he paid me." She laughed; it wasn't true. I suppose, she thought, I should be grateful. This sort of thing was bound to happen. Now it's over and I won't ever make the same mistake again.

But she sat for a while, brooding, resigning herself to having played a major part in a dreary business. She was so tired that even the mild activity of preparing for bed seemed more bother than it was worth. But it would shock her daughter to find her asleep on the couch in her dress, and she would be ashamed of herself, more ashamed than she was already. At last she roused herself.

The wind lashed the house with the same bitter fury she had quelled in her heart, and it suited her, as she walked through the dark rooms, to hear it rattling the doors and windows, blasting bits of branches and leaves against the glass so that they seemed held there by a magical power. She could see through the bamboo shades in her bedroom, and after changing into pajamas she sat for a few moments watching the big plantain tree straining against the force of the wind, its wide leaves plastered helplessly open along the spines like broken hands. The room was getting colder by the minute. She pulled on her warmest socks and, thrusting her legs under the covers, lay down wearily, feeling as her cheek touched the pillow a welcome sensation of relief and release. She threw her arms about her pillow and wept into it, amused through her tears at the comfort it gave her. Then she wept her way into sleep.

The sound woke her gradually. She was aware of it, in a state between sleep and consciousness, before she opened her eyes. It was a repeated sound. Her first thought was that it was coming from the wall.

Clink. Clink, clink.

She reached out and touched the wall, then turned and pressed her ear against it.

Clink. Clink, clink.

It wasn't in the wall.

She looked out into the darkness of her room. She could hear many sounds. It was raining, and she could hear the water rushing along the house gutters, pouring out over the porch where the gutters were weak. The wind was still fierce, and it whistled around the house, tearing at the awning (that was the dull flapping sound) and straining the ropes that held it in place. But above all these sounds there was the other sound, the one she couldn't place.

Clink. Clink, clink.

A metallic sound, metal against wood or concrete.

Yes, she thought, it's on the patio. The sound was irregular, but so continuous that it disturbed her. She got up and looked out the window, but all she could see was the plantain tree and the child's swimming pool, which was overflowing with icy water. The weatherman had predicted a freeze, and she did not doubt him now. In the morning the plantains would be tattered and in a day or two the long leaves would be thoroughly brown.

Clink. Clink, clink.

Perhaps a dog had gotten into the yard. Maybe it was the gate. She went into Nell's room and looked out the window. The gate was bolted; she could see it from that window. The rest of the yard looked cold and empty. There was a small corner, the edge of the concrete slab that she couldn't see from any window.

Clink. Clink, clink.

She diverted herself by contemplating her sleeping daughter. Nell lay on her back with her arms spread wide. Her long hair was sleep-tousled and her mouth was slightly open. She breathed shallowly. Anne arranged the blanket over her, kissed her cool forehead. My darling, she thought, touched by the sweetness of her daughter's innocent sleep. My beautiful girl.

Clink. Clink, clink, clink.

She might go out and see what it was. But it was so cold, so wet; the wind blew against the back door, and as soon as she opened it she would be soaked.

The sound stopped.

It was nothing. Some trash caught in a bush, blown free now.

She looked at the clock as she went back to bed. It was 3:00 a.m. She curled down under the blankets and pulled her pillow down next to her. It was a bad habit, she thought, clutch-

ing this pillow like the mate she didn't have. She thought of
Aaron.

Clink. Clink, clink.

It was nothing, she thought. Some trash caught in a bush.
She would throw it away in the morning. Now it was important
not to think, not about the sound and not about the party, or
her foolish infatuation, or the engaging smile of a young man
who cared nothing for her. These things didn't bear thinking
upon. It didn't matter, she told herself, and she knew why it
didn't matter, but somehow, as she lay in the darkness, her consciousness drifting into the less palpable darkness of sleep, she
couldn't remember why it didn't matter. Exactly why.

Clink. Clink, clink.

She woke up several times that night. Each time she heard
the sound, but she would not listen to it. Later she would recall
that though it was a small, innocuous sound, there had been
in it something so disturbing she had shuddered each time she
woke and realized that, whatever it was, it was still going on.

Eventually she woke and it was morning. Her daughter
stood next to the bed, looking down at her anxiously.

"It's too early," Anne complained.

"It's cold in my room. Can I get in bed with you?"

Anne pushed back against the wall and motioned the child
in under the blankets.

Clink. Clink, clink.

Nell put her arms about her mother's neck. "It's warm in
here," she said, curling down gratefully.

"Go to sleep," Anne replied. They fell asleep.

An hour later, when Anne woke and understood that she was
awake for the day, she found herself straining to hear the sound.

It had stopped. She didn't think of it again, not while she made pancakes for Nell, nor when she browsed leisurely through the morning paper, nor when she stood amid a week's worth of laundry, sorting the colors and textures for the machine. She collected a pile of clothes in her arms and balanced the soap box on top. Opening the back door to get to the laundry room was always a problem. She worked one hand free beneath the clothes and turned the knob. The door was opened but it had cost her two socks and an undershirt, which lay in the doorway at her feet. Bending down to get them would only mean losing more. Leaving the door open would let the heat out. She bent her knees, reaching down without bending over, like an airline attendant in bad weather. She retrieved the strayed garments, but the soap powder took the opportunity to fall open, and a thin stream of white fell where the socks had been. "Shit," she said, stepping out onto the patio. In that moment she saw the dead cat.

His body lay in the corner of the patio. In her first glance she knew so much about him, so much about his death, that she closed her eyes as if she could close out what she knew. He lay on his side, his legs stretched out unnaturally. His fur was wet and covered with bits of leaves and dirt. She couldn't see his face, for it was hidden by a tin can, a one-pound salmon can. Anne remembered having thrown it away a few days earlier. The can completely covered the animal's face, and even from a distance she could see that it was wedged on tightly.

"Oh, Jesus," she said. "Oh, Christ."

Anne put the laundry in the washing machine and went back to the yard for a close look. She crouched over the dead animal, pulling her sweater in tightly against the cold. He was a large cat; his fur was white with patches of gray and black. Anne recognized him as one of several neighborhood cats. Someone might feed him regularly and might look for him; she had no way of knowing. The can over his face made him look ludicrous. It would have been funny had she not listened for so many hours to his struggles to free himself. If I'd gone out, she thought, I could have pulled it off. Now she had to deal with the corpse.

When she went inside, she found Nell stretched out on her bed with her favorite comic books arranged all about her.

"There's a dead cat in the yard," Anne said.

The child looked up. "There is?"

"He got his face stuck in a salmon can."

Nell sat up and strained to look out the window.

"You can't see him from here. He's in the corner. I don't think you want to see him."

"I want to see him," she said, getting out of bed. "Where is he? Come show me."

"Put your robe on, put your slippers on," Anne said. "It's freezing out there."

Nell pulled on her slippers, hurriedly wrapped herself in her robe, and went to the door. Anne followed her disconsolately. They went out and stood side by side, looking down at the dead cat.

"What a way to go," Anne remarked.

Nell was quiet a moment; then she said in a voice filled with pity, "Mama, can't you take that can off his face?"

Anne hesitated. She was not anxious to see the expression such a death might leave on its victim's face. But she understood the justice of the request. She grasped the can, thinking it would fall away easily, but instead she found she had lifted the animal's head and shoulders from the concrete. The stiffness that was communicated to her fingertips shocked her; it was like lifting a board, and she laid the can back down gingerly. "It's stuck," she said. "It won't come off."

They stood quietly a few moments more. "Should we bury him?" Nell asked.

"No. Dogs would come and dig him up."

"What can we do, then?"

"I'll call the city. They have a special number. They'll come pick him up."

"The city?" the child said.

"Well, the Sanitation Department."

They went inside. "That's like the garbage men," the child observed. "You're not going to put him in the garbage can?"

"No. I'll put him in a plastic bag."

Nell considered this. "That will be good," she said. "Then some baby won't come along and see him and be upset."

Later Anne called the Sanitation Department. The man she spoke with was courteous. "Just get it to the curb," he said, "and I'll have someone pick it up. But he won't be there till this afternoon." He paused, consulting a schedule Anne imagined. "He won't be there until after three."

Anne appreciated the man's precision, and as it was still drizzling, she left the cat where he was until afternoon. Nell would be off visiting her father. Anne wanted to spare her the sight of the impersonal bagging of the creature, though she had noticed with some satisfaction that the child was neither squeamish nor overimaginative when it came to death. She understood it already as in the nature of things.

At noon the rain stopped and the sun appeared, but it was still bitterly cold and windy. Anne drove her daughter to her ex-husband's and stayed to fill in the parts of the dead cat story that the child neglected. It was hard not to make a joke of the absurdity of the accident. Even Nell saw the humor of it when her father observed that the salmon can would become a new object for dread and suicide threats.

"I can't take it anymore," Anne suggested. "I'm going to get the salmon can."

They laughed over it and then she went home. She didn't take off her coat and stopped only in the kitchen to pick up a plastic trash bag. She proceeded directly to the patio. Now when she opened the door there was no shock in the sight. She went straight to the body as if it had beckoned her.

She knelt down beside the cat. The pavement nearby was dry—the sun had taken care of that—but a ring of moisture like a shadow outlined the corpse. She slipped the bag over the animal's back feet and carefully, without touching him, pulled it up to his hips. But there it stuck, and she knew that she would have to lift him to get him into the bag.

She had a sensation of repugnance mixed with confidence. It wouldn't be pleasant, but she didn't doubt that she could do it. Five years ago she would have called on a man to do it and stayed in the house until the corpse was gone. Now there was no one to call, and no need to call anyone, for she could certainly put this dead body in a bag and transfer it to the curb. She was different now and better now. As a young woman she had been in constant fear, but that fear was gone. It was true that her loneliness was hard to bear; it made her foolish and because of it she imagined that rich, idle young men might be in love with

her. It was time to face it, she told herself. Her own youth was
gone; it was permanently, irretrievably gone. But it was worth
that confession to be rid of the fear that had been for her the
by-product of dependence. She shrugged against the dreariness
of this revelation and bent her will to the task before her.

She touched the cat's side, brushing away some bits of wood
that were stuck there. Beneath the wet, soft, dead fur was a
wall of flesh as hard as stone. This unpromising rigidity was
the cruelest of death's jokes on the living. She imagined that
rough treatment might snap the corpse in half, like a thin tube
of glass. She lifted the back a little and pulled the bag up to the
animal's middle. As she did this she became aware of her own
voice in the cold air, addressing the dead cat. "Well, my friend,"
she was saying, "I wish I'd known; I could have saved you this."

He was a pathetic sight, with his stiff, wet limbs, half in a
plastic bag, the red-and-black label with a great surging silver
fish across it all that distinguished his head. It was sad, she
thought, such a silly, useless death, though he was certainly not
the first creature ever to lose his life in an effort to avoid star-
vation. She touched his hard, cold side at the place where she
thought his heart might be; she patted him softly there. "Poor
cat," she said. "While I was tossing around in there worrying
about my little heartbreak, you were out here with this."

And she thought of the wall of her bedroom and how she
had fretted on one side of it while death stalked on the other
side. Tomorrow his prey might be something big; it might be
a man or a child. That night it had just been a cat. But he had
stalked all the same and waited and watched. It had taken the
cat hours to die, with death cold and patient nearby, waiting
for what he could claim; man or beast, it was the same to him.

But that was absurd, she thought. The unyielding flesh beneath her hand told her it was not so. The great fluidity, the sinuousness that was in the nature of these animals, had simply gone out of this one. Death had come from the inside and life had gone out. So that's it, she thought. She lifted her hand, held it before her, and gazed down into her own palm. "It comes from the inside," she said.

Anne pushed the bag aside and lifted the dead cat in her arms. She held him in her arms like a dead child and then she laid him in the bag and pulled the sides up over him. She carried him through the yard to the street. Later two men came by in a truck and took the bag away. The cat was gone. It began to rain again and grow colder still. That night, in that city, there was the hardest freeze in fifty years. Pipes burst, houses flooded, and the water pressure was so low that several buildings burned to the ground while the firemen stood about, cursing the empty hoses they held in their cold and helpless hands.

AMONG THE ARTISTS

HIS BLUE PERIOD

For anyone who has met Meyer Anspach since his success, his occasional lyrical outbursts on the subject of his blue period may be merely tedious, but for those of us who actually remember the ceaseless whine of paranoia that constituted his utterances at that time, Anspach's rhapsodies on the character-building properties of poverty are infuriating. Most of what he says about those days is sheer fabrication, but two things are true: He was poor—we all were—and he was painting all the time. He never mentions, perhaps he doesn't know, a detail I find most salient, which is that his painting actually was better then than it is now. Like so many famous artists, these days Anspach does an excellent imitation of Anspach. He's in control, nothing slips by him, he has spent the past twenty years attending to Anspach's painting, and he has no desire ever to attend to anything else. But when he was young, when he was with Maria, no one, including Anspach, had any idea what an Anspach was. He was brash, intense, never satisfied, feeling his way into a wilderness. He had no character to speak of, or rather he had already the character he has now, which is entirely self-absorbed and egotistical. He cared for no one, certainly not for Maria, though he liked to proclaim that he could not live without her, that she was his inspiration, his muse, that she was absolutely essential to his life as an artist. Pursuing every other woman who caught his attention was also essential, and making no effort to conceal those often sleazy and heartless affairs was, well, part of his character.

If struggle, poverty, and rejection actually did build character, Maria should have been an Everest in the mountain range of character, unassailable, white-peaked, towering above us in the unbreathably thin air. But of course she wasn't. She was devoted to Anspach and so she never stopped weeping. She wept for years. Often she appeared at the door of my studio tucking her sodden handkerchief into her skirt pocket, smoothing back the thick, damp strands of her remarkable black hair, a carrot clutched in her small white fist. I knew she was there even if I had my back to her because the rabbits came clattering out from wherever they were sleeping and made a dash for the door. Then I would turn and see her kneeling on the floor with the two rabbits pressing against her, patting her skirt with their delicate paws and lifting their soft, twitching muzzles to her hands to encourage her tender caresses, which they appeared to enjoy as much as the carrot they knew was coming their way. My rabbits were wild about Maria. Later, when we sat at the old metal table drinking coffee, the rabbits curled up at her feet, and later still, when she got up to make her way back to Anspach, they followed her to the door and I had to herd them back into the studio after she was gone.

I was in love with Maria and we all knew it. Anspach

treated it as a joke, he was that sure of himself. There could be no serious rival to a genius such as his, and no woman in her right mind would choose warmth, companionship, affection, and support over service at the high altar of Anspach. Maria tried not to encourage me, but she was so beaten down, so starved for a kind word, that occasionally she couldn't resist a few moments of rest. On weekends we worked together at a popular restaurant on Spring Street, so we rode the train together, over and back. Sometimes, coming home just before dawn on the D train, when the cars came out of the black tunnel and climbed slowly up into the pale blush of morning light over the East River, Maria went so far as to lean her weary head against my arm. I didn't have the heart, or was it the courage, ever to say the words that rattled in my brain, repeated over and over in time to the metallic clanking of the wheels: "Leave him, come to me." Maria, I judged, perhaps wrongly, didn't need her life complicated by another artist who couldn't make a living.

I had the restaurant job, which paid almost nothing, though the tips were good, and one day a week I built stretchers for an art supply house near the Bowery, where I was paid in canvas and paint. That was it. But I lived so frugally I was able to pay the rent and keep myself and the rabbits in vegetables, which was what we ate. Maria had another job, two nights a week at a Greek restaurant on Atlantic Avenue. Because she worked at night she usually slept late; so did Anspach. When they got up, she cooked him a big meal, did the shopping, housekeeping, bill paying, enthused over his latest production, and listened to his latest tirade about the art establishment. In the afternoon Anspach went out for an espresso, followed by a trip downtown to various galleries, where he berated the owners if he could get near them or the hired help if he couldn't. Anspach said painting was his vocation, this carping at the galleries was his business, and he was probably right. In my romantic view of myself as an artist, contact with the commercial world was humiliating and demeaning; I couldn't bear to do it in the flesh. I contented myself with sending out pages of slides every few months, then, when they came back, adding a few new ones, switching them around, and sending them out again.

On those afternoons when Anspach was advancing his career, Maria came to visit me. We drank coffee, talked, smoked cigarettes. Sometimes I took out a pad and did quick sketches of her, drowsy over her cigarette, the rabbits dozing at her feet. I listened to her soft voice, looked into her dark eyes, and tried to hold up my end of the conversation without betraying the sore and aching state of my heart. We were both readers, though where Maria found time to read I don't know. We talked about books. We liked cheerful, optimistic authors—Kafka, Céline, Beckett. Maria introduced me to their lighthearted predecessors, Hardy and Gissing. Her favorite novel was *Jude the Obscure*.

She had come to the city when she was seventeen with the idea that she would become a dancer. She spent six years burying this dream beneath a mountain of rejection, though she did once get as close as the classrooms of the ABT. At last she concluded that it was not her will or even her ability that held her back, it was her body. She wasn't tall enough and her breasts were too large. She had begun to accept this as the simple fact it was when she met Anspach and dancing became not her ambition but her refuge. She continued to attend classes a few times a week. The scratchy recordings of Chopin, the polished wooden floors, the heft of the barre, the sharp jabs and rebukes of the martinet teachers, the cunning little wooden blocks that disfigured her toes, the smooth, tight skin of the leotard, the strains, pains, the sweat, all of it was restorative to Maria; it was the reliable world of routine, secure and predictable, as different from the never-ending uproar of life with Anspach as a warm bath is from a plunge into an ice storm at sea.

Anspach had special names for everyone, always designed to be mildly insulting. He called Maria Mah-ree, or Miss Poppincockulous, a perversion of her real surname, which was Greek. Fidel, the owner of a gallery Anspach browbeat into showing his paintings, was Fido. Paul, an abstract painter who counted himself among Anspach's associates, was Pile. My name is John, but Anspach always called me Jack; he still does. He says it with a sharp punch to it, as if it is part of a formula, like "Watch out, Jack" or "You won't get Jack if you keep that up." Even my rabbits were not rabbits to Anspach but "Jack's-bun-buns," pronounced as one word with the stress on the last syllable. If he returned from the city before Maria got home, he came straight to my studio and launched into a long, snide monologue, oily with sexual insinuation, on the subject of how hard it was to be a poor artist who couldn't keep his woman at home because whenever he went out to attend to his business she was sure to sneak away to visit Jack's-bun-buns, and he didn't know what was so appealing about those bun-buns, but his Miss Poppincockulous just couldn't seem to get enough of them. That was the way Anspach talked. Maria didn't try to defend herself, and I was no help. I generally offered Anspach a beer, which he never refused, and tried to change the subject to the only one I knew he couldn't resist, the state of his career. Then he sat down at the table and indulged himself in a flood of vitriol against whatever galleries he'd been in that day. His most frequent complaint was that they were all looking for pictures to hang "over the couch," in the awful living rooms of "Long Island Jane and Joe" or "Fire Island Joe and Joey." He pronounced Joey "jo-*ee*." Sometimes if he suspected I had another beer in the refrigerator, Anspach would ask to see what I was painting. Then and only then, as we stood looking at my most recent canvas, did he have anything to say worth hearing.

I don't know what he really thought of me as a painter, but given his inflated opinion of his own worth, any interest he showed in someone else was an astonishing compliment. I know he thought I was facile, but that was because he was himself a very poor draftsman, he still is, and I draw with ease. Anspach's gift was his sense of color, which even then was astounding. It was what ultimately made him famous; then Anspach's passion for color was all that made him bearable. It was the reason I forgave him for being Anspach.

His blue period started in the upper right-hand corner of a painting titled *Napalm*, which featured images from the Vietnam War. A deep purple silhouette of the famous photograph of a young girl fleeing her burning village was repeated around the edges like a frame. The center was a blush of scarlet, gold, and black, like the inside of a poppy. In the upper corner was a mini-landscape: marsh grass, strange, exotic trees, a few birds in flight against an eerie, unearthly sky. The sky was not really blue but a rich blue-green with coppery undertones, a Renaissance color, like the sky in a painting by Bellini.

"How did you get this?" I asked, pointing at the shimmery patch of sky.

"Glazes," he said. "It took a while, but I can do it again." He gazed at the color with his upper teeth pressed into his lower lip, a speculative, anxious expression in his open, innocent eyes. Anspach fell in love with a color the way most men fall in love with a beautiful, mysterious, fascinating, unattainable woman. He gave himself over to his passion without self-pity, without vanity or envy, without hope really. It wasn't the cold spirit of rage and competitiveness that he showed for everything and everyone else in his world. It was unselfish admiration, a helpless opening of the heart. This blue-green patch, which he'd labored over patiently and lovingly, was in the background now, like a lovely, shy young woman just entering a crowded ballroom by a side door, but she had captured Anspach's imagination, and it would not be long before he demanded that all the energy in the scene revolve around her and her alone.

In the weeks that followed, as that blue moved to the foreground of Anspach's pictures, it sometimes seemed to me that it was draining the life out of Maria, as if it were actually the color of her blood and Anspach had found some way to drain it directly from her veins onto his canvas.

One summer evening, after Anspach had drunk all my beers and Maria declared herself too tired and hot to cook, we treated ourselves to dinner at the Italian restaurant underneath my loft. There we ran into Paul Remy and a shy, nearsighted sculptor named Mike Brock, whom Anspach immediately christened Mac. Jack-and-Mac became the all-purpose name for Mike and myself, which Anspach used for the rest of the evening whenever he addressed one of us. After the meal Anspach invited us all to his loft to drink cheap wine and have a look at his latest work. It was Maria's night off; I could see that she was tired, but she encouraged us to come. She had, she explained, a fresh baklava from the restaurant we should finish up, as it wouldn't keep. So up we all went, grateful to pass an evening at no expense, and I, at least, was curious to see what Anspach was up to.

The loft had once been a bank building. Anspach and Maria had the whole second floor, which was wide open from front to back with long double-sashed windows at either end. The kitchen was minimal: a small refrigerator, a two-burner stove, an old, stained sink that looked as though it should be attached to a washing machine, and a low counter with a few stools gathered around it. Their bedroom was a mattress half hidden by some curtains Maria had sewn together from the inevitable Indian bedspreads of that period. The bathroom was in pieces, three closets along one wall. One contained a sink and mirror, one only a toilet, and the third opened directly into a cheap shower unit, the kind with the flimsy plastic door and painted enamel interior, such as one sees in summer camps for children. In the center of the big room was a battered brick-red couch, three lawn chairs, and two tables made of old crates. Anspach's big easel and paint cart were in the front of the long room facing the street windows. The best thing about the place was the line of ceiling fans down the middle, left over from the bank incarnation. It was hellish outside that night, and we all sighed with relief at how much cooler the loft was than the claustrophobic, tomato-laced atmosphere of the restaurant.

Maria put on a record, Brazilian music, I think, which made the seediness of the place seem less threatening, more exotic, and she poured out tumblers of wine for us all. The paintings Anspach showed us fascinated me. He was quoting bits from other painters, whom he referred to as "the Massas," but the color combinations were unexpected and everywhere there was a marvelous balance of refined technique and sheer serendipity. These days he fakes the surprise element, but his technical skill has never failed him. When Anspach talked about paint, it was like a chemist talking about drugs. He knew what was in every color, what it would do in combination with other mediums, with oil, with thinner, on canvas, on pasteboard. He could give a quick rundown on all the possible side effects. Even then he didn't use much in the way of premixed colors; he made his own. His blue was underpainted with cadmium yellow, covered with a mix of phthalo green and Prussian blue and a few opalescent glazes that he called his "secret recipe." The images were recondite, personal. I was pleased to see that he was leaving the Vietnam subject matter behind with the cadmium red he'd given up in favor of the blue. The blue allowed him to be less strident, more interior. He pointed at a section of one large canvas in which a woman's hands were grasping the rim of a dark blue hole—was she pulling herself out or slipping in? The hands were carefully, lovingly painted, extraordinarily lifelike. "That," Anspach said, "is what I call painterly."

Paul turned to Maria. "Did he make you hang from the balcony?" he asked, for of course we all knew the hands were hers.

"Something like that," she said.

Later, when we were sitting in the lawn chairs and Maria changed the record to something vaguely Mediterranean, interrupted now and then by a high-pitched male voice screaming in agony, Anspach caught me watching her. I was looking at the long, beautiful curve of her neck—she had her hair pulled up because of the heat—and the prominent bones at the base of her throat, which gleamed in the dim lamplight as if they'd been touched by one of his secret opalescent glazes.

Anspach shot me a look like a dagger. "Miss Mah-ree," he began. "Oh, Miss Mah-ree, dat music is so nice. Why don't you do a little dance for us boys, Miss Mah-ree, Miss Poppincockulous, I know these boys would love to see the way you can dance, wouldn't you, Jack-and-Mac? Mr. Jack-and-Mac would especially like to see our Miss Mah-ree do a little dance to dat nice music."

Maria looked up. "Don't be silly," she said.

Anspach refilled his glass. Cheap wine brings out the worst in everyone, I thought. Then he swallowed a big mouthful and started up again, this time a little louder and with a wounded, edgy quality to his voice, like a child protesting injustice. "Oh, Miss Mah-ree, don't say I'm being silly, don't say that. Don't say you won't dance for us boys, because we all want you to dance so much to dat nice music, and I know you can, Miss Mah-ree, Miss Poppincockulous, I know you like to dance for all the boys and you can take off your shirt so all the boys can see your pretty breasts, because she does have such pretty baboobies, don't you know, boys. Mr. Jack-and-Mac and Mr. Pile, I know you boys would love to see Miss Mah-ree's pretty baboobies, especially you, Mr. Jack-and-Mac. Miss Mah-ree, don't say no to these nice boys."

Maria sent me a guarded look, then raised her weary eyes to Anspach, who was sunk deep in the couch with his arms out over the cushions, his head dropped back, watching her closely through lowered lids. "I would never do that," she said. "I would be too shy."

Anspach made a mock smile, stretching his lips tight and

flat over his teeth. "She's too shy," he said softly. Then he closed his eyes and whined, "Oh, please, Miss Mah-ree, don't be shy, oh, don't be too shy, oh pleasepleasepleasepleaseplease, my Miss Mah-ree, don't be shy to dance for us boys here to dat nice music, and take your shirt off, oh, pleasepleasepleaseplease, I know you can, I know you're not too shy, oh, pleasepleasepleasepleaseplease."

"For God's sake, Anspach," I said. "Would you leave it alone."

Anspach addressed the ceiling. "Oh, Mr. Jack-and-Mac, look at that, he don't want to see Miss Mah-ree dance, he has no interest at all in Miss Mah-ree's pretty breasts, can you believe that? I don't believe that."

Paul groaned and set his empty glass down on one of the crates. "I've got to be going," he said. "It's late."

Anspach leaned forward, resting his elbows on his knees. "Pile has to scurry home," he said. "It's much too late for Pile."

"Yeah, me too," said Mike. "I've got to be downtown early."

I looked at Maria, who was standing with her back to the record player. She hadn't moved during Anspach's tiresome monologue. She looked pale, ghostly, her eyes were focused on empty space, and as I watched her she raised one hand and pressed her fingertips against her forehead, as if pushing back something that was trying to get out. I too maintained that I was tired, that it was late, and pulled myself out of my lawn chair while Paul and Mike, exchanging the blandest of farewell pleasantries, followed Maria to the door. I stood looking down at Anspach, who was slumped over his knees muttering something largely unintelligible, though the words "too late" were repeated at close intervals. I was disgusted and angry enough to speak my mind, and I thought of half a dozen things to say to him, but as I was sorting through them Maria, turning from the doorway, caught my eye, and her expression so clearly entreated me to say nothing that I held my tongue and walked past the couch to join her at the door.

"I'm sorry," she said when I was near her.

"Don't be," I said. "You didn't do anything."

"He's just drunk," she said.

I took her hands and looked into her sad face. She kept her eyes down and her body turned away, toward Anspach, back to Anspach. "You look tired," I said. "You should get some sleep."

She smiled dimly, still averting her eyes from mine, and I thought, he won't let her sleep. As I walked through the quiet streets to my studio I blamed myself for what had happened. I should not have stared at her so openly, so admiringly. But couldn't a man admire his friend's girlfriend, was that such a crime? Wouldn't any ordinary man be pleased to see his choice confirmed in his friend's eyes? Of course the fact that Anspach was not, in any meaningful sense of the word, my or anyone else's friend gave the lie to my self-serving protest. That and the fact that what I felt for Maria was much more than admiration and I had no doubt it showed, that Anspach had seen it. He knew I wanted to take Maria away from him. He also knew I couldn't do it.

After that night I saw less and less of Maria. Sometimes she still came by in the afternoons when Anspach was in town, but she never stayed long and seemed anxious to be back in their loft before he got home. She had picked up a third grueling, thankless job, three days a week at an art supply house in Soho. The pay was minimum wage, but she got a discount on paint, which had become the lion's share of her monthly budget. Anspach was turning out paintings at an astounding rate, and the cadmium yellow that went into his blue was ten dollars a tube. The discount went to his head, and more and more paint went onto each canvas. He was cavalier about the expense, passing on his nearly empty tubes to Paul because he couldn't be bothered to finish them. Paul had invented a special device, a kind of press, to squeeze the last dabs of color from his paint tubes.

It was about that time that I met Yvonne Remy, Paul's sister, who had come down from Vermont to study art history at NYU. She was staying with Paul until she could find a place of her own, and the three of us soon fell into a routine of dinners together several nights a week, taking turns on the cooking. Yvonne was quick-witted and energetic, and she loved to talk about painting. Gradually we all noticed that she was spending more time at my place than at her brother's, and gradually we all came to feel that this was as it should be.

Yvonne was there that afternoon when I last saw Maria. She hadn't visited me in three weeks. She looked exhausted, which wasn't surprising, but there was something more than that, something worse than that, a listlessness beyond fatigue. The rabbits came running as they always did when Maria arrived, and she brightened momentarily as she bent down to caress them, but I noticed she had forgotten to bring a carrot.

Yvonne responded to her with that sudden affinity of kindness women sometimes show each other for reasons that are inexplicable to men. She warmed the milk for the coffee, which she did not always bother with for herself, and set out some fruit, cheese, and bread. When Maria showed no interest in this offering, Yvonne got up, put a few cookies on a plate, and seemed relieved when Maria took one and laid it on the saucer of her cup. Maria leaned over her chair to scratch a rabbit's ears, then sat up and took a bite of the cookie. "John," she said, her eyes still on the docile creatures at her feet. "You'll always take care of these rabbits, won't you?"

"Of course," I assured her. "These rabbits and I are in this together."

When she was gone, Yvonne sat at the table idly turning her empty cup.

"She seems so tired," I said.

"She's in despair," Yvonne observed.

○

Then a few things happened very quickly. I didn't find out about any of it until it was all over and Maria was gone. Anspach was offered a space in a three-man show with two up-and-coming painters at the Rite gallery. This coup, Paul told me later, with a grimace of pain at the pun, was the result of Anspach's fucking Mrs. Rite on the floor of her office and suggesting to her, postcoitus, that she was the only woman in New York who could understand his work. I didn't entirely believe this story; it didn't sound like Anspach to me, but evidently it was true, for within three months Mrs. Rite had left Mr. Rite and Anspach was the star of her new gallery, Rivage, which was one of the first to move south into Tribeca.

Paul maintained that Anspach told Maria about his new alliance, omitting none of the details, though it is possible that she heard about it somewhere else. Mrs. Rite was not bothered by the gossip; in fact she was rumored to have been the source of much of it. As far as Anspach was concerned, he had seized an opportunity, as what self-respecting artist would not, faced with the hypocrisy and callousness of the art scene in the city. He had decided early on to enter the fray, by bombast or seduction, or whatever it took, marketing himself as an artist who would not be denied.

Maria had narrowed her life to thankless drudgery and Anspach. She had given up her dance classes, she had few friends, and she had never been much given to confiding her difficulties to others. She was, as Yvonne had observed, already in despair. However she heard it, the truth about Anspach's golden opportunity was more than she could bear. Anspach told the police that they'd had an argument, that she had gone out the door in a rage, that he assumed she was going to weep to one of her friends. Instead she climbed the interior fire ladder to the roof, walked across the litter of exhaust vents and peeling water pipes, pulled aside the low, rickety, wire-mesh partition that protected the gutters, and dived headfirst into the street. It was a chilly day in October; the windows were closed in the loft. Anspach didn't know what had happened until the Sicilian who owned the coffee bar on the street level rushed up the stairs and banged on his door, shouting something Anspach didn't at first understand.

There was no funeral in New York. Maria's father came out from Wisconsin and arranged to have her body shipped back home. It was as if she had simply disappeared. I didn't see Anspach; I purposely avoided him. I knew if I saw him I would try to hit him. Anspach is a big man; he outweighs me by sixty pounds, I'd guess, and he's powerfully built. So I may have avoided him because I was afraid of what would happen to me.

Paul told me that a few weeks after Maria's death, Anspach moved in with Mrs. Rite, and that he'd sold two of the nine paintings in the group show. At his one-man show the following year he sold everything but the four biggest, proving his theory that the public was intent on hanging their pictures over the couch. Paul Remy saw the show and reported that Anspach's blue period was definitely over. The predominant hue was a shell pink, and the repeated image was a billowing parachute. This irritated me. Everything I heard about Anspach irritated me, but I couldn't keep myself from following his career, stung with frustration, anger, and envy at each new success.

In the spring Yvonne and I moved a few blocks south, where we had more room for the same money and a small walled-in yard, which soon became the rabbits' domain. They undertook amazing excavation projects, after which they spent hours cleaning their paws and sleeping in the sun, or in the shade of an ornamental beech. I kept my promise to Maria; I took good care of the rabbits for many years. They lived to be old by rabbit standards, nearly fourteen, and they died within a few weeks of each other, as secretly as they could, in a den they'd dug behind the shed I'd put up for Yvonne's gardening tools and our daughter's outdoor toys. After Yvonne finished school she moved from job to job for a few years until she settled in the ceramics division at the Brooklyn Museum. I took what work I could find and kept painting. Occasionally, always through friends, I got a few pictures in a group show, but nothing sold. Storage was a continual and vexing problem. My canvases got smaller and smaller.

Paul and I were offered a joint show at a new gallery on the edge of Tribeca, an unpromising location at best. The opening was not a fashionable scene: very cheap wine, plastic cups, a few plates strewn with wedges of rubbery cheese. The meager crowd of celebrants was made up largely of the artists' friends and relatives. The artists themselves, dressed in their best jeans and T-shirts, huddled together near the back, keeping up a pointless conversation in order to avoid overhearing any chance remarks about the paintings. I was naturally surprised when there appeared above the chattering heads of this inelegant crowd the expensively coiffed, unnaturally tan, and generally prosperous-looking head of Meyer Anspach.

"Slumming," Paul said to me when he spotted Anspach.

I smiled. David Hines, the gallery owner, had come to riveted attention and flashed Paul and me a look of triumph as he stepped out to welcome Anspach. Greta, a friend of Paul's who painted canvases that were too big for most gallery walls and who was, I knew, a great admirer of Anspach, set down her plastic cup on the drinks table and rubbed her eyes hard with her knuckles.

David was ushering Anspach past the paintings, which he scarcely glanced at, to the corner where Paul and I stood openmouthed. Anspach launched into a monologue about how we had all been poor painters together, poor artists in Brooklyn, doing our best work, because we were unknown and had only ourselves to please. This was during his blue period, a long time ago, those paintings were some of his favorites, a turning point, the suffering of that time had liberated him, he couldn't afford to buy back those paintings himself, that's how valuable they had become.

This was the first time I heard Anspach's litany about his blue period.

It was awful standing there, with David practically rubbing his hands together for glee and Paul emanating hostility, while Anspach went on and on about the brave comrade painters of long ago. Cheap wine, free love. *La vie de bohème*, I thought, only Maria didn't die of tuberculosis. I couldn't think of anything to say, or rather my thoughts came in such a rush I couldn't sort one out for delivery, but Paul came to my rescue by pointing out with quiet dignity that he and I still lived in Brooklyn. Then David got the idea of taking a photograph of Anspach, and Anspach said he'd come to see the pictures, which nobody believed, but we all encouraged him to have a look while David ran to his office for his camera. Paul and I stood there for what seemed a long time watching Anspach stand before each painting with his mouth pursed and his eyebrows slightly lifted, thinking God knows what. In spite of my valid personal reasons for despising him, I understood that I still admired Anspach as a painter, and I wanted to know, once and for all, what he saw when he looked at my work. Paul eased his way to the drinks table and tossed back a full glass of the red wine. David appeared with his camera, and after a brief conversation with Anspach, he called Paul and me over to flank Anspach in front of my painting titled *Welfare*. *Welfare* had an office building in the foreground, from the windows of which floated heavenward a dozen figures of bureaucrats in coats and ties, all wearing shiny black shoes that pointed down as they went up, resembling the wings of black crows. In David's photograph, two of these figures appear to be rising out of Anspach's head, another issues from one of Paul's ears. Anspach is smiling broadly, showing all his teeth. Paul looks diffident, and I look wide-eyed, surprised. When she saw this photo, Yvonne said, "You look like a sheep standing next to a wolf."

After the photograph session, Anspach stepped away from Paul and me and walked off with David, complaining that he had another important engagement. He did not so much as glance back at the door. He had appeared unexpectedly; now he disappeared in the same way. David returned to us with the bemused, wondering expression of one who has met up with a natural force and miraculously survived. He took from his coat pocket a sheet of red adhesive dots and went around the room carefully affixing them to the frames of various pictures. Anspach had bought four of mine and three of Paul's.

○

I don't attribute my modest success to Anspach, but I guess there are people who do. I attribute it to the paintings, to the quality of the work. I have to do that or I'd just give up. Still, there's always that nagging anxiety for any artist who actually begins to sell, that he's compromised something, that he's imitating the fashion. I'm not making a fortune, but I like selling a painting; I like the enthusiasm of the new owner, and I particularly like handing the check to Yvonne. It makes me lazy, though, and complacent. Some days I don't paint at all. I go downtown and check out the competition at the various galleries, drink a few espressos, talk with Paul, who isn't doing as well as I am but seems incapable of envy, of wishing me anything but good.

I sometimes wonder what van Gogh's paintings would have

been like if he had been unable to turn them out fast enough to satisfy an eager, approving public. Suppose he'd been treated, as Picasso was, as such a consummate master that any little scribble on a notepad was worth enough to buy the hospital where he died. Would that ear still have had to go?

○

Yesterday, as I walked out of a café in Chelsea, I ran straight into Anspach, who was coming in. I greeted him politely enough, I always do, but I haven't exchanged more than a few words with him since Maria's death. He pretends not to notice this, or perhaps he thinks it's the inevitable fate of the great artist to be tirelessly snubbed by his inferiors. He asked me to go back in with him, to have an espresso. "You know, I just sold a painting of yours I've had for five years," he said. "Your stock is going up."

It was chilly out, threatening rain, and I'd had an argument with Yvonne that morning. She'd told me that I was lazy, that all I did was sleep and drink coffee, which isn't true, but I had defended myself poorly by accusing her of being obsessed with work, money, getting ahead, and we'd parted heatedly, she to work, I to the café. I was not in the mood to have an espresso with Meyer Anspach. He looked prosperous, expansive, pleased with himself. His breath was warm on my face, and it smelled bitter, as if he'd been chewing some bitter root.

"It must be nice to have an eye for investments," I said. "It keeps you from having to buy anything you actually care about."

He laughed. "The only paintings I ever want to keep are my

own," he said. "I'm always trying to find a way around having to sell them."

"I get it," I said, trying to push past him. "Happy to be of service."

"Looks like I'm the one in service," he observed. "When I sell a painting of yours, it makes everything you do worth more."

This was an intolerable assertion. "Don't do me any favors, okay, Anspach?" I snapped. I had made it to the sidewalk. "I know perfectly well why you bought my paintings."

Anspach came out on the sidewalk with me. He looked eager for a fight. "And why is that?" he said. "What is your theory about that?"

"You want me to forgive you for Maria," I said. "But I never will."

"You forgive me!" he said. "I think it's the other way around."

"What are you talking about?" I said.

"You led her on, Jack, don't tell me you didn't. I was wearing her out and there you were, always ready with the coffee and the bunnies, and trying to feel her up on the subway."

"That's not true," I protested.

"She told me," he said. "She said you were in love with her, and I said, Okay, then go, but by the time she got around to making the decision, you were shut up with Yvonne. You closed her out and she gave up. That's why she went off the roof."

"If you'd treated her decently, she wouldn't have needed to turn to me," I said.

"But she did," he shot back. "You made her think she could, and she did. But you couldn't wait for her. You had to have

Yvonne. Well, that's fine, Jack. Maria wouldn't have made you happy. She was always depressed; she was always tired. She was never going to do better than waitressing, and sooner or later she was going to go off the roof. Yvonne is a hard worker, and she makes good money. You made the right choice."

"What a swine you are," I said.

He laughed. "You hate me to ease your own conscience," he said. "I was never fooled by you."

"Shut up," I said. I started walking away as fast as I could. I looked back over my shoulder and saw him standing there, smiling at me, as if we were the best of friends. "Shut up," I shouted, and two young women walking toward me paused in their conversation to look me over warily.

I went straight home, but it took nearly two hours. The subway was backed up; a train had caught fire between Fourteenth Street and Astor Place. I kept thinking of what Anspach had said, and it made my blood pressure soar. What a self-serving bastard, I thought. As crude as a caveman. I particularly hated his remark about feeling Maria up on the subway. I never did. I never would have. He would have done it, certainly, if he had been with her on those long, cold trips across the river, when she rested her head innocently against his arm; he would have taken advantage of that opportunity, so he assumed I had.

I tortured my memory for any recollection of having brushed carelessly against Maria's breasts. It made me anxious to reach in this way, after so many years, for Maria, and to discover that she was not alive in my memory. I couldn't see her face, remember her perfume. I kept having a vision of a skeleton, which was surely all Maria was now, of sitting on the subway next to a skeleton, and of rubbing my arm against the hard, flat blade of her breastbone.

I spent the rest of the morning trying to paint, but I got nowhere. I could see the painting of Maria's hands clutching the edge of a chute, and behind her, that ominous blue, Anspach's blue period, waiting to swallow her up forever. In the afternoon I picked up my daughter, Bridget, from her school, and we spent an hour at the corner library. When we got back home, Yvonne was there, standing at the kitchen counter, chopping something. Was she still mad at me from the morning? I went up beside her on the pretense of washing my hands. "Day okay?" I said.

"Not bad," she said, pleasantly enough. "How about you?"

I sat down at the table and started turning an apple from the fruit bowl round and round in my hands. "I ran into Meyer Anspach today," I said. "He said he sold one of my paintings."

"That's good," she said. She wasn't listening.

"He said Maria was in love with me. He said she thought I would wait for her to leave him, but I didn't, and that's why she killed herself."

Yvonne ran some water over her hands, then turned to me, drying them off with a towel. "Maria *was* in love with you," she said. "Are you saying you didn't know that?"

"Of course I didn't know that," I exclaimed. "I still don't know that."

Yvonne gave me a sad smile, such as she sometimes gives Bridget when she gets frustrated by math problems. Then she turned back to the sink. "How could you not have known that?" was all she said.

BEETHOVEN

"There's something Oriental about you," Philip said as I got out of the bed. This was in the sixties, before *Oriental* became the wrong word for Asian. As there is nothing remotely Asian about my appearance—I'm blond, blue-eyed—I concluded that Philip was referring to some perception he had about my character.

Philip was desperate, but I didn't know it yet. As I passed the easel and the paint truck on my way to the bathroom, I had to step over a stack of wallpaper books. This was Phil's latest innovation, painting on wallpaper samples. His friend Sid couldn't stop ridiculing him about the wallpaper, but Philip said Sid was just jealous. Though they appeared to dislike each other, Phil and Sid went out drinking regularly, and these evenings inevitably degenerated into bitter arguments that left Philip muttering until dawn. "Why do you go with him?" I asked once, to which he responded, with no hint of irony, "We're friends."

Phil was thirty; I was barely twenty. Everything about him

interested me. He was a man, not a boy; he was my introduction to the adult world I longed to enter, the real world, apart from college, which I'd left after one year, feeling the need to throw myself, if not upon thorns, at least upon something that would leave an impression. My parents, at first furious, then disappointed, had become resigned. I was required to visit them once a week, Sunday dinner, which was fine with me as I was eating poorly on my own and I enjoyed being idolized by my two younger brothers, who thought having a job and an apartment in the French Quarter was the absolute limit of sophistication. The fact that my job was waiting tables and my apartment a dark, roach-infested hole did not dampen their enthusiasm. After dinner they walked me to the bus stop, regaling me with stories about the trials of high school, which they made me promise never to tell my parents. When the bus came, I hugged them as if I was going off into a perilous adventure instead of just across town to meet Philip at a smoke-filled bar, to watch Philip work his way down one more rung of the ladder that stretched between desperation and despair.

I had begun to understand that my expectations of the world were unrealistic. I had imagined that, as a working single woman, I would attract the attention of a working single man, we would fall in love, and he would ask me to throw my lot in with him. Then I would leave my apartment and move into his. I wasn't picturing anything palatial; two rooms would have been acceptable, especially if there were windows. Philip's friend Sid lived with his girlfriend, Wendy, in two rooms. They had a tiny kitchen, a decent bath, and their bedroom opened onto a seedy patio. I assumed, for no reason, that the place had been Sid's first; that Wendy had come to him there. Later, of course, I found out the reverse was true. Now it strikes me that the most touching thing about myself in that period was this pathetic assumption, which must have come from reading fairy tales about princesses who, like rabbits, are always taken to their husbands' abodes for breeding purposes.

Philip's apartment constituted a serious obstacle to the maintenance of my supposition. We lived in the same run-down building. He was in the hot, stuffy attic at the top; I was at the bottom, near the narrow side alley where the perpetually overflowing garbage cans were lined up, lovingly attended by swarms of flies and the occasional rat. That was where I met Phil, struggling to drag his can out to the street. "I'll help you if you'll help me," I said. He started; he hadn't noticed my approach, and set his can down hard on the concrete, regarding me reproachfully. I stepped toward him into a thin slice of light that filtered through the wrought-iron gate from the street. "I don't need help," he said. Then, with the flicker of an apologetic smile—he'd been rude and now regretted it—he added, "But I'll help you when I come back."

After we got the garbage out, we went for coffee. We talked about what a jerk our landlord was, and I told Phil about my job. When we got back to the building, he asked me if I'd like to go up and see his paintings.

As I stepped across the threshold of Philip's attic apartment, I was conscious of entering a world where chaos was the rule; I glanced over my shoulder with a sense of bidding sweet reason goodbye. Phil leaned toward me as he pulled in the door, his expression mildly expectant, and I understood that he found nothing appalling in the broiling havoc of his domestic arrangements. The heat, freighted with turpentine fumes, assaulted me, as fierce as a roomful of tigers, but Philip brushed past me easily on his way to the air conditioner, an ancient, rusty metal box perched on a rotted sill, the wall beneath it permanently stained by a bloom of mildew. It came on with a gasp, a metallic groan, and settled down to a roar. Philip turned to me, gesturing to the machine. "It doesn't work too good," he said. "And it leaks on the guy's balcony downstairs, so he gets pissed off when I run it."

"Tell him to put a plant under it," I suggested.

"That's not a bad idea," he said. "That's actually a good idea."

I had taken one, then another step into the room and could now be said to be inside it. Because the windows were all dormers, the light lay in thick swaths, leaving the rest in deep shadow. It was twice as big as my apartment, but there was half as much space. As my eyes adjusted to the combination of brightness and gloom, I saw that there was a pattern to the disorder. Everything having to do with painting was in the light, with living in the shadow. There was also a difference in the quality of unidentifiable stuff lining the walls; some was in piles, some in neat stacks.

Philip disappeared behind a wooden screen draped with clothing. "Would you like something to drink?"

"Just water," I said, advancing another step. Near the screen was a card table with two metal folding chairs, which looked like a safe destination. The table was littered with newspapers, a plate of cigarette butts, a mug with coffee dregs in the bottom, and, incongruously, a bright orange satsuma. I took a seat facing the imposing easel in the brightest spot near the windows. There were canvases stacked about, only a few facing out. Their subjects were street scenes, buildings; there was a watercolor sketch of a stand of crape myrtles that looked highly competent to me. The unfinished canvas on the easel was a moody study of rooftops.

Philip appeared with two glasses of tap water. "No ice," he said. "The freezer doesn't work."

I took the glass, nodding toward the window. "Those are good," I said. To my relief, Philip showed no artistic prickliness or vanity, no skepticism about my critical expertise. "That's the view from the roof," he said of the work in progress. "When it gets too hot at night I go out there."

We sat and talked. After a while Philip put a record on the phonograph—it was the popular *After Bathing at Baxter's*—and I ate the satsuma. When the time came for me to leave for my shift, he escorted me downstairs to my apartment. On the staircase he rested a hand on my shoulder, in the shady patio he brushed my hair back with his fingertips, at the door he passed his arm around my waist and kissed me. It was a slow kiss, unlike any I had previously experienced, more tentative than exploratory, serious and courteous. "What time do you get off?" he said.

○

The venues for professional artists in our city were limited, and though I was not a student of the subject, I knew Philip didn't fit into any of them. He was not sufficiently avant-garde to show in the uptown galleries, where there were openings with wine and cheese and where the buyers were called "clients" and the paintings "investments." He wasn't bad enough to please the tourists who fluttered along with the pigeons on Jackson Square, having their portraits done in chalk or dickering over the prices of ghastly renditions of patios and bizarre bayou scenes in which the sky was an unnatural shade of green. He might have done commercial art; he had the technical skill, but he disdained such employment. He had learned his craft at the Neil McMurtry School of Art, a private academy run by the eponymous painter, who was occasionally commissioned to do large public works. I had whiled away many a Sunday morning in my childhood gazing up at four enormous toes which protruded from beneath the tablecloth at the Last Supper, part of an altar fresco executed by the esteemed McMurtry. The provenance of those toes was the subject of my earliest attempts at art appreciation. Were they attached to the Savior or the fellow next to him? My parents seemed to think McMurtry was the Louisiana equivalent of Caravaggio, but Philip said his work was overrated. Still, he recalled his time at the school with a romantic nostalgia. The sentence that began "When we were at McMurtry's . . ." generally ended with a sigh. He had met Sid at McMurtry's; the standoff that was their friendship had begun there, when they were both promising.

I knew, everyone knew at a glance, that Philip was very poor, but I believed, as I assumed he did, that this was a temporary condition. What money he had came from a small gallery on Decatur Street where the paintings were not so much displayed as crammed, often without frames, on every available inch of wall space. We were standing in this air-conditioned refuge one steaming afternoon in July when I first heard about Ingrid.

Philip was looking at a mawkish rendition of a sad clown,

a woman wearing a white costume with puffy black pom-poms for buttons, white face, red down-turned mouth, pointy white hat. The background was solid red, the same shade as the mouth. I've never liked anything about clowns, and this painting seemed designed to confirm my distaste. "This is Ingrid's," Phil said to the owner, Walter Stack, who looked up from a bin of canvases he was arranging according to size and said, "Sure."

"She still with Hazel?"

"Sure," Walter said. He returned his attention to the pictures.

Philip frowned at the frowning clown. "Hazel is all wrong for her," he said.

Walter abandoned the canvases and gave Philip a look I took to be sympathetic, though there was an edge of pity in it that made me anxious. He leaned a painting of a flowerpot—the paint was laid on like butter—against the counter and, nodding at the heavy cardboard portfolio Philip had pressed against his side, said, "What have you got for me? More wallpaper?"

Philip lifted the portfolio to the counter and opened it diffidently; his shoulders slumped forward in a way I had not seen before. He lacks confidence, I thought. "I have a few on the wallpaper," he said. "I'm finding that an interesting medium."

Walter began pulling out the various sheets, laying them side by side. "I sold the Beethoven," he said. "Do you have any more Beethovens?"

"Not this time," Philip said. "I could do another one."

"Do a few," Walter said. "I could sell maybe three or four."

"I can do that," Philip said. He turned to me, taking the small canvas he had wrapped in a pillowcase, which I held against my chest. He placed it carefully on the counter and pulled away the cloth. It was a painting of the rooftops outside his studio window. I thought it the best thing he had. Walter leaned over it skeptically, working his lips as if he were chewing something sour. "You see, I can't sell this," he said. "It could be anywhere. If you put the church in it, maybe. Tourists want stuff that says, 'This is New Orleans. I was there.' And they don't want anything dark. This is too dark."

Philip nodded, folding the pillowcase back over the canvas. I had the sense that this scene of crude rejection had taken place many times before, that he had, in fact, expected it, but it was new to me and it sickened me. "What about Beethoven?" I piped up, to my own surprise. "Beethoven doesn't say, 'This is New Orleans,' but you sold that."

Both men shifted their attention to me with the combination of interest and incredulity a cat might expect should it suddenly express an opinion. It pleased me to see that the balance in Philip's expression was weighted toward interest, whereas incredulity tipped the scales in Walter's alarmed and thorough regard. "Beethoven," he sputtered. "Beethoven says Beethoven. Everyone knows him, everyone loves him. He's like Einstein, or Marilyn Monroe." He dismissed me with a wave of his fleshy hand, adding to Philip, "Bring me Einstein or Marilyn and I'll sell the pants off of 'em."

As we staggered out into the blinding light on the street, Philip mumbled, "I can do a few more Beethovens."

"Who is Ingrid?" I asked.

○

Ingrid was Philip's former girlfriend, who had shared an apartment with him—not the current attic but a larger space in a building close to Jackson Square. This was convenient, as they were both doing portraits for tourists, pushing out their paint carts early in the morning, sharing the street with the horse carriages rather than risking the flood of refuse swirling across the sidewalks and the water curtains pouring off the balconies as the hose-bearing residents washed down their terrain in preparation for another sun-scorched day. It surprised me to learn that Philip had plied his art on the square, and he admitted that he had done it in desperation, and not for long, because he had no knack for pleasing tourists; they did not like his portraits or his person and haggled over the agreed-upon price or even refused to pay. "Ingrid is good at it," he said. "She has a real professional patter down. They eat it up."

"So she's still out there?"

"Sure," Philip says. "She has a license—the space right across from the Cabildo."

It didn't take much probing to learn that Ingrid, after two years of cohabitation, during which, Philip confessed, they had "fought all the time," had left Philip for a woman, a bartender at the Anchor, a sleazy establishment frequented by divers. This was Hazel, who was, in Philip's view, "all wrong" for Ingrid. He was perfectly candid in his assessment of this failed relationship and seemed relieved to talk about it. I felt hardly a twinge of jealousy, but I was curious to see this woman who had rejected Phil, and as it was easily done—I had only to alter my usual walk to the restaurant by a few blocks—the next morning I slipped from the alley into the cool shade of the Cabildo portico and, half hidden by a column, observed my predecessor in Phil's affections.

Or rather I observed her back, for she was facing the square, seated on a fold-up stool before her easel, her tray of pastels on a plastic cart next to her, one hand lazily conveying a cigarette back and forth between the tin ashtray on the shelf and her mouth. She wore a halter dress; her back, bony and tan, was bare. Her thick blond hair, poorly cut and none too clean, fell about her shoulders in clumps. On her easel, hung on the iron fence, propped against plastic cartons on the pavement near her feet, were samples of her wares, garish pastel portraits of famous personalities: Barbra Streisand, Einstein, Mick Jagger, Sophia Loren. Her specialty was a bizarre twinkling in the eye and a Mona Lisa serenity at the corners of the mouth. The backgrounds were all the same, a hasty scrawl of sky-blue chalk. As I watched, three tourists, a young man and two teenage girls, paused to examine Barbra Streisand. The artist ignored them for one last drag on the cigarette, then stubbed it out in the ashtray and addressed a remark to the group. I couldn't hear what she said, but she had shifted on her stool, and I could see her profile, which was all planes and angles, the cheekbones jutting over deep hollows, the nose bladelike, the chin a sharp wedge of bone. Her eyes, like those of her celebrities, had a chilling glitter to them. The tourists were not dismayed; in fact they lingered for some moments talking to her. The taller of the girls laughed twice; the young man appeared fascinated and ill at ease. Were they considering a portrait?

As I watched this scene, it occurred to me that Ingrid had no idea who I was and that there was no necessity for stealth. I stepped out from behind my column and sat down on the wide step next to an elderly black man who was tenderly unpacking a saxophone. This square was the most public of spaces, designed in order that strangers might eye one another at their leisure. The tourists had evidently asked for directions. Ingrid raised her arm and pointed toward the river. After a brief exchange, they walked away, the taller girl looking back with a shy wave as they went. I got up and wandered toward the square, pausing to smile upon a child emptying a bag of popcorn over the bobbing heads of an aggressive flock of pigeons. I turned back at the gate to the square, pretending an interest in the façade of the cathedral.

This put me very close to Ingrid, who was occupied in lighting another cigarette. Clearly a heavy smoker. She had the pinched skin around the nose, the bloodless lips. Probably a serious drinker too, judging by the glassiness of her eyes, the slight tremor in her hands. I pictured her kissing Philip, but it was difficult; she was so coarse, and she was several inches taller than he was. Two plumes of smoke issued from her nose. She's like some dreadful harpy, I thought. Waving the smoke away with one hand, she said clearly, "That's a nice skirt." Who was she talking to? I followed her eyes, which left the easel in front of her and turned with surprising force upon me, moving swiftly up from my skirt, over my waist, my breasts, to my astonished face. Her thin lips pulled back into a ghastly smile full of amusement at my discomposure, which was complete. I was so flummoxed I took a step backward and collided with the fence. "It fits you well," she added.

"Thanks," I said lamely, then recovered my footing and fled into the square. I didn't run, but I made directly for the opposite gate. I crossed the street quickly and threw myself down at the furthest table in the Café Du Monde.

So this was Ingrid.

○

Though I never actually saw Philip pick up a brush or pencil, in the next week his apartment sprouted a crop of Beethovens. There he was glowering from behind a chair, propped atop a stack of books, face-to-face with himself across the kitchen table. Phil had gotten a new supply of wallpaper sample books, which were scattered about the easel, splayed open to his various selections. Sometimes, when we were having coffee, he hauled one of these books into his lap and thumbed through it as we talked. The samples provided the atmosphere of each portrait, swirling paisley, pointillist, pastoral; Philip worked the designs right into his subject's coat sleeves and collar. But the face remained the same, instantly recognizable, the lunatic's thinning, unkempt hair, the overgrown brows, the pugilistic glare, the scowling lips, the brutish jaw, reminding his audience that this was the son of a drunken thug, the epitome of the Romantic, the scourge of the drawing room, the enemy of livery, the doom of the aristocracy, the death of manners.

"What is it you like about Beethoven?" I asked Phil one night when we were perched on the roof smoking cigarettes.

"The later quartets," he said. "Some of the symphonies. The Fifth, the Seventh, and the Ninth. Everybody likes those."

"No," I said. "Not the music. What is it about his face that you like?"

Phil considered my question. A mosquito landed on his

arm, and he brushed it off with the back of his hand. "It's easy to draw," he said.

As the summer burned on, I began to hate my job. I wasn't good at it, and my boss had noticed. I could never remember who had ordered what, and I could carry only two cups of coffee at a time, whereas Betty, who had worked there for years, could carry four. Once I set a tray of sandwiches and drinks down on a portable serving table and the whole thing tipped over onto the floor. I sometimes forgot to squirt the ersatz whipped cream on the bread pudding. If the diners were impatient or rude, as, because of my ineptitude, they often were, I became sullen. I worked for tips, we all did, and I wasn't doing very well.

One night, after a particularly miserable shift, during which I had knocked over a water glass while serving a bowl of gumbo to a miserly spinster, a regular who disliked me, Phil and I were sitting on the roof batting our hands at the humid, bug-laden air and drinking lukewarm beer. I complained about my job, about my boss and the harridans in the kitchen, about my dislike of the customers and my refusal to curry favor to get bigger tips. "It doesn't work anyway," I said. "They know I'm faking it, and they hate me for it."

"You should never fake it," he said. "If you can't be authentic doing whatever you're doing, you should do something else."

"I'm sure that's true," I said, though I wasn't sure at all. "But this is the job I have."

"You should read Sartre," he said. "Inauthenticity is a fatal disease. It kills you, one day at a time."

"So you think I should quit my job."

"The option is to take it seriously, engage in it, become it. While you're a waitress, become a waitress and nothing else."

This was the first and probably the only advice Phil ever gave me. I drank my beer and mulled it over. It didn't occur to me that Phil was unlikely to be the source of a recipe for successful living, and there was something in his formula—be engaged or be damned—that struck me as eminently reasonable. It still does. I had not, until that moment, identified myself simply as what I was, a waitress, and not a very good one. "It's not easy," I said, meaning my job.

"It's odd, isn't it?" Phil said. "You'd think it would be hard to fake it, but evidently it isn't." He held out his hand to the rooftops spread like open books all around us. "Sometimes when I sit out here," he said, "I think about what's really going on under every one of these roofs. That's the reason I like to paint this view, it's the lid of the problem. Look how close together they are. It wouldn't take much to burn the whole Quarter down; it's happened before." He extracted a cigarette from the pack in his shirt pocket, his lighter from his pants. "There's a flashpoint down there somewhere. Sometimes I think if I just dropped a match in the right place . . ." He lit the cigarette and exhaled a mouthful of smoke. I considered the vision, flames leaping from the windows, bursting through the rooftops, the screams of the desperate residents clinging to the rickety staircases, jumping from their wrought-iron balconies to the stone courtyards below.

"Then you'd see some authentic behavior," Phil concluded.

I tried taking Phil's advice, but my efforts to become a waitress only made me more disgusted with myself at the end of my shift, when I counted out the paltry bills in my apron pocket. Phil was poor too, but at least he was doing what he wanted to do. Except for the weekly visits to my family, I spent my spare time with him, and I was comfortable with him, as I had never been with the high-spirited college boys who were like thoughtless children spinning about in circles on the lawn, intent on disorienting their senses. Phil was frugal, modest, and he seemed to personally like me. When I arrived at his door, he was genuinely pleased by the sight of me. When we went out together, he was attentive; his eyes did not wander the room looking for something more interesting.

Walter Stack took five of the Beethovens, and in the next few weeks he sold three, which constituted a windfall for Philip. He was relieved to have the money; it was enough to pay his back rent and splurge on a bottle of wine, which we drank with the undercooked chicken cacciatore I whipped up in my gloomy kitchen. But something about this very limited success made Phil irritable and anxious. The fact that only three had sold was evidence that he need do no more, the craze was over. However, if the two remaining sold, as Walter expected they would, then he would be condemned to produce more, and the truth was, he was already sick of Beethoven. If he weren't careful he would be the guy who did Beethoven, which evidently struck him as an appalling fate.

"You don't have to do nothing but Beethoven," I protested. "Beethoven could be a sideline."

"I'm not a printmaker," Phil snapped. "I don't do editions. Every painting is different. It has to be. One leads to the other."

"Didn't Monet do a lot of water lilies?" I suggested hopefully. "And a series of Chartres Cathedral too. That was the same subject over and over."

Phil gave me a guarded look, which encouraged me. "Don't artists always do a lot of studies before they finish a big project? Maybe all the Beethovens are just the warm-up for the big one."

Phil drained his glass and poured out another full one. "That's ridiculous," he said.

"You like to paint the rooftops again and again," I persisted. "You've said yourself you don't tire of that."

"Well, that's the point, isn't it," he said. "Every time I look out the window, it's different. The light has changed; it's cloudy or clear, or raining. It's alive. Beethoven is dead."

That shut me up. I pushed the chicken around with my fork, sipped my wine, keeping my eyes down.

"And I'm not Monet." He said this resignedly, as if he didn't want to hurt my feelings.

I've never been much interested, as some women are, in trying to make something out of a man, in seeing his promise and compelling him to live up to it. I figured Phil was an artist and I wasn't, so he probably knew more about being one than I did. Everyone agreed that artists were, by their nature, difficult people. Maybe Phil's problem was that he wasn't difficult enough. He certainly wasn't egotistical, but he was stubborn. He did no more Beethovens that summer, and I said nothing more about it. He started doing self-portraits on the wallpaper samples, choosing some of the ugliest designs in the books, dark swirls and metallic stripes, paper for a child's room with romping pink elephants chasing beach balls. There was something sinister about these pictures. The likeness was good, but the eyes were wrong, unfocused and as lightless as a blind man's. As soon as they were done, Phil put them away in an old cardboard portfolio.

One evening when we were drinking beer with Sid and Wendy, Sid asked Phil what he was working on. "I'm in transition," Phil said. This answer struck me as unnecessarily vague; it wasn't as if Phil was not working. "He's doing self-portraits," I said. Sid stroked his well-kept beard, an irritating habit he had. "On the wallpaper," he said.

"Sure," Phil said. I started turning my coaster around on the table, waiting for Sid's pronouncement, which would provoke the usual argument, but Sid said nothing. When I looked up, he was signaling the waitress. "I'll buy a round," he said.

Phil drained the glass he'd been lingering over, his eyes fixed coldly on Sid's back. If Sid was buying, it meant we were in for a lecture.

"Thanks," I said to Wendy, who smiled.

"We're celebrating," she said. "We have good news."

Sid turned to us, his face radiating self-importance, but he left it to Wendy to satisfy our curiosity.

"Sid's taken a job at Dave Gravier's agency."

Even I had heard of the Gravier agency, which had produced the stylish Jazz and Crawfish festival posters that hung in upscale restaurants and shops all over town. "That's great," I said.

"It's just part-time," Sid said.

Phil fumbled a cigarette from his pack, his mouth fixed in a lopsided smile. The waitress arrived with our beers and a basket of tortilla chips, which Sid pulled closer to himself.

"So you sold out," Phil said softly.

Sid took a chip, bit it, chewed ruminatively as he rolled his eyes heavenward.

"And I knew you would," Phil added.

Sid swallowed his chip while Wendy and I exchanged speculative glances. "It's just part-time," Sid repeated.

"For now," Phil said.

"No, not just for now, Philip," Sid insisted. "I made it very clear to Dave that I am only willing to work for him three days a week because I'm planning a new series of paintings, large canvases, bigger than anything I've done before, and they'll be expensive to produce. So I'm willing to work part-time in order to increase my creative options, not, as you imply, to limit them, which means I'm not selling out. It's the opposite of selling out. I'm interested in doing important work, lasting work, and I can't do that by painting on grocery bags or feed sacks, or linoleum tiles I pull up from the kitchen floor. I need canvas and lots of it, big, sturdy frames, a lot of paint, and that stuff, as you may not know these days, my friend, because you are living in a dream, is expensive."

"Tell yourself that lie," Phil said, giving me a sidelong glance that presupposed my agreement.

"No," I said. "I see your point."

"An artist has to live in the real world," Sid informed us.

"Right," Phil snapped, stubbing his cigarette out in the ashtray. "And the real world has got to be a lot more comfortable than the one I'm living in. Which is what, would you say, some kind of antireality? A counterworld?"

"Money is freedom," Sid replied, ignoring, I thought, Phil's excellent point, which was that everything is reality—suffering, success, poverty, wealth, a rat-infested hovel or a mansion, it's all the same stuff. "And I need freedom to work. I'm not stymied. I'm not making excuses for myself, I'm not 'in transition,' I'm not afraid to work, and I'm not selling out to the establishment.

I'm grateful for the establishment. I need money, and now I won't have to worry about getting it and I can work in peace."

We were all quiet for a moment, listening to the fact that Sid had used Phil's expression "in transition" as the locus of his general contempt. I expected Phil to fire back forcefully, but he just swallowed half his beer, set the glass down carefully, and said, "You're clueless, Sid."

On the walk home, Phil was quiet. I chattered on about my visit with my parents, who were pressing me to go back to school, my dissatisfaction with my job, the roach problem in my kitchen, which boric acid wasn't touching. We trudged up the stairs to Phil's apartment, where the heat was packed in so tight it hurt to breathe. "For God's sake," I said, "turn on the air conditioner."

"It's broken," he said.

I leaned against the table feeling my pores flush out across my forehead and back. "When did that happen?"

"This morning." Phil had stripped his shirt off and was bending over a stack of wallpaper sample books.

"We can't stay here," I said. "Let's go to my place. At least I have a fan."

"You go," he said pleasantly. "There's something I need to do here."

"Are you going to paint?"

He gathered up a few of the sample books and carried them, weaving slightly, to the kitchen table. Then he pulled one of the jumbo garbage bags from the roll under the sink. "I'm getting rid of these," he said.

"Tonight?" I said. "Can't it wait until tomorrow?"

"No," he said.

I took up a dish towel and wiped it across my forehead. "It's too hot, Phil," I complained. "And I'm too tired."

"I don't need help," he said. "Just go to bed. I'll see you in the morning."

The thought of the comfortable bed in my clammy room off the alley was appealing. I rarely slept there because it was too narrow for both of us. The sheets were clean; the *tick-tick* of the oscillating fan always reminded me of sleeping at my grandmother's house when I was a child. "I'm going," I said.

Phil scarcely looked up from the bagging of the sample books. "Goodnight," he said. "Sleep well."

○

A few days later Phil and I stopped by Walter Stack's gallery to see if the remaining Beethovens had sold. Phil had nothing new to offer; as far as I could tell, he had stopped painting and he was running out of money. "What is this? You're coming here empty-handed?" Walter complained as soon as we were inside the door.

"I'm working," Phil replied. "I'll have something in a few days."

I scanned the crowded walls and spotted Beethoven scowling out beneath a charcoal rendering of Charlie Chaplin. The famous-dead area, I presumed.

"I was wondering if you'd sold any of the Beethovens," Phil asked. Something in Walter brought out a diffidence in Phil that made my stomach turn.

"I did sell one," Walter said. "A lady from Oregon who plays the piano." He turned to the cash register and punched the buttons until the drawer sprang open. I smiled at Phil; surely this was good news, but he was looking past me, out at the street, with an expression of such excitement mixed with fear that I turned to see what he saw. Two women were maneuvering an oversized portfolio through the heavy glass door. The one at the back was a tall, muscular redhead; the other, pushing in determinedly, was Ingrid.

"Look," Walter said. "Now here's a working artist. What have you got for me, beautiful?"

Ingrid's hawkish eyes raked the room, drawing a bead on Phil, who was pocketing the single bill Walter had pulled from the register. "Hi, Phil," she said, pleasantly enough.

"Hello, Ingrid," Phil replied. He stepped away from the counter, close to me, and I assumed he was about to introduce me. Having cleared the door, the two women passed us and lifted the portfolio to the counter. While Ingrid unfastened the ribbons along the side, her friend engaged Walter in light banter about another dealer. I craned my neck, hoping to get a look at Ingrid's offering, but the counter was narrow and she was forced to hold the cover upright, blocking my view. Walter looked down doubtfully at whatever was displayed, working his jaw. I turned to Phil, thinking he must be as curious as I was.

He was leaning away from me, his weight all on one leg, his shoulders oddly hunched, and as I watched, he raised one hand and pressed the knuckles lightly against his lips. The color had drained from his face, and he swayed as if he might collapse, yet there was a vibration of energy around him, a kind of heat. His dark eyes were fixed with a febrile intensity on Ingrid's back, bathing her with such a combination of sweetness, longing, and terror that I thought she must feel it. Or hear it. Indeed, his expression aroused in me sensations similar to those evoked by the commencement of certain melancholy music: a shiver along the spine, the silencing of the inner colloquy, all the senses arrested by an unwelcome yet irresistible revelation of suffering.

Ingrid didn't feel it. She was engaged in bargaining, which was pointless, as Walter took everything on consignment and set the prices himself. Her friend brought up the other dealer again, suggesting that he would make a better offer, and Walter, obligingly, pretended outrage. Phil's hand had dropped to his side, but otherwise he didn't move. He was so rapt in his contemplation of Ingrid, so unconscious of everything else, including me, that when I touched his arm it startled him and he gripped my hand tightly. "Phil," I said. "Let's go now," and I led him, unprotesting, into the street. The group at the counter, absorbed in their transactions, took no notice of our departure.

Outside, the light and heat assailed us, and we clung to each other until we reached the covered sidewalk on Decatur Street. "Do you want to go for a coffee?" I asked, and Phil nodded. His eyes were wet, but his color had returned and he gave me a weak, convalescent smile. "We'll go inside," he said. "It will be cool in there."

That night we brought my fan up to Phil's apartment, but it was still too hot to sleep. I tossed and turned. Phil left my side without speaking and climbed out the window to smoke a cigarette on the roof. Anxiety was my bedfellow, a many-headed hydra snapping at me with undisguised fury. My future unfolded before me, a black hole of thankless, boring work. What are you going to do? I asked myself repeatedly, urgently. At length I got up and went to the kitchen. The moon was full; there was a shaft of creamy white across the ugly floor, lighting

my way to the refrigerator. I poured a glass of water and sat
naked at the kitchen table, looking about in a panic. There was
more room without the wallpaper books, and Phil had cleared
off his easel, which struck me as suspicious and portentous.
What would happen next? What was Phil going to paint on
now? Doubtless Sid was right and Phil had been using the wallpaper not for the interesting creative possibilities it afforded but
because the books were free and he was too poor to buy canvas,
or even cheap board. My eyes rested on the mottled linoleum at
my feet. Would Phil take Sid's suggestion and start prying the
tiles up off the floor?

This thought cast me down very low. I had left school
because I wanted to live in the real world, and now I was doing
just that and I didn't like it at all. My childish fantasy of an
untroubled and companionable relationship with a man who
valued me was clearly the worst sort of naïveté, though oddly
enough I'd gotten what I wanted. Phil was easy, kind, and I did
not doubt that he cared for me. But in the gallery that day I had
seen him unmanned by an unrequited and impossible passion
for a woman who cared nothing for him. It wasn't his weakness that had shocked me; it was the invincibility of his ardor,
which clearly could brook no dissembling, even in public, even
in front of me. To be either the subject or the object of such a
humiliating, destructive force was not a condition I could ever
tolerate. "There's just no future in it," I said to myself, purposefully vague about the pronoun reference. Was "it" my life with
Phil? Or was "it" the whole catastrophic enterprise of romantic
love?

Eventually Phil climbed back in the window and found
me there, naked, clutching my water glass and staring into the

blackness between us. He went to the refrigerator and looked inside. "I've got a cold beer we could split," he said.

"That sounds good," I said.

He brought the beer to the table and sat down across from me, opening the can with a can opener. I finished my water and held out the glass for my share.

"You can't sleep," Phil observed.

"It's too hot," I said.

"Do you want to go out?"

"No."

"Okay," Phil said. We sipped our beer.

"I just don't see what you're going to do now," I said.

"What do you mean?"

"Well, with the self-portraits, and no more wallpaper and no more Beethoven. I don't see how you'll make a living."

"I'll think of something," he said.

"Maybe Sid has the right idea. You could get some part-time work. That might take the pressure off."

He smiled. "I don't want to take the pressure off," he said. "The pressure is part of it."

"Part of what?" I said. "Being miserable?"

"I'm not miserable."

I considered this.

"But you are," he said.

"I hate my job," I said.

"Then you should quit."

"And do what?"

For answer, Phil finished his beer, got up, and took the empty can to the sink. He came behind me and began rubbing my shoulders. "You're very tense," he said.

I let myself go limp beneath his hands. "I know," I said. He worked my neck between his fingers and his palm, up and down until I let my head fall back against his chest. He leaned down to kiss me languidly. "Is it too hot to do this?" he asked, sliding his hand around my back and over my breast.

"No," I said. "I want to." Then, as I followed him to the rumpled mattress, I felt, in spite of everything, of the heat, of my disillusionment and frustration, of my fear of the future, in which, we both knew, Phil would no longer figure, a perverse but unmistakable throb of dark desire.

THE UNFINISHED NOVEL

"Rita's back," Malcolm said. We were drinking iced coffee at a café on Esplanade, watching the traffic ooze through the heat haze. "She's living near here."

Rita. My God, Rita. She came at me from the past, from that first winter in Vermont, her thin woolen coat blowing open over a short cotton skirt, bare legs, picking her way across a snowbank in her high-heeled, open-toed shoes. She won't last a year here, I thought then, and I was right.

"Is she alone?" I asked.

"Oh, I think so. She's changed a lot. I didn't recognize her."

"In what way?"

"She's gained a lot of weight. She looks pasty, not healthy."

This surprised me. Rita had been thin, willowy, long limbs, big hands, boyish hips.

"What's she doing?"

"It's hard to tell. She was pretty vague. She wanted me to believe she was involved in some top-secret mission for the Pueblo Indians."

"Wow," I said. The waiter appeared with our check, which I snatched away from Malcolm.

"Thanks," he said.

"My pleasure."

"You haven't changed," he observed.

I come back to New Orleans every few years and stay only long enough to convince myself it's time to leave, which takes between two weeks and three months. Whenever I return, my friends are always quick to observe that I haven't changed, which I take to mean I still have most of my hair. Malcolm, who once sported a full crop of coarse black thatch, has lost most of his, save a monkish tonsure he has the good sense to trim close. He has a well-kept beard, compensation for what's gone on top, and he's developed the beard-stroking habit, which annoys me. As a young man he was dissolute, a womanizer, heavy drinker, chain smoker, not promising, but to everyone's surprise, including his own, he prospered. He has a successful furniture business, a devoted wife, several children, an expensive car, and a large, tastefully appointed house near City Park. Having never read a novel, he has no opinion about the ones I've written, and since he has no curiosity about my private life, his success has allowed us to remain friends. He neither resents nor envies me.

I paid the bill while Malcolm swatted at a fly grazing on the remains of his brioche. "She asked about you," he said.

"What did she want to know?"

"If I was in touch with you. If I knew where you were."

"I hope you didn't tell her."

"Well, I did. But you're bound to run into her sooner or later, so it doesn't matter. If women want to find you, they always know how to go about it."

"How much weight would you say she's gained?" I asked.

"A lot." Malcolm laughed. "But she still has beautiful hair."

Not a week passed before I walked into the post office and got in line behind Rita Richard. I didn't recognize her. What I saw was the wide back of an overweight woman, not a sight to provoke my interest, but there was something about this one that seemed familiar. Her curling, golden hair resisted the confines of an oversized clip. A cheap flowered blouse, stretched tight across her shoulders, was tucked haphazardly into the straining waistband of a differently flowered, voluminous skirt. Her ankles bulged around the thin straps of cruel, high-heeled sandals. Perhaps it was the shoes. Did some molecule floating around in my brain remember caressing those ankles, long ago, when there was a tantalizing space between the strap and the smooth bone of the instep? Whatever it was, I knew it was Rita, and my first instinct—if only I had succeeded in following it—was flight.

I took a few cautious steps backward; at the same moment the line moved forward and a teenager who had just come in, his view obscured by the large package he intended to entrust to the U.S. mail, collided with me. The ensuing apologies, excuses, and reassurances naturally engaged the attention of everyone in the place. As I helped the boy regain control of his package, I was aware that Rita had turned to see what the fuss was about, that she had recognized me, and that she was waiting for the matter to be settled, which, no matter how I tried to extend it, was quickly accomplished. The boy went ahead; Rita stepped behind, smiling at me confidently. I was at pains to disguise a complex of emotions: consternation, shock, anxiety, and through it all the pang of recognition—this unappealing creature was certainly Rita, but how altered!

"Hello, Maxwell," Rita said. "I heard you were in town."

"Rita?" I said. "Is it really you? I thought you'd gone out West and become a stranger."

She laughed at this weak joke, and it was Rita's laugh, knowing, intimate, flirtatious. "I did," she said. "But now I'm back."

"How amazing to run into you," I faltered.

"Not really," she said. "It's a small town. Sooner or later we all come back."

"But to stay? Are you here to stay?"

"Oh, yes. I won't be leaving again. What about you?"

"It's just a visit for me."

"Of course. You're too famous to live here."

This was the kind of dismissive remark I get a lot in my hometown. I'm not famous by any means, but I have a small reputation, or so I flatter myself, and I am able to live in modest comfort on the proceeds of my books. "Oh, I'm not famous," I said, but Rita wasn't interested in my answer. From somewhere within her skirt she had produced a purse, much too small for a woman her size, and she proceeded to dig in it, talking all the while, until she pulled out a battered checkbook from which she tore off a page. "I live a few blocks from here, on St. Ann," she said. "Here's the address. I'd like to talk to you about something—it's a sort of proposition." Here she gave me her raised-eyebrows, compressed-lips expression, suggesting the stifling of a naughty thought. "A business proposition. Will you come see me? Here's the address."

She held out the paper, which I eyed warily. "It's a deposit slip," she said. "It has my address on it. If you don't want to come see me, you can just make a deposit."

And be done with it, I thought. If only it were that simple. I took the flimsy paper; I couldn't see any way not to.

"It's not far from here," she said again.

"I suppose I could come by," I said.

She brought her hand up to her neck, pulling her fingers through the curls that were loose there, her light eyes fixed on me. It was a gesture so familiar and, in the new context, so perverse, it unsettled my reason. I had the sense that this woman was an impostor, that she had studied Rita, the real Rita, who was at that moment perfectly alive in my memory, as palpable as my own tongue in my mouth.

"How about tomorrow?" she said.

"No, I've got appointments all day." This was in fact true.

"Thursday?" Now she was amused, watching me squirm. I decided to limit her pleasure and my own suffering. "Thursday would be fine," I said. "In the afternoon, around three."

"I'll be there," she said.

Yes, I thought. I don't doubt you are there most of the time. "I'll see you then," I said, consulting my watch.

She looked concerned. "Don't you want to mail your letter, Maxwell?"

I gestured at the line, which was now down to one. Rita stepped aside, suggesting that she would generously yield her place to my urgent necessity, but I had only one thought and that was to terminate this interview. "I'll do it later," I said, and I fled like one pursued. Indeed, Rita did pursue me. As I was pulling out of the parking lot, I saw her standing at the plate-glass window, watching me stolidly as I drove away.

Among the dark strands of my dismay at having been so smoothly apprehended by Rita was a glittering thread of

vindicated spite, for she had once made me very unhappy. I
gloated over the details of her appearance, her run-down shoes,
the missing top button of her blouse, her general air of shab-
biness, failure. I had done well, and Rita decidedly had not.
Who would have predicted such an outcome twenty years ago,
on a certain freezing night in Vermont, when I shadowed Rita
along a windswept alley, desperate to stop her from going in at
a certain door?

I'd first met Rita in college. She was a year behind me;
perhaps we had a class together, but she was not part of my
group. She passed as an exotic when she got to Vermont, but
in our sultry, provincial hometown she was just another tall,
pretty waitress who slept around, drank too much, and never
stopped smoking. She was rumored to write poetry, and once,
at an open reading, I'd seen her read half a dozen perfectly for-
gettable lines, pausing to take a drag on a cigarette midway
through. I had a girlfriend, the winsome Rachel Paige, who
was entirely devoted to me and to my burning ambition to leave
New Orleans and become a writer. It wasn't until I got my
acceptance to the graduate writing program in Vermont that
Rachel realized she had courteously helped me right out of her
life, but to her credit, she was not resentful. Perhaps by then she
was sick of me.

I spent the summer before I left working as a bartender and
pointing out to anyone in earshot that I couldn't wait to leave
town. My conversation was tiresome. I hated the whole gestalt
of the southern storyteller, the homespun crank who populated
his stories with characters named Joleen, Angina, and Bubba-
Joe-Henry, all of whom drove pickup trucks, drank Dixie beer,

and knew everything there was to know about pigs. I was eager to shrug off my southernness like a reptile's skin and ascend to the realms of Transcendental bliss. I intoxicated myself reading Emerson and Thoreau; I wanted what they had, all of it, the self-reliance, the days as gods, the different drummer, the excitement about ideas, the passionate love of nature, of writing, and of books. I wanted to write with the force Thoreau, reading Aeschylus, called "naked speech, the standing aside of words to make room for thoughts." I affirmed with Emerson the maxim that "to think is to act." Southerners, in my view, substituted stories for ideas, and it was to me like offering marshmallow to a starving tiger. I was sick of it.

Of course, when I got to Vermont, I settled down and wrote stories like everyone else. Even if "naked speech" had been within my capabilities, it wasn't likely to sell, and I was, above all, a realist about the requirements of the market. But my characters had names like Winston and Edna, they worked at bookstores, they concerned themselves with ethical questions. By my second year their inquiries were impeded by blizzards or locals who spoke in monosyllables. I let my beard grow out, discovered the virtues of flannel shirts, wool socks, lined rubber boots. My accent, never strong, faded; my hands were chapped. I enjoyed the not inconsequential pleasures of chopping wood. I had left the South behind, purposefully and finally, and I rejoiced in my new identity.

This was why I experienced a shudder down to my duck boots when, on the first day of the spring semester—which was a long, long way from spring—I walked into my workshop classroom to find Rita Richard bent over in her chair, trying to dry her feet with a handkerchief. She looked up at me through a flutter of thickly painted eyelashes and said, "Are you surprised to see me, Maxwell?"

I was so thoroughly taken aback that my response was an unchivalrous "What are you doing here?"

Rita finished her foot care and pulled her shoes back on with a grimace. Brendan Graves, with whom I drank beer most weekends, shot me a look of exaggerated inquiry. Did I know this singular creature? "I'm in the program," Rita said. "I applied too late for fall, so they let me come in now."

"I didn't know you wrote," I said.

"Well, I don't talk about it. But I do."

Our conversation was interrupted by the arrival of our professor, a writer of small reputation who is probably still laboring in the merciless groves of academe. I excused myself and took my seat across the table from Rita, next to Brendan, who quickly wrote, *Who is she??* on his notebook and pushed it toward me.

From New Orleans, I wrote back. *An acquaintance, no more.*

Before the professor had finished the roll call, everyone in the class had this information. Rita's southern shtick was on full display. When he called her name, she lifted her palm and pulled her head back as if he'd offered her something distasteful. "It's Ree-shard," she said. He nodded, tried it, came out with "Ray-chard," and she corrected him, sweetly, patiently, until he got it right. "I'm from New Orleans," she said. "That's how we say it there, but only if it's your family name."

He paused, giving her a long look over the top of his reading glasses. He was a handsome man, weathered, lots of curly gray hair, tweedy jacket over a sweater embroidered with cat fur. "New Orleans," he said. "You're a long way from home."

"I am just a little anxious about the snow," she said with a chirpy insouciance that sent a chuckle rippling around the table. "I wish I could just grow a beard, like Maxwell has." All eyes turned briefly upon me. In that moment, I hated Rita.

"That's right," the professor said. "You're from New Orleans too, aren't you, Max? I'd forgotten. And you two know each other?"

"Yes," Rita said. "Maxwell and I go way back."

"It's Max, Rita," I said. "Not Maxwell. Just Max."

Rita laughed. "Will I have to change my name too?"

"Well," the professor said, "you'll have to work that out with Max." He cast me the nervous smile of a man who avoids even the outskirts of a quarrel and continued the roll call.

That spring, every Tuesday from four until six-thirty, I sat across the table from Rita in a steadily intensifying state of mystification. After the first day my expectations were naturally minimal. I was prepared to spend my time in class alternating between outrage and humiliation. I was determined to keep my distance from her. The first discussions in these venues are necessarily tentative and anxious, the air laden with portentous questions: Is the professor competent, hostile, does someone talk too much or not at all, is there a peer whose writing one actively despises, do we take a break, is coffee allowed, is the room over- or underheated?

There were eight of us, so it was not until the fifth meeting that we had each exhibited our wares and established a pecking order. Rita's turn came up at the end of the first rotation, by which time most of us had been treated to her personal critique. She invariably began with some specious disclaimer: "Now I know this isn't mine, but if it were," or "I may have gotten too involved in this story," after which she laid out her argument with the confidence of a general presenting a foolproof strategy for battle. Her recommendations were original and intuitive; she was able to enter into the writer's intentions with an open, inquisitive mind. My initial relief at not having to take issue with her every week gave way to admiration; she really had the requisite knack. It was clear that she read every piece several times. When we passed in the manuscripts to the author at the end of the class, I noticed that hers were copiously annotated, her comments neatly printed in the margins in purple ink.

By the time my own story came up for review, I was as eager to hear Rita's reaction as the professor's. Of course, though I had found her to be critically acute about the efforts of our peers, I didn't think Rita's remarks about my work were particularly useful. She made a few suggestions for structural changes that, if not improvements, presented provocative options. She observed, as others have over the years, that my female characters were shallow, lacking complexity and dimension. She said this with a laugh that made the professor inquire whether, in her opinion, this vacuity presented a serious problem. "No," she said. "I don't think it matters at all. In fact, I think it's intentional, at least I hope it is." Here she gave me her faux-naïf smile. "It mirrors forth the myopia of the narrator, doesn't it?"

Twenty years have passed and I can reproduce that sentence exactly as I heard it. I can still feel the soft osculation of Rita's voice, the full two syllables she gave to the word *mirrors* as she swept back the ever-encroaching mass of her curls and raised her eyes to mine. Ostensibly she was giving me credit for having created a contemptible persona, but the coolness of her eyes on my suddenly burning cheeks left me with the sensation of having been rendered pitifully transparent. I looked away, at my own hands, at the table, at the professor, who studied the open pages of my manuscript, compressing his lips to contain a smile. Just you wait, I thought.

That very evening I carried to my chilly apartment the first thirty pages of Rita's work in progress, a novel or, as she put it, "Maybe a novel?"

I made a cup of coffee and sat down at the desk, uncapping my red pen, intent on vengeance. An hour later I laid the pen across the unmarked pages and rested my head in my hands.

○

St. Ann is a long street that runs from the French Quarter all the way to Bayou St. John. On either end, near the river and near the park, it's respectable enough, but there is a stretch that curves around a derelict canning factory that is decidedly unsavory. As I followed the numbers descending into this area, I was increasingly conscious of my car, a late-model Volvo, which announced to the loitering residents the status of its owner as an alien, possibly a landlord. Because I had to keep one eye out for the house numbers and the other on the minefield of potholes in the road, some so deep the wheel sank in to the hubcap, my progress was slow. The houses were all rickety structures, single or double shotguns, raised on chunky brick piers, sagging in various directions, all in need of paint. Some of the porches were packed with junk; a few sported melancholy potted plants or plastic garden chairs. The sidewalk undulated over tree roots, cracked in places and sprouting fierce patches of weeds. Erosion had worn away the edges of the road, leaving a ditch in which all parking was on an angle.

I spotted the correct number, four iron digits nailed into the porch column of a house as shabby as its neighbors, and guided the Volvo cautiously into the ditch. A worn-out man in an undershirt, sitting on the front step of the neighboring house, got up and went inside. From a narrow alley between his house and Rita's, a cat came stealthily toward my car. I got out and stood gazing at the house front. Rita's porch was bare. One side was obscured and softened by the bright green curtain of a plantain tree, and there was a vine curling in the rails, some adventitious weed intent on destruction. On a neighboring porch a huddle of teenagers shouted at one another in their secret language, doubtless making plans to flatten my tires or scratch the paint with a broken bottle, such as the one glinting in the ditch at my feet. I pressed the remote device in my pocket, and the car emitted a brief yelp and click as the locks closed down. The cat let out a screech, which sounded dire, though it didn't move from its station on the sidewalk. I like cats, so I walked around the car to speak to this one. As I approached the animal slunk away, but I determined that it was in poor condition, spectrally thin, with a sparse coat and ears so infected by mites they were malformed.

I'd had the air conditioning on in the car, and the heat enveloped me, closing over my face like a hot iron mask, so severe and sudden I gasped for breath. I could see that Rita's door was open behind the screen, which meant there was no air conditioning. I scanned the side for a window unit—maybe she cooled only one room—but there was nothing. How does any-one live in this heat? I thought. Then, from under Rita's porch, from the plantain's grove of stems, from beneath a dust-clad azalea in the neighbor's yard, from the alley of the house next door, from the open window of the rusted Dodge Dart corrod-ing in the ditch behind my Volvo, there issued a legion of cats.

They didn't press me, they didn't even approach, but their intention was clearly to appraise me, to determine whether I might be, in any sense, a potential source of food. Their collec-tive gaze was chilling. If our respective sizes had been reversed, I would have stood in fear for my life. I looked from one to another; they were uniformly thin and scant of coat; every one of them had the encrusted, deformed ears that denote severe infection. I resisted an impulse to get back in the car, drive to the nearest vet, and purchase a gallon of ear-mite cream and a dozen Havahart traps. Hostility toward the human residents of this street animated me. Of course they were all poor, but couldn't they see this suffering in their midst and organize to do something about it? Wasn't there one among them who sym-pathized with these luckless scavengers, which surely provided them the service of keeping their vicinity rat-free?

Rita, for example. I cast an accusing eye at her door. She was standing there in the semidarkness behind the screen, look-ing back at me. She's certainly getting enough to eat, I thought, and I scowled at her as she pushed the door open and stepped out into the light.

"Hello, Maxwell," she said. "I thought you might not come."

At the sound of the screen door, the cats scattered. "Some-thing should be done about these cats," I said, going up the cement steps to her porch. "They've all got ear infections."

"They're feral cats," she observed. "You could never catch them."

"At least the SPCA could be notified," I insisted. "The cats in Rome are in better shape than these."

"Are they?" Rita said, without interest.

I was about to extol the virtues of the Roman cat association, which cares for the feline populations of various public areas, but before I began I looked at Rita, who so impossibly filled the doorway, and the shock of her transformation struck me anew. I searched for some dissembling remark. "It's very hot," I said.

"It's a little better inside." She stepped back, opening the screen door, and I looked past her into the house. When my eyes adjusted to the gloom, I realized I was looking into her bedroom. I was fixed between curiosity and foreboding, and stymied by the unsettling feeling of having done this before. It wasn't déjà vu, it was an actual memory: Rita, the real Rita, with her slender wrists and light, penetrating eyes, opening another door while I hesitated, stamping snow from my boots. "For God's sake, Maxwell," she was saying. "Come on in. You know you're dying to." As I had then, I summoned my courage and stepped inside. Rita came in behind me, pausing to latch the screen. "Go on through to the kitchen," she said. "There's a fan in there."

The shotgun house, so named because a rifle fired at the front door can hit a target, presumably fleeing for his life, on the back porch, is a singularly ungracious yet practical architectural development. The rooms are lined up with central doors opening from one to the other; the kitchen is always at the back. They are composed of from two to six rooms; most have four; Rita had three. My impression of the place, as I made for the promised fan, was of disorder and penury. The bed was a double—Rita would need the space—pushed into a corner, gray sheets rumpled, the single pillow afloat near the center. There was a chipped table pushed up against the metal footboard, on which a small television perched amid heterogeneous stacks that included books, dishes, and bags of chips. The next room was furnished with tables, though none for dining. They were pushed into the four corners and piled with more junk. Some of it was pottery of a brickish hue, much of it broken. As in the front room, the shades were drawn, the air stifling. There wasn't a chair in sight.

The kitchen, while not welcoming, was a relief. A ceiling fan whirred overhead, churning the oppressive air. The back door was open, letting in a block of softened light. This room had wooden shutters, which were partly opened and latched, admitting the light in muted slashes. The furnishings were minimal, the appliances venerable, the countertops covered in chipped red linoleum, as was the floor; everything was clear and clean. In the center of the room a porcelain-topped table and two sturdy white chairs suggested the possibility of a tête-à-tête.

Rita followed me, taking down two plastic glasses from a shelf as I sat at the table. "Would you like some lemonade?" she asked.

"I would, yes," I said. She opened the refrigerator, and I had a view of the largely empty shelves. She took out a plastic pitcher and set it on the table with the glasses. "So, Maxwell, how long will you be in town?" she said.

"Not long," I replied. "It's too hot."

She poured out two glasses of lemonade—it was freshly made, not from a can—pulled out the other chair, and sat down across from me. "Sorry, I don't have any ice," she said.

I took a swallow from the glass. It was good, not too sweet. Rita watched me, but I wasn't able to meet her eyes. I looked instead at her thick fingers wrapped around the glass. The nails were neatly filed, painted a babyish pink.

"So I heard you were married," she said, "but I don't see any ring."

"I was," I said. "It didn't work out."

"Any children?"

"No."

"Me neither," she said wistfully, which surprised me, as I had not imagined for one minute that Rita wanted children. I made no response, and a brief, studied silence fell between us. "So you're a famous writer now," she said.

"I wouldn't say I was famous."

"Well, you are around here."

I shrugged. "What about you?" I said. "What are you doing?"

"Oh," she said. She brushed her hair back in the familiar gesture that forced me to look at her face, that puzzling combination of Rita and not-Rita. "I'm still writing. I've almost finished the novel. It's over a thousand pages, though. I guess I'll have to cut it to get it published."

So that was it, I thought, the "business proposition." I was to help her find a publisher for a book she had been writing for twenty years.

"I work so slowly," she said. I did a quick mental calculation: less than fifty pages a year. "I've been busy with other things, of course. And my health has not been good."

"But you're nearly done," I said. "That's great."

Rita took a sip of her lemonade, allowing another heavy pause between us. "Do you think so, Maxwell?" she said. "Do you really think it would be great if I finished my novel?"

It was always games with her, I thought, and I was sick of playing already. There was a time when she could have baited me in this way for an hour or so and I would have gone along, reassuring her of my good intentions toward her, driven by lust to excessive civility, but those days were gone. What I really wanted now was to get as far away from her as I could. "What is it you want from me, Rita?" I said.

"I want to show you something."

"The novel," I said, keeping my voice interest-free.

She laughed. "No, Maxwell, not the novel. It's not finished yet." She pushed her chair back noisily and stood up, leaning on the table with the care of someone who expects to suffer in the process. I noticed a hectic flush rising from the fold of her neck to her cheeks, and a rough exhalation escaped her, not a groan but harsher than a sigh. "It's in here," she said, leading the way to the darkened, cluttered room. I followed her, consoling myself with the observation that this brought me closer to the street. Rita switched on a floor lamp, which shed a dull light over a table laden with pottery. She took up a piece and held it out to me. "It's this," she said.

I accepted it, as I was evidently intended to, and turned it over in my hands. It was a section of a bowl, poorly made of hard, red clay, the rim imprinted with uneven scoring, such as might be made with a stick. The clay was of uneven thickness, but smooth and cool to the touch. There was something about it, a lack of artifice, a naïveté that was not without charm. "What is it?" I asked.

"It's a thousand years old," Rita said, taking it from me. She took up another piece, a flat disk, chipped at one corner, scored at the edges like the other. "Look at this one."

"Really?" I said. "How do you come by it?"

She smiled her it's-a-secret smile, her wouldn't-you-like-to-know smile, which had always infuriated me. "I'm the agent for it," she said. "It's extremely valuable. This stuff here is worth a million dollars, and there's more to be had when I go back to New Mexico."

I laid the disk on the table, careful to place it well away from the edge. So Rita, lovely Rita, hadn't just gained a lot of weight, she'd also lost her mind. Did she really think I would believe a million dollars' worth of antiquities had somehow made its way through history to a rickety table in this mildewed shack in the City That Care Forgot? Actually one could hardly find a better place to hide it—her neighbors were doubtless criminals, but they weren't likely to steal a bunch of broken crockery. I ransacked my brain for something to say, something that would release me from this suffocating room.

Rita picked up another bit, a platelike piece, and raised it toward the lamp. "This is my favorite," she said.

I was struck by the alteration in her profile, which had once been very fine, though she'd always had a weak chin. Now she had no chin. Malcolm was right: Her skin was sallow, unhealthy; the crescents beneath her eyes looked bruised. Time had gone hard on her, worn her down, *her*, who had been so rebellious, so uncompromising. As she set the plate back among the curious rubble, my irritation turned to sadness, and I resigned myself to accepting whatever story she had to tell. It wouldn't be true, any of it, but it would be revealing. "Where did you get this stuff, Rita?"

"From the Zuni," she said. "I was out there with them for a long time. They're a matriarchal culture, you know, they don't much trust men. I got pretty involved, trying to help them deal with the Bureau. I'm the only white woman they trust. The museums are wild to buy this stuff, but the council is afraid they'll get cheated, so I agreed to handle it for them."

"Is that where you went when you left Vermont?"

"No," she said. "Not right away." She turned to me with an absurdly coquettish smile that suggested she detected the subtext of my question—when you left me in Vermont, when you ran away from me.

"Danny and I went to Alaska first. You can make a lot of money up there. We worked in a fish canning factory."

"Good lord," I said. "I hope you finally bought a pair of practical shoes."

She laughed. "I did. I had to. It was very strange up there. It's light all the time. The factory runs in twelve-hour shifts, everyone drinks a lot of coffee. In an odd way I liked it, but maybe it was because Danny was happy there." She waved her hand across the room. "It's all in there," she said, "in the novel."

I followed her gesture through the gloom to a table strewn with debris: piles of audiotapes, a Walkman, envelopes stuffed with paper, several bags of chips—did she live on potato chips?—crumpled tissues, a stapler, a coffee cup, and in the midst of it all, with a narrow space cleared all around like a castle brooding over a moat, a stack of four white stationery boxes with a pair of reading glasses neatly folded on top. On the floor, leaning against one of the table legs, was the battered typewriter case I recognized across the expanse of twenty years. It had spent a month of its mechanical life on the kitchen table in my cramped apartment in Vermont. I'd written a brief note on it once, which came back to me in its entirety: *Back at 10. adore you.* M. "So you're still using the Olivetti," I observed.

"It's a real problem with the novel," she said. "I was in Arizona for a few years, and my landlady there let me use her computer, so some of it's on a disk. But most of it is typed. Somebody told me editors don't even look at typed manuscripts anymore, they want everything in an e-mail. Is that true?"

I considered Rita's question. The old anecdote about Thomas Wolfe's manuscript arriving at Max Perkins's office in an orange crate came to mind. "They'll still look at manuscripts, but they don't like it," I said. "And it goes against you, right at the gate—it proves you're out of touch."

This amused Rita. "Out of touch!" she said. "That could be the title of my book. That's the point, isn't it?"

"Is the title still *Dark Witness*?" I said.

"You've got a good memory, Maxwell."

"I know," I said.

She wiped the back of her hand across her forehead. "It doesn't have a title right now." A thousand pages, I thought, and no title. Her forehead and upper lip were damp. It was stifling in the room, and she was rubbing the palm of one hand with the thumb of the other, an odd habit I attributed to nervousness.

"So when you left Alaska, you went to New Mexico," I said.

"Not directly. We went down to Spokane and stayed there for a while, downtown in this old hotel, until we ran out of money. Danny went off the deep end; she really lost it in Spokane, and she wound up in the rehab center, so I was broke and they threw me out of the hotel. I didn't like Spokane. Spokane is really America. That's where they test products to see if Americans will buy them. One day I just packed up the backpack and the Olivetti and hitchhiked to Arizona. That was tough. I almost got killed doing that. Truckers should pretty much all be rounded up and shot. Except the women."

I imagined Rita, the real Rita, standing on a highway in the rain, somewhere out there, out West, with her backpack and her typewriter case, dropping her raised thumb to her side as the eighteen-wheeler fastens her in its blinding headlights and she hears the rapid downshift of the gears. It would come to a stop well past her; she'd have to run to meet it, clamber up through the steam rising from the tires into the dark interior of the cab. "Women truckers?" I said.

"Sure," Rita replied. "There are women truckers, Maxwell. It's a real subculture. They're mostly farm girls who couldn't take the abuse and got out. A woman trucker saved my life. She loaned me the deposit on a little place in Tucson. She tried to talk me into being a trucker too. They make good money and you're really on your own, but that life didn't appeal to me."

"No," I said.

"I mean, I could have done it, but it just seemed so pointless. So I found this place in Tucson, a little house on a ranch, and the landlady, Katixa Twintree, she said I could work on the ranch for part of the rent. I got a job waitressing down the road, so I was okay there for a while. Katy is half Basque, half

Indian, quite a fierce individual. She had a girlfriend, Mathilde, French, a real bitch. Katy is fantastic. I was completely in love with her, and Mathilde was completely jealous of me, so it was a mess. I couldn't sleep at all. I was writing a lot. Katy asked to read it; she was very excited by it, that's when she loaned me her computer, which made Mathilde insane. There was a huge scene. Katy just let Mathilde and me fight it out, she is so wise, and Mathilde left. So then I moved in with Katy, and I guess that's the happiest I've ever been. Katixa Twintree was it for me, the love of my life."

As Rita told me this ridiculous story, my eyes wandered around the dim room, trying, without much success, to make out what was actually in some of the stacks of rubble on the various tables. At her concluding remark—which I took to be rather pointedly directed at me, as if she imagined she still had the power to wound me—my attention returned to her, and I saw that she was so moved by her own history there were tears standing in her eyes. This irked me. "So why aren't you still with her?" I asked coldly.

She gave me a wan smile. "I guess she was too good for me, Maxwell," she said. "Just like you." She brought her hand to her chest and the color drained from her face; even her lips turned greenish. She took a few steps toward the bedroom. "I have to lie down," she said.

I followed, my irritation replaced by a flutter of panic. "Are you all right?" She gained the bed, falling across it with a groan, facedown. I stood in the doorway gazing at the unappealing bulk of her. Her sandals, slipping from her feet, made two sharp raps on the floor. Her skirt was pulled askew, revealing the network of broken veins inside her knees. Her ankles were bruised, swollen, and the soles of her feet were filthy. As I watched, she rolled heavily onto her side so that she was looking back at me. "Would you get me a glass of water?" she said.

I went to the kitchen, relieved to have a mission, poured out the remains of Rita's lemonade, rinsed the glass, and filled it with water. "I've got to get out of here," I said softly. There was a back door; I could easily have snuck out that way, but it was a dishonorable course. As she always had, Rita was putting me through a moral exigency. I thought of my cozy house in Vermont, and of Pamela, my neighbor, my friend, and my lover, who would know exactly how to preserve her integrity and still get the hell out of Rita's kitchen. I longed for her, not to hold her close but to be in her kitchen, to sit at her polished oak table while she prepared our afternoon coffee, to hear her aimless conversation as I watched the slanting sun flicker among the bright leaves of the geraniums blooming lavishly in the window. Light, light, I thought. Not this shuttered obfuscation, not this universe of lies. I turned off the faucet and carried the dripping glass through the sweltering gloom to Rita's bed.

She had turned onto her back and propped herself against the pillow, her skirt neatly spread over her legs. She was breathing slowly, consciously, her hand still open across her heart. She took the water without comment and drank half the glass, then motioned for me to set it on the table at the foot of the bed. This allowed me a close view of the clutter around the television, which included a plate of desiccated cottage cheese peppered with something that looked suspiciously like mouse droppings.

"Thank you," Rita said.

"Are you better now?"

"I'm not getting any better," she said.

I made no response to this self-dramatizing statement. It occurred to me that the whole thing, from the invaluable pottery through the unfinished novel to her physical frailty, was a lie. She was making it up as she went along. There was no "business proposition," she had just wanted to get me into her wretched life and see if she could make me feel responsible for it. Outside a catfight flared up, a brief interlude of yowling, then it was quiet and the only sound was Rita's measured, phlegmy breathing.

My eyes settled on a stack of paperbacks next to the disturbing cheese plate. They were cheap romance novels, their lurid covers featuring women in distress, barely constrained bosoms, swollen lips, streaming hair. "How can you read this stuff?" I said.

Rita sniffed. "I just read it to pass the time. It's harmless. It's better than television." I picked up the book on top, anxious to avoid the vision of Rita, sprawled before me, defending her intellectual pursuits. The passionate but terrified damsel on the cover had pale eyes and a mass of golden curls, very like Rita. I wondered if this had influenced her choice. The title was something absurd.

"Will you do something for me, Maxwell?" Rita said.

I put the book down, careful not to upset the stack. "Is it the business proposition?"

"Yes," she said. "There might be something in it for you."

"I'm really fairly busy, Rita," I said.

"It wouldn't take much of your time."

"Is it to do with the pottery?"

"Yes. It is. There's a gallery uptown that deals in pre-Columbian stuff. I wrote to the guy and sent him some photos, but I don't have a phone so I had to ask him to write back, but he hasn't done it. He's probably suspicious because I don't have a phone. I'm not well enough to go clear up there—I don't have a car, and the bus stop is nearly a mile. Besides, if someone like you went to talk to him, well, he'd take it seriously."

"But I don't know anything about pre-Columbian art," I protested.

"You don't need to know anything. You just have to tell him you've seen the stuff in the photos and you know me and it's not a hoax or a scam. He'll be excited about it; he'll be over here like a shot trying to get it for nothing. It might be good if you were here when he comes, so he won't try to take advantage of me. I know what this stuff is worth."

"So, basically, you just want me to vouch for your character, is that it?"

"Sure," she said. "That's it."

I had not thus far looked Rita in the eye, but at this point I did. She held my gaze in that icy, still, calculating way I remembered, which had once so unnerved me that I gave in, looked away, agreed to whatever she wanted. There, disguised by puffy flesh, were the same limpid windows to her mercenary heart. Did she remember how she had reduced me to shadowing her, to crouching in the snow outside a window, too mortified to move? Did the two hundred dollars, a full month's rent, that she took from the envelope in my sock drawer weigh more than a feather on her conscience? Even now, in desperate straits, alone, unloved, and unlovable, she looked upon me with thinly disguised contempt. A hint of a smile lifted the corners of her mouth. What was I going to do? Let her down? Wouldn't that just be typical.

"How recklessly you've lived," I said.

"Well, Maxwell," she said, disengaging her eyes from mine, "we can't all be successful."

I sneered. "Is that your best shot?"

"I could give you maybe five percent of the deal," she said.

I laughed. "You really are incorrigible, Rita. Do you seriously imagine you have anything I want?"

She brought her hand back to her heart. The color in her face drained again, but not because she was struck by my irrefutable assertion. Her voice was confident. "You'd give your soul to have written my novel," she said.

I glanced away, to the room where the boxes gathered dust in the gloom. It occurred to me that they might be empty.

"Go ahead," Rita said. "Have a look. You know you're dying to."

I turned back, regarding Rita narrowly. Another suspicion had come to mind, that I would find myself in those pages, or Rita's version of me. Of what happened between us. She raised her head from the pillow, her lips parted in a menacing smile.

"I really don't have the time," I said, consulting my watch.

She dropped back onto the pillow. "You always were such a coward."

"Right," I said. "Let's leave it at that. Great seeing you, Rita." I headed for the door, fully expecting some further indictment of my character, some final cut, but she was silent. As I unlatched the screen and stepped into the blinding wall of heat, she moaned, turning ponderously toward the wall. I closed the screen behind me and went out to the street, scattering cats in my wake.

o

I had lied to Rita. I wasn't particularly busy; in fact I was at loose ends that day, as I had been for weeks. My work wasn't going well; I was avoiding the desk. As I wandered about my rented apartment, the confrontation in that depressing house began to take on color and depth, until I was convinced something had happened. I called Malcolm, who agreed to meet me for drinks near his store. I was eager to talk about Rita with someone who had known her when she was what I now thought of as the "real" Rita, the bewitching Rita, who had disappeared for twenty years and reappeared as a slovenly harridan to reproach me with the desert that was her life. Her parting remark, a continuation of an argument we'd had long ago, rankled me. Clearly, in Rita's view, my success only proved the justice of her charge: As a writer I was eager to please, as a man I was afraid to live.

"Well, look where it got you," I said to the specter of Rita, hovering about me as I changed my shirt. I caught sight of my torso in the wardrobe mirror; was there a thickening at the waist? Pamela had been after me to join the local gym. "Exercise," I said. "Healthy food, hygiene, air, light, life."

"How well did you know Rita?" I asked Malcolm. We were conveying our full martini glasses to a toadstool-sized table in the bar.

"You mean when we were in college?" he said. We sat down and pulled our chairs in close. "I guess I knew her about as well as I could." His smile was wry; of course he'd slept with her.

"Did you ever read any of her writing?"

"No," he said. "We weren't that intimate. I didn't know she was interested in that sort of thing until she left to go up there . . . where you went."

"So she was secretive about it."

"She was." Malcolm speared an olive. "Was it any good?"

"It was different," I said.

"In what way?"

In what way? In a way that made us all sick with envy. Even the professor was torn between his excitement to have such a student and his despair at his own turgid prose. Rita's plot was simple enough, a love triangle, a tale of abandonment and revenge. But it wasn't the plot that took the reader by storm; it was the style. "Brutal yet elegant," the professor suggested, which was about right, about as close as I could get. Rita sat there, placid and opaque as a cat, while we heaped on the praise. "It's the speed that gets me," one of us opined, "it's like lightning." "The world is so sensual," another exclaimed. "It's lush and hot, but somehow it's invigorating." My turn came around. What did I say? "Original, intriguing." Something like that. After class Rita came up to me and asked if I'd go have a drink with her and say a bit more. "Yours is the only opinion I really value, Maxwell," she said. "Just between us, you're the only one up here who can write worth a damn, including Simon." Simon was the handsome professor; Rita was rumored to be having an affair with him. I took her arm, gratified. Later, when I cared, she would retract this statement. When it suited her, Rita would tell me that I was, in her opinion, just another talentless hack.

"So, did she ever get anything published?" Malcolm asked.

"No, I don't think so."

"Then it couldn't be too good, right?" he concluded.

"Right," I agreed.

After our third round of martinis, Malcolm called home to say he wasn't coming for dinner and we walked over to Galatoire's, where I switched to whiskey and ate a piece of fish. Several old acquaintances stopped by our table to tell me I hadn't changed. One, a pretty, vapid realtor who had sung in a band in college, enthusiastically informed me that she had seen one of my novels in a bookstore. Malcolm told me about his children: One was doing well, another had stolen a car from a priest. Well, borrowed; he took it back the next morning. We left the restaurant and went to several bars. It felt good, drinking, exchanging witticisms about the scene, laughing, eventually shouting. At the end I left Malcolm on the phone, begging his wife for a ride home, and stumbled across Esplanade to my apartment in the Faubourg. I'd forgotten about Rita, my novel, Pamela, my waistline. I burst into Donna Elvira's aria about how much she wants to tear out Don Giovanni's heart. A dog, investigating a garbage can, paused, offered himself as an audience. *Sì,* I sang. *Gli vo' cavare il cor. Sì.* The dog, evidently impressed, sat down. "That's Donna Elvira," I confided, moving on. "She's been betrayed."

I turned the corner to my street. The door was, I reminded myself, the third on the right. It was dark, but I could make out the concrete steps and flimsy iron rails, what my neighbors called "the stoop," on which, in pleasant weather, they were inclined to sit and chat with the passersby. Sociable town, I thought. It really wasn't a bad place at all. Gradually it dawned on me that there was something on my stoop. It appeared to be an enormous cloth bag, stuffed and drooping over the rail. To my horror it moved, it rose, it came at me out of the darkness. "Maxwell," Rita said. "You've been drinking."

"Exactly right," I said, veering past her. "Exactly right, and now I'm going to sleep." I pulled my keys from my pocket, but too eagerly; they slipped through my fingers and clattered to the pavement. Rita, for such a large person, was quick. She snatched them up and went ahead to the door. "Poor Maxwell," she said, "you need help." In a moment the door was open and she stood inside looking out at me.

"I need help," I agreed. I waved my arms and stamped my feet. "Help! Help!" I shouted. "A woman has broken into my house."

Rita came down quickly, shushing me. "Stop, Maxwell. You'll wake your neighbors." She tried to take my arm, but I brushed her away. "You really shouldn't drink," she said. "You never could hold it."

"Get away," I said. "Stay away from me." She had placed herself between me and the stoop.

"Stop it, Maxwell," she said. "You're acting like you don't know me."

"I *don't* know you," I cried. "You're not Rita. You've killed her somehow, out there, out West. You studied her and you know a lot about her, but you're not Rita. You're an impostor." I dodged around her, reached the steps, but somehow when I got inside she was so close behind me I couldn't shut the door.

I plunged into the dark interior. Rita followed, closing the door and flicking on the light switch. "I need a drink," I said.

She leaned against the bookcase, watching me, breathing heavily, her lips parted and her tongue protruding. Panting, I thought. Like a dog. I availed myself of the whiskey bottle on the sideboard and poured out a glass. How was I going to get rid of her now that she was inside, blocking all the space between me and the door? "Why are you here, Rita?" I said, keeping my voice calm.

"I felt so bad after you left today," she said. "I didn't mean what I said. I was angry at you because you didn't want to help me." Her voice was shaky, edgy. If she started crying I would never get rid of her.

"Okay," I said. "Apology accepted."

"I didn't think you would come, and I wasn't ready for how it made me feel to see you again, so I said stupid things. And you were so cold, Maxwell. You never used to be so cold."

"I've changed," I said.

"And now you tell me you think I'm an impostor, that somehow I've killed myself."

"I didn't mean it. I'm drunk. And I'm tired. I want to sleep."

"I need to sit down," she said. She advanced to the couch and collapsed among the cushions. It was an uncomfortable product of the folded-futon school with a decidedly backward pitch, which she accommodated by leaning forward and planting her feet wide apart. Her big skirt billowed over her ankles so that only the pink toenails peeked out. She patted her hair down absently. "Could I have a glass of water, Maxwell?"

I sipped my whiskey, contemplating my options. Should I

drink more in the hopes of becoming comatose, or try to sober up and devise a plan to get her out of my living room? I was drunk enough to be stupid, I was sure of that. Rita was looking around the room, appraising the furnishings. "It's nice in here," she said. "It's cool, too." Her eyes came back to me, settling upon me with a proprietary complacency that sent a warning chill through my circuitry. "You've really done well for yourself, Maxwell. I knew you would."

I poured water from the seltzer bottle into a glass and handed it to her. "No ice," I said. "Sorry."

Rita took the glass and drank half of it. "Seltzer," she said. "I haven't had that in a long time. Do you have any vodka to put in it?"

"No vodka," I said. "Only whiskey."

Rita held out the glass. "That would be fine," she said. "Whiskey and soda is a good drink."

I poured a thimbleful into her glass, keeping my eye on my own hand, which seemed detached from me, a long way out there. "Just a little more, if you don't mind," Rita said. I poured in enough to turn the water golden. Rita took the glass and sipped at it, making a sucking sound that was loud in the stillness of the room.

"The thing is," she said, "what I told you wasn't true. I felt bad about that. I wanted you to know the truth."

"Why does it matter?" I said.

"I think it matters," she said. "I think of myself as an honest person. The truth is, Katixa wasn't the love of my life. I thought she might be for a while. I was pretty worn out after Danny, and Katy was strong and quiet, and she was excited about the novel. Danny never read any of it; she wasn't much into reading."

"Danny was into barroom brawls, as I recall," I said.

"That's true." Rita laughed. "Danny liked to fight. Katy was the opposite; she was always calm. But after a while I realized she didn't really know anything about books. She was excited about my novel because she'd never really read one before. To her I was a genius. I couldn't talk to her about it, about where I was going with it, what I was doing. Writing is such lonely work—well, you know."

"I do," I said, pouring myself more whiskey. The comatose option was looking attractive.

"At that point I thought maybe my problem was that I couldn't be happy with a woman. So I got disenchanted with Katy and pretty soon I was bored with the ranch and every animal and every person on it except Bolo, the Mexican, a real Indio. One day he had had enough of it too, because Katy was suspicious of us and making his life hell, so he said, 'Let's get out of here,' and I went with him."

"So that was it," I observed.

"Was what?"

"Your problem. You couldn't be happy with a woman." I was standing behind her, and she turned to look at me, clutching her glass, her eyes flashing in the old way, with the pleasure she took in telling a tale. She gulped her drink and plunged on.

"I still don't know. Maybe it was. Bolo and I stayed together for a while, drifting around, until we just drifted apart and I wound up on the reservation. While I was there I thought about my life a lot and I realized there had only ever been one person who loved me in the way I wanted to be loved, and that was because he was smart enough to value the best thing about me, which is my writing, because he knew, among other writers, among my peers, I was good—I was doing good work."

"And that person would be me," I said.

"Sure, Maxwell. That's what I realized. You were the love of my life, but I didn't know it then. I was too young. I didn't have any experience. I didn't know enough to know it."

"You knew enough to steal my rent money."

"Are you still mad about that?" she said testily. "Is that why you're so cold to me?"

"I'm not mad about it. But I'm curious to know, since you're such an honest person, how you justify stealing from the person you now recognize as the love of your life."

"There's nothing intrinsically dishonest about stealing money, Maxwell. Money doesn't have anything to do with integrity; that much is clear. Just read a newspaper. You knew I took it, and you knew why."

I appeared to myself as I was that day, impossibly naïve, rushing into the frigid apartment, calling her name, but only once, because it was instantly clear that everything was altered; her typewriter, her shelf of paperback books, her furry slippers were gone. It was an hour or two later when, in an agony of suspicion, I opened the empty envelope in my sock drawer. Of course, I thought, of course. "You took it because you didn't give a damn about me," I said. "And you're right, I did know that."

She sipped her drink, arranging her skirt in an absent, coquettish way that infuriated me. "I was desperate," she said.

A chill arising from that night when I'd understood how

thoroughly and willfully she had betrayed me thickened the air between us, and it had a fierce, sobering effect. "Aren't you always desperate, Rita?" I said. "Aren't you desperate right now? Isn't that why you're here? To see if you can use me somehow, because you're so desperate?"

"I don't understand," she said, gasping for air. She leaned forward over her knees so far I thought she might fall on her face. "I'm not well," she said breathlessly.

I watched her, pitiless as a god. She was a pathetic woman who meant nothing to me. "I'm calling a taxi for you," I said, taking up the phone. As I spoke to the dispatcher, Rita sat up again and commenced mopping her brow with a handkerchief she extracted from her sleeve. When I hung up, I lit into her again. "What you don't understand," I said, "is that there's nothing noble or brave about the way you've lived. You didn't finish your novel because you didn't know how to finish it. No one kept you from finishing it, because no one cared whether you finished it or not. You made everyone who might care suffer because you knew you would never finish it." I'd wounded her. The sweat pouring from her brow mingled with tears. A series of racking sobs convulsed her. "It doesn't take twenty years to write a novel," I continued. "It might take five or seven, but not twenty."

"It's almost finished," she pleaded.

"I'm almost finished," I said. "But not quite. You're a liar and not a very careful one, Rita, you always have been. You lie about things that don't matter. Do you think anyone believes you've got a million dollars' worth of art objects in that shack you live in, that you have the confidence of some Indian tribe, that you're here selflessly laboring on their behalf?"

Rita was hardly listening to me; she was too absorbed in her own suffering. Her handkerchief was a sodden ball she dabbed at her flushed face; her mouth was ajar. The sight of her, perspiring on my couch, enraged me. "Get up, Rita," I said. "Get up and get out of here." I wrestled my wallet from my pocket and peeled off a fifty-dollar bill. Rita struggled to her feet, gripping the sofa arm with both hands, and made a tottering progress toward the door. I was ahead of her, throwing it open.

"It's not fair," she said, through her tears. Her hand came up fast when she saw the money I held out to her, my arm stretched fully to escape actual contact with her flesh. She took the bill and looked out at the street, which was humid, hot, and dark, then back at me. "I've read all your books, Maxwell," she said. "I'm a much better writer than you'll ever be."

Something happened then; it was the worst thing that happened. She was looking past me at the couch and I had the sensation she might push her way back to it. As I stepped forward to block her, she must have turned toward me, because I bumped into her and knocked her off balance. I saw a flash of mixed confusion and consternation cross her features, and then she was falling forward, over the steps. Not many steps, but she fell for what seemed a long time, without a sound save the dull thud of her body against the concrete. She lay still, facedown on the sidewalk, the mass of her flowered skirt rising over her like a tent.

There was a moment, before I could move, when I considered closing the door and going to bed. But of course I did no such thing. I leaped down to the pavement and bent over her, whispering her name. A hand came out from somewhere and grasped my ankle. Another unworthy impulse, to kick free of her, passed, as she turned onto her side and looked up at me dazedly. "Are you hurt?" I said.

"I don't know," she replied.

I offered my hand, which she gripped with surprising strength, pulling herself to a sitting position. I was as close as I had been to her, close enough to recoil from the rank smell of unwashed flesh and fetid breath coming off her. "You slipped," I said.

Groaning from somewhere deep within, she pitched forward to her hands and knees and billowed up beside me. To my relief the taxi turned the corner, pulled up at the curb. Rita stood panting beside me, still clutching the bill I'd given her. "You pushed me," she said. The cabdriver got out and opened the door for her.

"This lady has had a fall," I told him, ushering Rita inside. She didn't resist. "Are you sure you're not hurt?" I said, but Rita wasn't looking at me. She was folding up the bill I'd given her and sticking it into her sleeve. It occurred to me that the driver might not be able to change a fifty and some further unpleasant scene might occur, so I handed him a twenty and told him to keep the change. This caught Rita's attention. "That's too much," she said.

"For God's sake, Rita," I said. "It's my money."

"It's too much," she repeated.

The driver frowned at her. "I'll give her the change," he said. "I'm not trying to rob nobody."

"She's very upset because of the fall," I said, slipping him another bill, both of us careful to keep our hands beneath the window. "She lives on St. Ann, close to the old cannery."

"Sure," he said. "Don't worry. I'll take over now." I looked in at Rita. The cab was air-conditioned, the light was on. She was arranging her skirt, brightening up. There was a skinned patch on her temple, bruising rapidly, and the palms of her hands were scratched; that was all I could make out. A taxi ride was something of a novelty to her, and she was now concentrated on controlling every aspect of it. "Goodnight, Rita," I said. She looked up, fixing me with cold eyes. "You pushed me," she said. I backed away and the cabbie slid into his seat. Giving me a jaunty salute, he pulled the door closed and carried Rita away, into the night.

The next morning I battled my way through the precincts of an impressive hangover to the computer screen, where I spent an hour tracking down a ticket to Vermont. I called Malcolm, who expressed no surprise at my decision. "Too hot for you," he said. "You'll be back in January." Next I called Pamela, who detected some urgency in my tone, something amiss. "You sound upset," she said. "Is everything okay?"

"I'm just drinking too much. I'm not getting any work done. It's too hot and I miss you."

"I miss you too," she said. "It's lovely here. My tomatoes are ripening. There was a moose in the road this morning, heading for the hardware store."

My spirits lifted. "Tomatoes. A moose," I said. "Sounds like paradise." Pamela agreed to meet me at the airport. I packed my suitcase, called the landlord and then the taxi. The driver was not the one who had rescued me from Rita; I made sure of that by calling a different company.

○

Two weeks later the boxes arrived. The postal slip had the New Orleans zip code, so I thought I'd left something behind and the landlord had sent it on. But when the postman pushed the sizable package across the counter, I saw that the return address was Malcolm's. "It's heavy," the postman warned me. He was right.

Malcolm had put the flimsy stationery boxes in a sturdier carton, previously used to transport a case of wine. He'd shoved a little newspaper around the sides and laid a folded sheet of paper with my name printed on it across the top. I knew what was in the boxes the moment I lifted the flaps, but a firm impulse of denial allowed me to read Malcolm's note with more curiosity than apprehension. I admired the unexpected legibility of his cursive hand. He'd had a Jesuit education.

Dear Max, he wrote. *I'm sorry to tell you that Rita Richard has passed away. The circumstances were grisly. She called me just after you left, asking for your address in Vermont. When they found her, my phone number was in her purse, which is how I got involved. We had to get rid of everything in her house. These boxes, addressed to you, were among her things.*

When you get this, give me a call and I'll tell you all about it. Hope you are well. Your friend, Malcolm.

Rita had scrawled my name and address on the lid of the top box, obviously intending to package them at some later date. Her handwriting was scratchy; the pen she'd used was running out of ink. I could see her, bearing down on the name of my town, on the zip code, determined that I should not get off easily, that I owed her something yet.

I lifted the boxes and put them on the floor next to my

desk. A sensation of dread, such as Epimetheus must have felt when his bride told him who had manufactured her luggage, stole upon me, and I recalled that in some versions of that story it is he, and not the lovely, curious, deceitful Pandora, who opens the box, thereby unleashing all the evils of this world.

I felt, as I had not in her living presence, perilously vulnerable to Rita. Purposefully I strode away from the boxes to the kitchen, where I paced back and forth. After a thorough examination of the contents of the refrigerator, I picked up the phone and called Malcolm.

No one knew exactly when or how Rita had died; her neighbors had nosed her out. By the time Malcolm arrived, the police were zipping her into a body bag; they were wearing gauze masks and had brought in blowers to air out the rooms. They had found her, face up, on the floor in the second room, between the pottery shards and her novel. Malcolm explained that he was little more than an acquaintance, which provoked the detective. Why would she have your phone number in her purse? he wanted to know, and when Malcolm said she had called looking for a friend's address, he repeated the question. The landlord arrived, visibly flustered. Rita had failed to pay the rent for two months and he had sent her an eviction notice. The police came through, dragging Rita in the bag like an unwieldy carpet. The landlord turned white, rushed out to the porch, and vomited into the azalea bush. This made the detective suspicious. How well did the landlord know Rita? he wanted to know. In fact he'd never even seen her, he insisted. He'd inherited the house at his mother's death a year previous; Rita was already in it. Usually she paid her rent on time. The landlord was shaky, so they all went into the kitchen for a glass of water. There they discovered the garbage, alive with maggots. The landlord had to go outside and sit on the back steps, his head between his knees. "I don't see why you're so upset if you didn't know this lady," the detective observed.

"It's my house," the landlord protested. "There's a corpse rotting here, who knows how long, the place is crawling with maggots. Of course I'm upset!"

"You're mighty sensitive for a landlord," the detective said.

After some conversation it was discovered that Malcolm and the landlord had both gone to Jesuit, two years apart. Malcolm had played football with the landlord's brother. "Dickie Vega," Malcolm said. "You remember him. This guy is his older brother, Jack Vega."

The detective took their names and addresses and told them he would be in touch. The police were sealing off the house until the results of the autopsy came in. Malcolm and Jack Vega agreed to walk over to Matuzza's and have a beer.

The autopsy report said that Rita had died of natural causes; therefore, the detective told Malcolm, he was closing the case. He had determined that Rita had no living relatives, so the city would undertake the disposal of her remains. He had also learned that Rita had a criminal record: She'd stolen a truck in Nevada.

"What kind of truck?" I asked Malcolm.

"Big. A semi. They found it in Texas."

Jack Vega had a Dumpster dropped off at the house, and he and Malcolm went through Rita's possessions. "Just junk," Malcolm said. "There was a checkbook with about twenty dollars in it and a fifty-dollar bill on the table by the bed; that was it. No insurance policy, no personal mail, just bills, clothes, a bunch of broken pottery, some books, and those boxes I sent you. I had to do the garbage—Jack couldn't go in there."

"So you threw all the pots out," I said.

"It was junk. It was all broken."

"She thought it was valuable," I said.

"Right," Malcolm said.

When I got off the phone, I sat at the kitchen table drumming my fingers. So that was it, the end of Rita. A bloated corpse rotting on the floor of a dilapidated shack. Total worth: seventy dollars and some broken pots. How long did she lie there, in the sweltering heat with the slatted light creeping in across her body, later withdrawing, leaving her in the dark, with the skittery night creatures, the roaches, the mice, her unfinished novel? I called Malcolm again. "Did they estimate when she died?" I asked.

"Yes. It was the day after she called me, looking for you."

"And when was that?"

"It was after you left."

"So, a few days later."

"No. I guess it had to be the next day. She knew you were gone, though. She said she'd seen you the night before and you'd forgotten to give her the address. I figured she made that up."

"No," I said. "I didn't see her. I was out with you that night."

"I knew that. I knew she was lying. She lied all the time, but it didn't do her any good."

"No," I agreed.

"So, what's in the boxes? Love letters?"

"I don't know. I haven't opened them yet."

"I thought about throwing them out with the rest of the junk, but Jack said we should respect the wishes of the dead.

That doesn't mean you can't throw them out. Maybe you should. Maybe you don't want to know what's in them."

But I knew what was in them. In my study I stood with my toe pressed against the boxes. I pushed against them, but they didn't budge. "You pushed me," I heard Rita say.

I was painfully conscious that I had lied to Malcolm. I wasn't afraid of being caught in the lie; no one was interested in Rita's last night on earth. The coroner's verdict, natural causes, meant no mysteriously ruptured organs, no suspicious bruises or contusions, and Rita was ill, anyone could see that; she'd said as much herself. I discounted the possibility that the fall Rita had taken at my apartment had contributed to her demise. What bothered me about the lie I'd told Malcolm was that I couldn't take it back without appearing suspicious. I was stuck with it.

Just as I was stuck with the boxes. I backed away, to my chair, where I sat regarding them steadily, as if I expected them to move. I considered my options, assessed the ebb and flow of curiosity. Once I opened them, I thought, Rita would be back in my life with a vengeance. Did I have a moral obligation to allow this to happen? They contained, I could not doubt it, her life's work, all she had to show for herself, and she had directed them to me as the person most likely to vindicate that life, which had ended in ignominy. She was right to choose me; I was situated to be of use. I could send the manuscript to my agent, or directly to my editor, and it would receive a fair reading. Neither of them would be delighted to receive a thousand loose pages typed on various machines with no backup, by an author who was unknown and dead, but they would look at it and, if it was as good as Rita said it was, consider the risk.

And what if Rita's novel was a success? It wasn't unprecedented. Virgil, Emily Dickinson, Franz Kafka, Fernando Pessoa, John Kennedy Toole, to name a few, had left the business arrangements to their friends and relatives. Pessoa's chest contained thousands of loose pages. Kafka had outdone everyone by extracting a promise from his friend Max Brod to burn everything at his death, burn *The Castle*, burn *The Trial*, but Brod, to the relief of posterity, had broken that promise. I'd visited Kafka's grave in Prague and laid the requisite pebble on the slab to hold the wispy Czech in place, and another on the loyal Brod's tablet nearby. What kind of friend made such a request? Kafka was dying for years. He had plenty of time to burn whatever he wanted burned. Didn't he possess a stove, a box of Czech matches?

If Rita's book was published, my part in that process would be a feature of the packaging. Like Brod's, my celebrity might rest upon it. I would be the generous writer of little note who went to bat for a work of genius by an artist who had died precipitately, crushed by the indifference of a heartless industry. The public eats that stuff up: the fantasy that artists—unlike, say, businessmen—are driven by warm fellow feeling. In their devotion to the religion of art, they are ever seeking, without self-interest or crude competitiveness, to celebrate genius, wherever it can be found. There wouldn't be any money in it for me. To maintain my status as a selfless benefactor, I'd have to give all the proceeds to a worthy cause—the Zuni might be a good choice, whoever they were, or some lesbian-gay alliance. I might get some interviews out of it. Who was this fascinating author? How did the manuscript come into my possession? I'd be free to reinvent Rita any way I chose: a courageous adventuress, a seductress, a poète maudit, a helpless victim of her own integrity and her impossibly high standards, a self-serving user, a tramp, a liar, a thief. Rita would belong entirely to me.

This scenario amused me, though it was doubtless far-fetched. The fact that twenty years earlier everyone in a small writing program in Vermont had agreed that Rita was gifted didn't mean she had parlayed her gift into a masterpiece that would take the publishing world by storm. It was more likely that the novel was a disjointed, flawed narrative, an overblown, self-absorbed chronicle of Rita's battle with the world. There might be flashes of brilliance, but no discipline.

One way to find out. All I had to do was open a box.

How close to finished was it? Was there, in its pages, some exaggerated version of myself, of those few months, so long ago, when Rita and I gave up on sleep in favor of drinking and sex? Would I find myself dissected, a squirming, quivering creature, flayed and pinned open on a page, my panicked heart throbbing for all to see?

I got up and took a closer look at the boxes. In the top corner of each one was a number, one through four, an effort at order. She had, I knew, written my address sometime between her return home in the taxi that night and her death, a period of not more than forty-eight hours. There might be a note to me with a more precise description of her wishes, perhaps an apology for having insulted me and some mollifying language designed to make me feel guilty if I failed to comply. Wouldn't that be just like Rita?

I slipped my fingers under the edge of the top box and eased the lid up with the care and trepidation of an expert trained in munitions disarmament.

Twenty years ago, for a poor graduate student on a stipend of four thousand dollars a year, two hundred dollars was a lot of money. I bought my clothes at secondhand stores, attended college functions for the free food, otherwise subsisted on vegetables, and drank draft beer with my peers at the local pool hall for a dollar a pitcher. My father was long dead, and my mother, who lived on a small pension from the U.S. postal system, didn't approve of my decision to leave Louisiana in search of an unlikely career. Even if she'd had the money, I was too proud to ask her for help. Within a few days everyone knew Rita had left not only me but the town, and I was the subject of pitying looks and kind remarks, which galled me. I certainly wasn't going to augment my image as the local cuckold by revealing that Rita had robbed me as well. As I straddled Rita's novel, the recollection of that humiliation assailed me, stayed my fingers, straightened my spine. I stood there, drinking it in, a bracing, bitter potion from the past. How had I made up the loss?

I'd gone to the real estate office and arranged to pay twenty-five dollars for that month and an extra twenty-five on the regular rent for the next seven months. I searched the local paper for part-time work, but there wasn't much. Because I was teaching and taking classes, my hours were limited; the town's economy was depressed, and I didn't have a car. Eventually I found a minimum-wage weekend job selling tickets at the movie theater in the mall out on the highway. There was a bus that let me off in the parking lot. It wasn't bad. I got all the popcorn I could eat and I could see the movies for free. I cleared about twenty dollars a week, which made a big difference in my lifestyle. I bought a good pair of duck boots, and because I could pay for the pitchers more often, my entrance at the pub was greeted with hearty enthusiasm.

I wrote a story about a guy who works at a movie theater. He becomes obsessed by a beautiful young woman who comes in alone every Saturday night, buys two tickets, and sits through two films, the seven and nine features, whatever they are. He starts to make up a life for her, a reason why she has to be away from home and off the street from seven to eleven every Saturday. It can't be because she loves the movies; most of them are idiotic. He starts following her after the shows. He knows where she lives, where she buys her groceries, what café she meets a girlfriend in, where she buys her clothes. Finally she has him arrested for stalking. He loses his job. It turns out she's a freelance movie critic. It was called "The Flicks," and it was the first story I placed in a reputable quarterly, *The Oliphant Review*. I was paid ten dollars, plus copies.

I never told anyone Rita had robbed me. It was one of those secrets I kept because it was pleasurable to keep it; I have a few. Years later, in a novel, I had a male character steal money from a lover in a similar fashion. My character pauses in the midst of the heist and considers taking only half the money—he knows how poor his lover is—but I doubted that Rita had given me that much consideration. It was a failure on my part to imagine a character as heartless as Rita.

The phone rang; it was Pamela. Did I want coffee? I wanted to get away from those boxes, but I didn't tell Pam that, perhaps didn't know it myself until I was safe in her kitchen. The windows were open, there was a vase of bright zinnias on the ledge, the light was lambent, the air fragrant and cool. Pamela in her man's shirt spattered with paint, her hair mussed, her eyes unfocused from the hours of close work at her easel, leaned over me with the coffeepot and pressed her lips against my neck. "Have you been working?" she asked.

"Yes," I lied. After the coffee I lured her into her bedroom, where we passed a few amiable hours. Then we were hungry and decided to go out for sushi. We were pleased with ourselves for wasting the afternoon on sex. We ate a lot of raw fish and drank several bottles of sake. After that we walked around the town, looking in the shop windows, greeting neighbors out with their dogs, and stopped at the bar for a nightcap. It was midnight when I left Pamela at her kitchen door and crossed the lawn to my own. In the course of the evening I'd forgotten about Rita's novel. But when I turned on the light in my study, there it was, a reproachful cardboard cairn near the trashcan. I considered the possibility that sake and whiskey were incompatible substances, that in some sense this explained the difference between East and West. If mixed in a glass, would they separate? I put this question in the same to-be-explored category as the contents of Rita's boxes. My desk didn't send out even a beckoning vibration as I wandered past it on my way to my bed.

In my dream Rita was young again, but I was as I am now. It was a snowy scene and she was teasing me to race her to a fence post across a field. She didn't have a chance, I told her, she was wearing open-toed shoes with high heels and I had on sturdy boots. But she insisted. She was lovely, her eyes bright, cheeks flushed. Her hair, stuffed under a fur hat, burst out over her forehead in golden ringlets. "Come on, Maxwell," she said. "If you're so sure of yourself, what have you got to lose?" At length I agreed. She took off, surprisingly quick in those impossible shoes, and I followed. My feet were heavy. I ran in dream slo-mo while Rita dashed ahead. As I hobbled along I came across one of her shoes, then the other, abandoned in the snow. When I looked up she was sitting on the fence, laughing. I clutched her shoes to my chest. It was snowing hard; I could barely see, but I could hear her, laughing, and calling out to me, "I win, Maxwell. I win."

The telephone was blaring. I fought my way free of Rita's taunting and snatched the receiver, pressing it to my ear, distracted by a sudden sharp pain in my groin. "Maxwell," Rita said. "Did you get my novel?" In the process of throwing the phone away from me, I lost my balance and slid off the edge of the bed to the floor. When I opened my eyes, I was flat on my back, looking up at the red point of the phone charging light, which went on only when the receiver was firmly lodged in its cradle. I looked down at my erection, fading fast after having been squashed when I rolled over on it to answer the call. "Rita," I said. "God damn you."

In the morning my mood was blacker than my coffee. Rita was stomping around in my head like a devil with a pitchfork, and not Rita lite, but Rita as she was on the last night of her life, with her harsh breath, her forearms like hams, her petulance, her frank, flamboyant destitution, Rita who had suffered and lived and stolen large machinery, Rita the accuser, the avenger.

I could hear the boxes chortling on the floor.

o

I was twenty-five that year. Rita was just twenty-one, but she was way ahead of me, erotically speaking. My experience had been that some women liked sex, others endured it, and others were looking to make some kind of deal. Rita was avid, rapacious; it was sport to her, yet I never doubted for a second that she was in deadly earnest, in it to prove to herself that she was the gold medalist. Now it strikes me that she was suicidal, trying to get some man to kill her, but I didn't have a clue about the dark side of anything then. I was an innocent, and Rita knew it.

So did Danny Grunwald, the scary little dyke Rita left me for, who reigned in an unofficial way over a pool table at Cues, the bar we frequented, daring "suckers" to play a game with her, swilling cheap bourbon and probably shooting something besides pool. Now and then she picked fights with tough men twice her size, went out in the alley and came back bloody, pleased with herself. She liked to tease Rita about me. "Hey, gorgeous, what are you doing with that loser?" "What has he got that I don't have, honey? I'm sure it ain't that big." That sort of thing. I thought that Rita's laughter was embarrassment, that she was as appalled as I was.

That night we'd been drinking for hours. Rita was tense and, before I knew it, furious at me for joking with a fellow student at the table next to ours. The fight went on back at my apartment, all night and into the next morning, when I took a shower and went to the college to teach my class. I knew Rita had a class in the afternoon, so I didn't expect to see her until evening, by which time we would both have been sober for more than twelve hours and in a condition to patch up our quarrel over a plate of vegetables and a pot of strong coffee. But the hours slid by and Rita didn't appear. I read all twenty of my students' writing exercises—describe a situation in which you regretted your behavior. There were always a few who had no regrets; invariably these were boys. Why were girls so full of regret? One, a clever one, regretted taking my class.

At length I was hungry. I chopped and steamed the vegetables, made the coffee, ate at the table while reading a Chekhov story for my Modern Masters class. Finally it was 10:00 p.m. and no Rita. I put on my boots, coat, hat, scarf, gloves, and went out into the icy world in search of her. I figured she would be at Cues; if not, I could drink with friends.

She had been there, but she was gone, no one knew where. Things I failed to notice: sympathetic looks on the faces of my friends, absence of Danny Grunwald. Hours later I slogged back to the apartment, certain she would be there—she had an early class in the morning—but she wasn't. I fell asleep on the couch. When I woke, the sun was up and Rita was passing through the room on her way to the shower.

"Where were you?" I inquired from the cushions.

"Wouldn't you like to know," said Rita.

I got up and we argued a little more over breakfast, but we were both too tired to keep at it. She offered some obvious lies, she'd been at the library, time slipped away, she'd met up with friends, gone out until it was too late and she was too drunk to walk home. We went to the college together, parted amiably enough, agreed to meet at the diner for dinner; it was payday. I waited there for an hour before I ate a grilled cheese and went out to find her. It was snowing. I tried the library, which was bloody unlikely, and then Cues. As I came into the block, I spotted Rita leaving the bar, walking briskly away from me.

She looked so purposeful I didn't call out to her. I wanted to know where she was going. I scurried along, close to the wall in true detective style. She turned into an alley halfway down the block. Stealthily I followed. It was a narrow street of one-room cottages with half-closed porches, lined up one against the other. They had been built for factory workers long ago, when there was a factory. Now they were run-down, derelict, but occupied. The residents stowed their wood on the porches, and the smoke from the stovepipes hung over the narrow passageway, coating the walls, the trashcans, the banked snow, the passersby with grime. Rita stamped her feet at the entrance to one of these, stepped up to porch, opened the door without knocking, and went inside.

I stood in the snow for several moments, unable to make up my mind to move. I had a fair idea of what I would find if I followed Rita, if I knocked on that door, and I wasn't up to it. I made my way back to Cues and joined a table of aspiring writers, most of whom would eventually find employment in the tech industry. I drank half a pitcher of beer, glowering at the pool table, where a cordial game was under way, absent the belligerent heckling of Danny Grunwald. One among us pointed out that our professor's new novel had gotten a lackluster review in the daily *Times*. It was generally agreed that his books were boring.

I was thinking about the stovepipes on the shabby houses in the alley. My apartment, which I'd rented in blissful August ignorance, had a fireplace that warmed an area of about four cubic feet in front of it. I knew now, too late, that a woodstove was the indispensable appliance in this climate; one could sooner go without a refrigerator. Whenever Rita and I visited friends who had a stove, we stayed late. At home we sat at our typewriters wrapped in blankets; at night we took our clothes off after we were under the covers in bed. In the morning, against the advice of the authorities, we warmed the kitchen by leaving the oven door open. If I had a woodstove, I concluded, Rita might be with me now.

Maybe that was it. Maybe Rita had just gone to the little house to warm up. I finished my beer. Energized by this crackbrained theory, I bid farewell to my friends and stumbled out into the snow, around the corner to the smoking cottage. I wanted to tell Rita that we would move right away, as soon as I could find a place with a woodstove.

The porch was piled with carefully stacked, evenly split wood, a professional job. The ax hanging from a nail on the wall had an edge that gleamed. I didn't doubt that Danny could swing it. The wood filled the space; only an area in front of the door was clear. This door, obligingly, had a curtainless window in it. Heedless as a fish biting down on a lure, I stepped up to it and looked inside.

It was a scene out of Bosch, complete with demons and, belching from the cast-iron stove that squatted in one corner, the flames of hell. The furnishings were meager: a card table, two metal folding chairs, a sagging sofa the color of dried blood, and a side table with a red-shaded lamp that partially obscured my view of the main event. This was going forward on a bare mattress in front of the stove. Rita was naked, on her hands and knees, back arched, hair wild, features contorted in the ecstasy that so often resembles pain. Behind her, equally naked, Danny Grunwald was gleefully occupied, ramming something cylindrical into Rita's delicate parts. She laughed

and talked as she worked. Mercifully, I couldn't make out what
she was saying, but I could imagine it, which may have been
worse, though I doubt it. Her eyes, which had always struck me
as piggish, glittered like burning coals, and her tongue flicked
sprays of saliva into the air. She was built in square blocks, with
large, sagging breasts attached at the front. Her skin, in that
diabolical light, looked like meat. They were both turned away
from me, so I was free to look as long as I wanted. What exactly
was that instrument Danny was using on Rita? Which orifice
was she penetrating with it? I pressed my face against the glass.
Rita dropped her head forward and made a bucking movement
with her hips. Danny leaned over her back and grasped one of
her breasts.

The voyeur spying on lesbians, who is detected and invited
to join in the fun, is a stock feature of pornography. Men would
pay to watch a man in my position; I knew that, but the last
place I wanted to be was on the other side of that door. I don't
deny that the sight of Rita disporting herself excited in me
feelings hitherto unknown. It was hot, all right, but the heat,
which became every moment more unendurable, wasn't in my
cock, it was in my brain.

I stepped back, clutching my head. Wiring was shorting
out in there; I could hear it, sputtering and popping. I had to
sit on the step because my knees were rubbery. A pile of snow,
dislodged from the eaves by my collapse, dropped down on my
neck. Great, I thought, and then, who cares? I didn't bother
to brush it away. I was busy experiencing, for the first time,
the bracing shock of total betrayal; there really is nothing so
cleansing. Born alone, die alone, love a mirage, life a cruel joke,
death standing in the wings, the one who really wants you, the

only one who cares. I was in pain, but I didn't feel like crying. I had the sense that something hidden had been revealed, not about Rita, who was clearly, from here on out, the "other," the "not me," but about myself. My expectations had been banal. I was stupid.

Eventually I got up and walked back to my apartment. I tried to read Chekhov, who had a lot to tell me about betrayal, but I couldn't concentrate. I turned out the light and sat in the dark, fell asleep on the couch again. Sometime before dawn Rita came in. I didn't ask her where she'd been, which provoked her to trot out a veritable circus of lies. "Rita," I said, "I was on the porch tonight, watching you through the window."

This was a hammer blow, and she staggered beneath it. Come on, I thought, tell me I didn't see what I saw. After a moment she said, "Danny thought someone was out there."

"Well, Danny was right."

Then we had tears, apologies, protestations, vows; it went on for a long time. She wanted me to go to bed with her, which I told her was impossible; I was fresh out of anything hard enough to satisfy her. More tears, buckets of tears, suicide threats. When she was exhausted we got into bed and fell asleep with our clothes on. Toward morning I woke up, found her straddling me, thought, What the hell, and did it. We got up, wary as cats, ate breakfast, minimal, polite conversation, and I went off to my class. At the door Rita kissed my cheek and said in her most earnest manner, "Maxwell, you have to forgive me."

I didn't forgive her, but I thought of her during the day, and that part of me that had hardened toward her thawed around the edges. Simon, the handsome professor, stopped me in the hall to say he was hosting a dinner party for a visiting writer, just a few faculty, selected students. "We thought of you and Rita." This cheered me up. Real food, I thought, probably meat, wine from regular-sized bottles. "That would be great," I said. "I'll tell Rita."

The snow stopped, the sun came out. I had a few student conferences, all about their regrets or the lack of them. In the afternoon I walked across the campus, pondering Rita. What was she? Did she know herself? When I got to the apartment, I flung my bag on the couch and called her name. Just once. That's when I noticed the Olivetti was gone.

○

I took my coffee into my study and stood at the desk, looking down at Rita's boxes. In some bizarre, chimerical fashion, she was in them, impatient for me to make up my mind and get to her. "Come on, Maxwell. You know you're dying to." Not just yet, I thought. I grabbed my notebook and went out to the screen porch. It was a strategy. When it was sunny out and the desk did not entice me, sometimes it worked. I laid out my arsenal—pen, notebook, coffee—and sat looking out at my yard. Birds were chirping; the air was warm and damp; my geraniums, the only flower I can grow successfully, sparkled in the early morning light. Pamela's deep purple clematis, cared for on her side of the fence, billowed over and made a lush display on mine. My eyes rested upon an oblong flagstone half hidden by a spirea bush, the grave of Joey, my late companion, dead, by my reckoning, three years now, felled in his youth by a cancerous growth resulting from injections the vet said he needed to keep him alive. He was a big cat, fourteen pounds, powerful but shy and goofy, not much of a hunter; his prey slipped through his paws. Sometimes when he tried to jump up on a chair or when he was tearing up the stairs, he missed his mark and landed on his side or his butt, always with an expression of discombobulation that made me laugh. His last months were hard. The tumor grew so large it pushed up into his neck, making it difficult for him to turn his head. Still, the vet said, he wasn't in pain, he was eating, cleaning himself. Occasionally he tried to catch a bug or stalked a squirrel. He tired easily but didn't sleep much. In the afternoons he searched me out and leaned against my leg until I took him up and held him in my arms. Then he would sleep for a few minutes, always waking with a start, as if he'd been dreaming and waked into an unfamiliar world.

His death was sudden and awful. The tumor, evidently full of fluid, collapsed, sending a blood clot to his brain, or so the vet speculated when it was too late. For perhaps fifteen minutes he screamed in agony, crashing against the walls, tearing at the air; I couldn't get near him. Then he was still but breathing hard, the air rasping in his throat, his eyes wide, swarming with terror. By the time I got him to the vet, he was gone.

I was angry about it all, angry at the vet, angry at myself, angry at death. I brought Joey home, got out my shovel, and dug his grave. I wanted it big and deep, and I dug for a long time, until I was standing in a hole above my knees. At the start I wept, but as I worked I began to take an interest in doing a good job. One could do worse than be a gravedigger, I thought. I wrapped his body in an old pillowcase, laid it in the hole, down in the earth where nothing could disturb him.

Then I shoved all the dirt back in on top of him. Pamela gave me the stone; she had it left over from a path she'd made in her own garden. Later she planted the spirea, which required no maintenance.

Down in the earth. The phrase arrested me. I took up my pen to write it down, feeling it might be the start of something. To my chagrin, the pen was dry. "For God's sake," I said. I pitched the pen in the trash as I passed through the kitchen on my way to the desk. The boxes were waiting, quoting Rita: "Among other writers, I was good. I was doing good work." It struck me anew as an uncharacteristically modest remark for Rita to have made, but she was in her conciliatory mode, trying to convince me that I should care what happened to her, now that no one else did. I chewed the end of my pen. It was sad, Rita's life, especially the end, dragged off in a sack by the police, her corrupted body disposed of at the public expense. Did they bury her somewhere, in some paupers' field, or was she incinerated along with other undesirables, the vagrants no one claimed, shoved promiscuously into a furnace, like the doomed dogs and cats at the pound? And then what? Did they scrape the ashes into plastic bags and cart them off to the landfill?

Whatever they'd done, that corporeal substance, once beautiful, later unlovely, containing the turbulence that was Rita, was no more. For twenty years she'd been a dim figure from my personal past, and there had been moments—not many—when I wondered what had become of her. Now I knew. She had entered the historical past, that densely populated terminus for which we all hold a ticket. She wasn't going to call, she wouldn't turn up at my door, she couldn't know what I did with the heap of cardboard and paper she had directed to me in an effort to entangle me further in her miserable fate. What, after all, did I owe her?

Pursuing this question, I went back to the porch. I was thinking of Franz Kafka and Max Brod. I'd heard somewhere that when Kafka read his dark stories to the very small group of his admirers in Prague, he was so convulsed by laughter he could hardly get through a sentence. It occurred to me that Brod had disregarded Kafka's wish that his work be consigned to ashes not because he couldn't bear to deprive the world of the complete works of his friend but because Kafka was just that, his friend, someone with whom he had shared pleasant hours of camaraderie, conversations, laughter, someone he missed. Publishing the manuscripts was a way to extend the friendship he had enjoyed, to keep his brilliant, quirky, ironic friend alive.

Though we had briefly been lovers, there was no sense in which Rita and I were friends. She had seldom been even routinely kind to me. I didn't miss her. If offered the opportunity to call back to life Rita or Joey, I knew I would choose, without hesitation, the cat.

Sound thinking, salubrious, this was the way to go at it, out in the warm, clear light of day, without sentimentality or superstition. I sat down to the notebook, calling up the phrase that had tantalized me earlier: down in the earth.

I'd been mistaken. It wasn't the beginning of something new; it was the end of this story. I looked out over my property; I'd want a spot as far from Joey as possible. There was a mass of invincible pachysandra thriving in the sandy soil near the fence. I could pull it aside and lay it back on top when I was done. It would grow in by fall.

I was calm; I wasn't vengeful. I'd give Rita a chance. I

would put the boxes in a hard plastic case—I had a number of them I used to store my own manuscripts—space-age stuff that would withstand a century or two of the old diurnal roll. I swallowed the last of my cold coffee. Then, with a sense of purpose and well-being, I went out to the shed to get my shovel.

THE OPEN DOOR

At breakfast Isabel said, "You hate men because you want to be one."

"Oh please," Edith replied, buttering her toast so hard it broke. The only sliced bread the baker had was the equivalent of zwieback, unless you wanted salted pizza dough. "Spare me the deep psychology."

Isabel shrugged. "I don't mind," she said. "I like men too."

Edith poured hot milk into her coffee, thinking how pleasant it would be to throttle Isabel. "You're just lucky I'm not one," she said.

Isabel turned her attention to the newspaper, folding and flattening it next to her plate. As she read, she stroked her thick forelock back against her temple, a gesture that sometimes filled Edith with desire, but this morning it was just one more irritating thing about Isabel. This trip was a mistake. Edith should absolutely have refused the invitation, but there was nothing to be done about it now. She must just get through it somehow.

Last night's reading had been a fiasco. The audience was

made up of women who had come to flirt with one another and couldn't be bothered listening to the poet they had paid to hear. When she looked up from her text, Edith saw Isabel whispering into the ear of a voluptuous blonde dressed in red elastic and stiletto heels. At the reception Edith was trapped by a tweedy Italian academic who confessed herself to be a passionate lover of Emily Deek-in-son. "Wild-a nights, Wild-a nights," she intoned, closing her eyes tight and holding her glass of prosecco out before her like a microphone. Edith looked past her to see Isabel and the blonde clutching one another's forearms to keep from collapsing with laughter. Afterward, in the taxi, Isabel opened the window, which she knew Edith hated. "It's so warm," she said, rosy and flushed from the wine and the attention, leaning her head back against the seat; she was practically purring. Edith looked out the other window and saw the Colosseum whirl into view like a murderer leaping from the shadows. Isabel saw it too, and regarded the monstrous rubble dreamily. "How I love Rome," she said. "Couldn't we live here someday?"

Not on your life, Edith thought as she watched Isabel brush her toast crumbs off the newspaper onto the carpet.

"I see the government is dissolving again," Isabel observed without looking up.

○

Twice in two days Isabel had accused Edith of hating men. Did this mean she was thinking of leaving Edith for a man? An Italian, no doubt, one of these swaggering babies who Isabel would claim understood her because they were both Latins. While Edith had to spend the morning at the university talking with students who had read her poems in bad translations, Isabel was lounging in some piazza with this man, chattering about how wonderful Rome was and how impossible it was to live in a college town in godforsaken Connecticut, what a word, and of course the man would try to say *Connecticut,* fail miserably, and they would both laugh until they wept.

Edith answered another question about Emily Deek-in-son. Yes, she was an early influence. All American poets had to address that astonishing gift sooner or later; and then a young woman raised her hand and asked a very specific question about a translation of one of Edith's poems, which this student thought was inaccurate. It was the word *choke* in a poem titled "Artichoke," which the Italian translator had rendered *cuore,* "heart." Edith found this an entirely interesting and appropriate question. She explained that the word *choke* meant the tough, matted center of the vegetable, an inedible part, not the heart, which was soft and delicious. The English word had a verb form as well, *to choke,* which meant "to strangle." Edith grasped her neck between her hands, pretending to choke herself.

"*Strozzare,*" the student said. "We have a pasta called *strozzaprete.*" The audience laughed while Edith waited for the translation. "Priest strangler," the student said. Edith beamed at her. "Exactly," she said. "You could say 'priest choker.' "

At the reception Edith kept an eye out for this young linguist, and when she made her shy approach, sipping nervously at her cup of Coca-Cola, Edith motioned her in, cutting short a conversation with one of the organizers of the event, who was explaining how important it was to promote the free exchange of culture. "Your question was interesting," Edith said. "What is your name?"

"Amelia," the girl said. She was thin and awkward, her dark hair cropped short and her myopic eyes made large by the thick lenses of her glasses. "I am an admirer of your poems for many years now."

"I wish you were a translator," Edith said. "You have obviously given more thought to the difficulties than some professionals."

"It is difficult," Amelia agreed. "Especially poetry like yours, which is so passionate."

Edith patted the young woman's bony shoulder. "Thank you," she said. "Thank you for saying that, Amelia."

It was what Isabel had said, years ago, when she finally read a manuscript of Edith's poems. Well, it was almost what she said. "It's surprising," she said. "I think of you as cold, but these poems are passionate."

Edith had mulled over this qualified praise for some time. To Isabel a person who did not act upon every impulse was cold, and it didn't occur to her that the systematic repression of powerful emotions resulted in a hard surface that contained a core of molten lava. She had no interest in the Victorians, whom she dismissed as prudes. Edith's reticence was a source of amusement to her. She liked to parade around the house in scanty gowns; after her bath she sat naked on the chair in the bedroom, rubbing scented oils lovingly into every inch of her flesh, as serene and rapt as a child in its mother's arms. She was affectionate in an overpowering, leonine way, grabbing Edith by the waist or arm or even by the neck and hauling her in for unexpected hugs and kisses, and if she detected any flinch or tremor of reluctance, she would push her captive away, saying, "Oh, you are so cold. What will it take to warm you up?"

Better she should ask, Edith thought, what it took to make me so cold. She knew all about Isabel's happy childhood; she was the darling of her Italo-Spanish parents, who traveled widely, always moving in bohemian circles, the mother a painter, the father a successful photojournalist. But when Isabel politely asked about her childhood, Edith knew she had no real interest in the subject, so she said only, "It was a farm in the Midwest, completely boring." She didn't describe the poverty, both spiritual and physical, the bone-aching work which was her lot from the time she could lift a plate, the battle zone of the shabby domestic scene, the parents whose hatred for one another found expression in rage at their children for being born, the strong possibility that when she was grabbed by the arm, the waist, the neck, what she was about to receive was not an expression of affection.

"I didn't come to life at all until I went to college," Edith said, and left it at that, sparing Isabel the details of those painful years as well: the paralyzing social awkwardness, the repulsive sexual encounters with young men whose sole desire was to insert their penises into a woman's, any woman's, mouth, the yearning after beauty, the discovery of poetry, of a world so utterly exotic and exciting that she had to take it in slowly, like a starving child who longs to gorge but can barely manage a spoon of gruel. She entered the classroom too awed to speak and sat quietly in the back, her heart racing as the professor elucidated what was to her the syntax of flight. She still remembered the night, alone in her dorm room, when she read an Elizabeth Bishop poem and collapsed across her bed in tears of such agony and joy that she could hardly get her breath. This was life! This was light! This was hope, even for her!

And then she fell in love with Madeleine, the brainy editor of the student literary magazine, and then it became possible to be a feminist, to stand with other women against the oppressive maleness that made history one long description of the battle for territory, and then she began to write poems of her own, and the black ink flowed like the black nights of her childhood, replete with nightmares, terror, and blinding flashes of light. The poems were edgy, shocking; they took on the world she hated and reduced it to rubble. The first professor she showed them to called her into his office and sat looking at her incredulously for a moment before he said, "I can't believe you wrote these, Edith. You seem so mild-mannered."

Edith smiled at this recollection as she stood at the mirror combing her hair back and gathering it into the twist she had taken to wearing because Isabel said it made her look like a French aristocrat. Poetry made manners possible. It was her vengeance; she needed no other. She applied a gloss to her lips and darkened her eyebrows, which had gone nearly white in the last year. She felt a quiver of anxiety about the evening ahead. She had skipped a talk at the conference so that she and Isabel could have dinner alone together in a place where no one knew a thing about them.

○

At the restaurant Isabel enthused about the pleasures of Rome, how beautiful, exciting, and charming it was, how lively the populace, how stunning the women and fashionable the men, how she felt she had come home at last, and Connecticut was some other planet where she had been taken hostage and forced to pursue her art among aliens.

"Is there much of a dance scene here?" Edith asked, pouring out another glass of the excellent wine the waiter had recommended.

Isabel pursed her lips. Of course it wasn't New York, but yes, there was. She had spent the afternoon at a studio run by an old school friend, and she could report that everything was highly professional. The company had just come back from a successful tour of Japan.

Italian dancers in Japan, Edith thought. That would be worth seeing.

"The Romans know how to live," Isabel continued, "sensibly and well. Yet it's remarkably inexpensive. Our apartment, for example; nothing remotely comparable could be found in New York, Paris, or London for the price."

This was true, Edith admitted. All the Americans who had accepted the lodgings arranged by the conference were jealous. They were stuck in an ugly modern building in an uglier suburb, an hour from the university by a crowded and unreliable bus. Isabel had taken one look at the address on the conference brochure, pronounced it impossible, and gotten on the phone to her various Italian connections, some of whom, Edith knew, were former lovers. The apartment belonged to the sister of a man Isabel had seduced when she was in school, many years ago, as she pointed out, and now safely married to a Milanese. He visited Rome only a few weeks a year; there was no possibility that she would even see him. They had the place for a month, staying on two weeks after the conference ended. It was in a six-story art deco building near the Vatican, complete with marble floors, tall windows, and surprisingly modern plumbing. It even had a sunny study, which opened onto the courtyard, where Edith sat with her espresso each morning drawing pictures of flowers in the margin of her blank page.

"The apartment is great," Edith agreed. "Though I couldn't live with the street racket for much more than a month."

Isabel rolled her eyes up to show her impatience, then spoke to the waiter who had arrived with a platter of fried vegetables. He was a cherubic young man, all curls and chubbiness, with an expression of solicitous serenity that Edith envied. He listened to Isabel's chatter, nodding agreement while his eyes wandered over the table, checking the levels of the wine and water bottles, then settling on Edith's face. He knew that she was an American, that she didn't speak Italian. At the start of the meal, he had enjoyed a brief exchange with Isabel in which she had told him they were from New York. It was easier, Isabel explained when he had gone; no Roman had heard of Connecticut. Now, as Edith allowed herself to be examined by the mild-eyed young man, Isabel asked, "Do you want grilled fish?"

"No," she said. "I want pasta."

"La pasta," the waiter exclaimed, evidently pleased. He ran down the list of offerings, most of which Edith understood: with peas, with shrimp, with salmon, with tomatoes and garlic, with porcini mushrooms.

"Funghi porcini," Edith said, and Isabel too looked gratified.

When the waiter left them, Isabel reached out and patted her hand. "Isn't this a great restaurant? I haven't been here in twelve years, but nothing has changed."

"It's very nice," Edith agreed. She knew this was an inadequate response, but she felt oppressed by Isabel's hard-sell campaign to make her agree that everything in Rome was superior to everything in America. It was an interesting place to visit, certainly, but there was much that Edith found horrific: the packs of thieving children who would take the shirt off one's back if they could get it; the kiosks displaying walls of the vilest pornography; the embarrassing television shows where even the news announcers wore low-cut tops with push-up bras and seemed intent on seducing their audience; the ceaseless roar of the traffic; the young men on motor scooters cruising through even the narrowest streets, so that one had to be prepared to press against the wall at every moment; the ubiquitous cell phones, often two or three at a restaurant table, with the diners all shouting into them; the monuments to tyranny and superstition every twenty feet or so.

And then there was the strain of watching Isabel, who was practicing denial with the terrified concentration of a fiddler in a burning building. She was glancing appreciatively around the room; it was cavelike but bright, because the walls were white. There were racks of wine bottles cleverly stored in various alcoves. "It's lovely," Isabel said, soaking in the agreeable atmosphere. "And the food is excellent. I could eat here every night."

But you can't, Edith thought. And when you can't, what happens then?

○

Isabel and Edith had lived together for ten years, sometimes harmoniously, but sometimes not. They met at a party given by one of Edith's colleagues at the college where they were employed, a painter who flattered herself that her wide range of acquaintance made her parties newsworthy events, though in fact she invited only people from the college who were connected to the arts and had some small professional standing as well as endless opinions with which they had long ago succeeded in boring one another past rage. Edith had just won a prize for her second collection of poems, *Sullen Vixens*, and she was being congratulated by a Victorian scholar whose insincerity was a marvel to see, as Edith knew he had tried mightily to block her tenure. As she accepted his fake enthusiasm, she saw Isabel smiling up at her from a wicker couch in the sunroom. Isabel in the sunroom! She was wearing something diaphanous, a dark blood-red, billowy in the skirt but fitted in tight folds across the bodice, leaving her shoulders and neck exposed. She had one arm stretched across the back of the couch, and she was leaning forward to fish a few nuts from the bowl on the coffee table. There were a lot of big plants ranged around the room and several of the painter's brightly colored canvases on the walls, so Isabel appeared to be sitting in a tropical jungle. She had her dark hair pulled back tightly; her lipstick was blood-red, like her dress. Edith thought of a Frida Kahlo self-portrait she had seen once, but this picture of a woman she did not yet know was free of the heavy neurosis of that portrait: It was as if Frida had taken a look at herself and been actually delighted by what she saw.

Later Edith asked her hostess who the woman in red was. The painter raised her eyebrows as high as she could get them and pressed her lips together in a bizarre grimace, which she evidently thought proved she knew Edith well and understood the erotic significance of her question. "Wouldn't you like to know," she announced joyfully. "Well, I will tell you. She is the new instructor in the Dance Department, Isabel Perez. She's from Costa Rica originally, I think, or maybe Paraguay. I can't remember. Come along and I'll introduce you."

And so they met. The painter introduced Edith as "our wonderful poet who has just won a very important prize. We are so proud of her." Edith, made miserable by the idiotic falsity of this introduction, could only nod and stretch out her hand, which Isabel took gingerly, saying that unfortunately, she knew nothing about poetry. There was just a trace of an accent, not much more than the odd incorrect stress. Edith could think of no response to this observation, so she smiled and nodded her head, hating the painter from the bottom of her heart. As soon as she could, she slipped away to the drinks table and poured out a full glass of bourbon.

When she looked back into the other room, she saw that Isabel had gotten up from the couch and was talking animatedly to a tall black man in a white suit, Mabu Adu of the French Department. She could tell by the way Isabel was working her mouth that they were speaking in French.

Edith shivered. She had not hoped to meet anyone even mildly interesting at this party; she had certainly not expected to fall in love. She found it difficult to stop looking at Isabel. Michael Mellon, her fellow poet, a nonentity from nowhere, rushed up to her and confessed that he had been thrilled by the news of her prize because it was so rare these days for work one actually admired to receive any recognition at all. He felt positively vindicated. "In fact," he said, "Ellen told me to calm down. She said I was acting as if I'd won the prize myself!"

Edith accepted her colleague's praise at face value. The poor man had been instrumental in bringing her to the college, taught her book in his classes, and, as she knew from various sources, had made an impassioned speech at her tenure review meeting, calling her one of the best poets of her generation. She did not doubt that he was the only person in the department who had not actually writhed in pain at the news of her selection. "What a generous man you are, Michael," she said. "Your friendship is as good as a prize to me." He blushed, and glanced about to see who was witnessing this acknowledgment of his worth. Edith followed his look and saw Isabel very near, her head tilted to listen to some pleasantry from Mabu, her eyes resting on Edith, the slyest of smiles lifting the corners of her mouth. I wonder what she looks like having an orgasm, Edith shocked herself by thinking. She returned her attention sharply to her well-wisher, who was asking her a question about a promising student whose honors thesis he was directing.

They talked a few minutes more; then, when Michael spotted his wife arriving—she had dropped the children off at the soccer clinic—he excused himself and hurried away. Edith took a swallow of her bourbon and watched in amazement as Isabel disengaged herself from Mabu and made straight for her side. When she got there, she said in a silky voice just above a whisper, "What thought were you having about me just now?"

Had Edith heard correctly? Isabel's perfume, spicy and warm, wrapped around her like a sensual embrace, and Edith held her glass still only with an effort. "I was thinking," she said, "that I would like to take you to lunch."

Isabel frowned. "But where? Everything in this town is so dull."

"We could drive to the city."

"Yes," Isabel agreed. "I know some wonderful places there."

Much later, in very different circumstances, it occurred to Edith that this brief and magical exchange only proved how absurdly easy Isabel was.

○

Edith stood glowering at the books on the English bookshop table. How was it possible? Two collections by her archenemies, Lulu and Mark Zinnia; one by her former girlfriend Lydia, whose poetry was always described as lyrical, though Lydia actually had the sensitivity to language of a baseball bat; and one by Malva Plume, a mawkish sentimentalist who "celebrated the body." There was also a small stack of *The Monk's Alarm Clock*, the surrealist J. P. Green's newest, which Edith had read and liked. That was it for contemporary American poetry. On the fiction table nearby, Edith spotted the Marilyn Monroe book and the new one in which Mussolini visits New York. She picked up Lulu's book and opened it to the picture on the back flap, taken, of course, by Mark. Lulu was sitting on what looked like a swing; there was a heavy chain next to her face. Her slightly protruding eyes were focused entirely on the camera. Beneath it was a list of the prizes she had won. Edith opened to a poem at random and scanned a few lines. Lulu was anxious about Mark's bad cold. Edith laughed and snapped the book closed.

The Zinnias were a golden couple, astonishingly successful given the meagerness of their talents and the tedium of their lives. They never stopped congratulating themselves. Whenever they took a little trip, like this one, there was a whole spate of poems about the trip. They wrote poems about their spoiled, mean children as if they were visiting deities. Edith recalled the last time she'd seen the vicious daughter, a dumpy, overweight child who sat down on the ottoman next to Edith, balancing a plate of brownies and a plastic glass of punch, and asked with an insinuating smirk, "Are you and Isabel going to get married?"

Before the rift the Zinnias had been friendly to Edith, inviting her to their crowded parties, where the wine was cheap and the flower arrangements were large and composed of weeds. Edith politely attended their readings, keeping her mind firmly on something else—a novel she had read or a mental image of Isabel's naked back. What she knew about their personal lives she learned from their poems.

Edith placed Lulu's book back on the stack next to her husband's. She really had not thought when she wrote "Tame Poems" that Lulu would recognize herself as the subject. "Tame poems, docile, bleating lambs, / no threats, no surprises." Edith thought it harmless enough, and general as well, though there was one line near the end that clearly referred to Lulu's poem "You Protect Me."

But as soon as the poem was published in an obscure journal, everyone at the college seemed to know about it. Michael Mellon took her aside after a department meeting and told her that Lulu was devastated. There were no more party invitations. Mark cut her at the graduation; Lulu was too sick to attend.

Publishing "Tame Poems" proved that Edith was angry and rash. Michael told her that Mark announced at a dinner party that Edith was eaten up with jealousy, because he and

Lulu were devoted to each other, whereas Isabel was flagrantly unfaithful to her. The Zinnias were powerful in poetry circles; they edited anthologies and sat on prize committees. That year Mark edited a big anthology. Edith was conspicuously absent from this collection.

Isabel laughed at the whole business. "Wonderful," she said. "There are never any chairs at those awful parties, and the food is always fish paste on white bread."

One summer night shortly after the anthology snub, Isabel and Edith sat on their front porch splitting a bottle of champagne to celebrate Isabel's return from a course of master classes in the city. Isabel was in high spirits. "Let's walk," she said, pulling Edith up by both arms. "Let's stroll past the Zinnias' and see if they're having a party." It seemed an amusing idea, and Edith slipped her arm through Isabel's thinking that Mark and Lulu had never known a single moment as joyful as this one, strolling out into the quiet, tree-lined street, giddy from champagne, the warm night air, and each other's company. What if there was a party and the guests standing on the porch looked out to see Edith and Isabel, indifferent to their feast, nocturnal and svelte, like panthers slinking past a gathering of stupid, yelping hyenas? Who would envy whom?

But when they got to the house, there was only one dim light on near the back. "What is it, ten o'clock?" Isabel said. "And the Zinnias are snug in their beds." This was funny too. Edith pictured Lulu and Mark in matching flannel pajamas, plaid, or with pictures of teddy bears on them, curled up under the covers in their narrow four-poster. Long ago Lulu had insisted that Edith and Isabel take themselves on a tour of the house, and Isabel had snorted at their rickety antique bed with its thin pillows and grandmotherly quilt. "The scene of a grand passion," Isabel said, even going so far as to sit on the edge, pronouncing it "rock hard, completely unforgiving."

"Wake up, Mark and Lulu," Isabel sang out as they stood looking up at the dark house. "Your house is not on fire." Edith chuckled, then said, "Hush. They might wake up." Isabel drew her closer to the house while she laughed and made a mock struggle. "No, no, be careful, be quiet," she said, stumbling over a yard hose. "We don't want to wake the great American poets." When they were past the porch, Isabel said, "I have such a great idea," and she pulled Edith behind a bush so that they were hidden from the street and right up against the wall of the house. "What is it?" Edith said. "What are we doing here?" Then Isabel put her arms around Edith's waist and held her close, kissing her neck and shoulder. "My Edith," she said. "You are so adorable when you are tipsy."

"Me?" Edith protested. "You drank much more than I did."

"But I am never drunk," Isabel said, kissing her on the mouth. Edith closed her eyes and gave in to the embrace. It was true, she thought, Isabel was never drunk.

Edith's blouse was unbuttoned and Isabel's halter top was around her waist when the light went on and Mark stepped out onto the porch. "What's going on out here?" he said in the tough voice of the outraged homeowner protecting his domain. Did Mark have a gun? Edith thought. Isabel took her hand and whispered, "Run!" They burst past the bushes, clutching their clothes to their breasts and running hard until they got to their own porch. Then they staggered inside and fell on the couch, laughing like bad children.

Wild-a nights, Edith thought. The bookstore clerk approached and asked if he could be of assistance.

"I'm looking for a book of poetry," Edith said. *"Unnatural Disasters*, by Edith Sharpe."

"We don't have that," the boy said indifferently. He had a long face, pockmarked skin, and a prissy British accent. "We don't carry much American poetry." He walked away to another customer, who was going through a stack of travel books.

Edith went out into the street, still so absorbed in her thoughts about the Zinnias that she nearly collided with a *motorino* parked on the thin strip of cobblestone that passed for a sidewalk. When the awful business with Isabel's student Melanie blew up, Mark was as hateful and stupid as the rest of them. But one afternoon Lulu had come into Edith's office, closing the door behind her and leaning against it. "I just want to tell you," she said, "that I don't think these charges against Isabel are entirely fair."

"Of course they aren't," Edith said. "But no one really cares about that much, do they?"

"Melanie Pringle was my student last year."

"Did she make a pass at you?"

Lulu's eyes widened at this thought. "No. But she's no innocent." Then, clearly horrified by what she had just said, she pulled the door open and slipped out into the hall.

o

"Turn it off, turn it off," Edith said, rising from her chair in desperation. "I can't look at any more breasts."

Isabel scowled. "You are so puritanical," she observed. She changed the channel to a panel show in which three women were perched on a narrow couch gibbering into one another's cleavage. Edith stalked toward the kitchen. "It's not puritanical to detest seeing women degraded to nothing but mammary glands on stilts, which appears to be the highest goal of the female in this ridiculous country."

Isabel studied the television screen. "You're jealous because they are so beautiful and they enjoy being beautiful."

"Oh, for Christ's sake," Edith said to the stove. "I am not jealous of women who choose to be bimbos." She pulled the coffeepot from the rack and poured water into the base. "Do you want coffee?" she shouted.

Isabel clicked off the television. "Yes," she called back.

Edith struggled with the espresso packet, attempting to open it with a dull knife. "There are scissors in the drawer," Isabel advised her from the doorway. Edith looked at her, scowling as the knife pulled free of the packet and the coffee exploded across the counter. "Surely you can see these women are just cows in need of milking?" she said, reaching for the sponge.

Isabel smiled. "They do love their breasts," she said. "And why shouldn't they? They're lovely. I've never wanted large breasts myself; that's impossible for a dancer. It just doesn't work to have anything bouncing around. But if I had breasts as pretty as Giovanna Bottini's, I certainly wouldn't wear mannish suits like the news announcers in America."

"Who is Giovanna Bottini?"

"The one with the talk show."

Edith tightened the top of the *caffettiera* as hard as she

could, set it on the burner, and lit the flame with the sparker. So Giovanna Bottini was not the woman at the reading. "How can you have a talk show if everyone is preoccupied with presenting her breasts and no one listens?" she said gloomily. "It's depressing. It's like the poetry reading. Why have a poetry reading if no one is going to listen? Why not just have a party and spend the money on food?"

"Oh yes," Isabel replied. "It's so much better to sit in an icy little room reading to dreary overweight women in parkas who tell you how liberating it is for them to think about how much you despise men."

"I don't despise men, Isabel, as you well know. I have many friends who are men. I hate the patriarchy and with good cause, as a purely cursory reading of history will prove."

The coffeepot began to hiss. "I'll heat the milk," Isabel said.

When they had carried their cups to the table, Isabel pursued the subject. "Why do these Italian women bother you so much?" she asked seriously. "You don't mind it when I wear almost nothing and leap about on the stage. Why isn't that depressing?"

"It's completely different," Edith said. "You're an artist. It's not your body you put on display, it's your art. You've made your body into something sublime with which you express an ideal of beauty that has nothing to do with tits on parade."

Isabel considered this for a moment. "No, that's not true," she concluded. "For me, dance is entirely sensual and erotic. I don't care about ethereal ideals of beauty. I use my body as a medium for the expression of extreme states of desire."

Right, Edith thought. She set her cup down carefully in the

saucer. "How can you say that to me?" she said, glaring at her own hand. She was never able to look at Isabel when she was angry.

Isabel allowed the harshness of this question to darken the air between them. "What are you talking about?" she asked.

Edith kept her eyes lowered, running through the menu of cutting replies that appeared behind her eyes.

Isabel answered her own question. "You're talking about Melanie Pringle," she said. "All this is about Melanie Pringle, isn't it? All this hostility toward sexuality and beauty. I thought if we came here we could get away from all that and have a pleasant time together, but I see you've packed Melanie up and brought her along."

"Just don't tell me about your extreme states of desire," Edith said, "and maybe I won't be reminded of what they cost us."

"There was nothing extreme about it," Isabel protested. "She waited in the dressing room until the others were gone and she put her arms around me and kissed me."

"What made her think she could do that?" Edith asked coldly. "She must have been pretty confident about what your response would be."

"She's a beautiful, rich young woman," Isabel replied. "No one tells her no. She's made out of confidence, that's all she is. And when she realized I didn't care for her, she got angry and decided to destroy me."

"Was that the reason?" Edith sniffed. "That's reassuring."

"It's a stupid mess, she's a stupid girl, but it has nothing to do with us. We can't let her drive us apart. Now that would be folly."

Edith felt something in her chest contracting, as if her heart had turned into a fist. "I guess it just doesn't occur to you that I might feel humiliated," she said. "That having my colleagues all fall silent when I enter a room because they've been talking about you, because they feel sorry for me, that having Lulu Zinnia, for God's sake, look at me with pity because I live with you, that I find that humiliating, and that this stupid mess, as you call it, has everything to do with us. It will probably be the end of us, especially if you lose your job."

"You care what Lulu Zinnia thinks more than what I think!" Isabel exclaimed. "How can you possibly care what a tedious, bourgeois housewife like Lulu Zinnia thinks of you? You despise Lulu; you've insulted her publicly. You despise most of your colleagues, and rightfully so, they're a pack of hypocrites. What does it matter what they think of us? They already have so many horrible thoughts about us just because we're together, what will a cunning new twist add? Do you want to be like them, Edith? Tell me now, because I need to know. Do you want us to bind ourselves to their narrow, empty morality so that you can hold up your head and not feel humiliated by people you despise?"

"I don't despise Lulu. I despise her poetry," Edith corrected.

"All the more reason to dismiss her cheap sympathy."

Edith drank her coffee, though she didn't taste it. "It's not that I care what they think. I'm afraid of what they can do. You know what's in the works; you know what's going to happen when we get back. If you get sacked for harassing a student, you won't be able to find a job anywhere."

"I'm not going back," Isabel said abruptly. Edith shrugged and blew out her breath. "I'm not," Isabel insisted. "I'm not going to go on trial and be judged by those lifeless puppets.

And anyway, I can't go back now. I've accepted a position here, starting in the fall."

Edith was so astounded she clutched her head between her hands. "What have you done?" she whispered.

This is what Isabel had done. While Edith had been absorbed in the conference activities, Isabel had been talking, talking, talking, and making plans for them both. Her college friend had offered her a position at his academy, which operated partly for students but was also the studio of a professional company. "I won't be teaching overweight girls who lurch around like frightened sheep," she said. "These are real dancers." She had also made inquiries at the university, where Edith's appearances had been wildly popular. A new program in feminist studies was being planned for the advanced English students, and Isabel's informants assured her that if Edith showed an inclination to accept a position, one would be offered.

"It's not that simple," Edith said. "I've been at the college for fifteen years. I have tenure, a good retirement plan. I can't just throw all that over for a job that may have no future."

"You're in a job that has no future now!" Isabel exclaimed. "If you stay there you'll end up like the rest of them, with their policies and their committees and their horror of sex and joy and life. You'll dry up like a prune. Think how happy we could be here. We'll find an apartment with a terrazzo. No snow, no disgusting galoshes and parkas! You'll be like a flower opening in the sun."

"There's more to life than good weather and coffee," Edith said drily. "And I don't want to be a flower."

"You're being impossible," Isabel said, getting up from the

table. She went to the window, where she stood looking out into the noisy street. Overhead they heard the screech of furniture being dragged across the floor; they had heard the same sound every evening of their stay, though they never heard anything dragged back. Edith sat at the table, hunched forward, her hands folded before her, and she thought, I'm sitting like an old woman. She straightened her spine and looked at Isabel.

It all felt dismally familiar. They were at the middle point of an argument they had been through a thousand times: reason versus passion, vitality versus stability. Sometimes, when Isabel was so frustrated and stymied by her career that she became depressed and Edith had to buck her up, they had even switched sides. But this time a resolution of these irreconcilable differences would have to be found, because it was not just philosophies that were at odds but material possibilities.

Edith observed the sad tilt of Isabel's still firm chin, the downcast eyes, the line of her elegant nose casting a shadow like a blade across her cheek. She was forty-one years old, and she was panicked. Edith herself was a threat to her, being part and parcel of the intolerable status quo. Now she'll tell me America is killing her, Edith thought.

Isabel came from the window and rested her hands on the table, leaning into them. "I can't live in that place," she said. "It's like being slowly asphyxiated. I feel alive here. Rome is full of disorder and messiness, all the things Americans are terrified of because they prefer death to life. That's why they are so in love with machines, which are dead, and why they prefer communicating with one another using code names so they can't be identified."

Even as she was annoyed by this argument, which she had heard before, the sideline about technology amused Edith; it was so like Isabel to deploy her grievances in squadrons.

"If you care for me at all, you won't ask me to go back there," Isabel concluded.

"Wait," Edith said. "I wasn't aware I had any choice in the matter. Would you go back if I asked you?"

Isabel looked into her eyes with such desperation that it hurt Edith to see it. "I don't know," she said.

Edith pictured Isabel sitting at the end of a long table as a group of men somberly considered the charges against her. It crossed her mind that Melanie Pringle was not entirely an accident, that Isabel had, in some unconscious way, been looking for Melanie. "I don't think you should go back," Edith said. "I think you've done the right thing."

"Then you'll stay with me here?"

"I hate it here, Isabel."

"I've lived ten years in a place I hate for you," Isabel retorted.

"That's just not true. You've been trying to leave the college since the day you got there. You didn't stay for me, you stayed because the only other position you were offered was in Arizona."

"I would have gone to Arizona if it hadn't been for you," Isabel said. "That's how much I hate it there."

"I just don't think I can work here," Edith said. "I haven't written a word since we've been here."

"That's all you really care about," Isabel snapped. "Your bitter, hateful poems." Then she burst into tears.

Edith was unmoved by Isabel's tears. Her head was aching

and she was nauseated. "So the poetry has to go too," she said. "What do you think will be left of me?"

"I didn't say you shouldn't write it," Isabel whimpered. "I said you shouldn't care about it so much."

Edith thought her head would burst at this remark. "Suppose I tell you to stop caring about dance," she said.

"I didn't say you should give it up!" Isabel protested, drying her eyes on her sleeve.

"There's nothing you won't say when you're not getting what you want," Edith said. She pushed her chair back and staggered away from the table.

"Where are you going?" Isabel asked coldly.

"To get some aspirin," Edith said. "My head is killing me."

○

Your bitter, hateful poems, Edith thought. She was sitting at a table in the small, whitewashed anteroom of the lecture hall, attaching strips of sticky paper to the pages of her books. There were four books, plus a loose manuscript of uncollected work. She was putting off looking at the date of the most recent poem.

She had more and more difficulty writing, and she knew it was not entirely the fault of European travel. Perhaps, she told herself, she was going through a transition, and exciting, original work lay ahead. She need only be patient and alert, waiting to hear the new voice, to recognize the new path. Poems that came less easily would be more telling.

Or perhaps the truth was that she had exhausted the vein of her poetry and there was nothing left to draw from it, nei-

ther blood nor gold. There had been a time when her head
was always filled with phrases and lines, presenting themselves
wantonly for her inspection like contestants in a beauty pag-
eant, and she went to her desk with a strange, nearly erotic
excitement. Were these poems hateful? It was true that the
metaphors reviewers used to describe them frequently included
sharp edges: knives, razor blades, a surgeon's scalpel. Here, in
fact, was a sonnet titled "Incision," which was ostensibly about
their cat Jasper's neutering, though there was some play with
the word *incisive,* and the wounding, emasculating power of
language. She would read that one; it would remind Isabel of
Jasper, whom she missed.

They had argued late into the night. For the first time in ten
years they had gone to sleep in anger, though Edith thought she
remembered Isabel's hand seeking her own, perhaps in sleep.
In the morning they hardly spoke, both puffy-eyed and bleary
over their coffee. It was the last day of the conference and Edith
had a full schedule. Isabel planned to lunch with a friend, then
arrive at the university in time for the reception before the reading. As she was packing up her books, Edith said, "You don't
have to come, you know. You've heard it all before."

"Don't be ridiculous," Isabel said. "Of course I'm coming."

Edith turned a few pages, scanning titles, looking over the
compact display each poem made on the page. The window
next to her table was open, and the warm air was damp, musty,
with a torpid movement that was more like an exhalation than
a breeze. August must be an inferno, Edith thought, and smiled
as the legend *The Divine Comedy* passed across her brain. Outside someone shouted a greeting to someone else, and there was

a burst of laughter. The students were affectionate with one another and almost absurdly respectful of their professors. One of the coordinators had told Edith that all exams were oral; the students had to sit before a group of their professors and answer questions. Like the Inquisition, Edith thought. Italy had a lot to offer.

She patted her upper lip, where a few drops of moisture had gathered. Here was the poem "Icescapes." She had written it after a terrific storm when she and Isabel had not been able to get out of the house because the doors froze shut. It was a poem about jealousy; Isabel had flirted outrageously with a visiting poet at a dinner the night before. The dinner, then the storm. All night they had listened to the trees cracking, branches hurtling down like ice swords, and in the morning, when they looked out the window, it was as if the world was made of glass. She would definitely read this poem, which would seem exotic to her Roman audience. Carefully she laid a strip of paper against the margin of the page and wrote the title on the list for Amelia, who would be reading the translations with her. Wouldn't the double entendre on the words *ice pick* get lost in translation? This seemed amusing, the idea that richness, nuance, got lost in translation. Where did it go? She imagined the land of what was lost in translation, imagined herself in it.

She was happy doing this, making these choices, browsing through this world of her own making; she felt at ease, at rest. Tonight's audience, Amelia had told her, would be larger than on the first night, and a greater proportion of it would be serious students of English who were familiar with her work. She felt the pleasant excitement she often had before a reading, hoping her delivery of the poems would be illuminating, giving her audience a sense of greater intimacy with the words on the page.

Could she do what Isabel wanted? Could she stay here and leave everything she knew behind? She looked out the window, at the dark leaves of a tree and the fresher green of a vine curling over the sill, patiently working the frame loose from the wall. There was something in the vine that was not a leaf. As Edith focused upon it, it moved. It was a lizard, small, bright green, with a pink throat, opening and closing over its glassy eyes the mauve double folds of its curious eyelids. It took one cautious step onto the dusty stone ledge.

Edith watched the lizard, fairly holding her breath at the strangeness of it. She had the sensation that some reliable anchor was being cut away and she was now completely adrift. A line from a gospel song she had heard—but where? when?—ran through her confused thoughts: "Praise God, the open door. I ain't got no home in this world anymore." Where am I? she thought. She had a sharp recollection of the field outside her parents' house, a hot summer day; she was sitting on the porch, angry voices raised behind her, gnats batting against her face, the hum of insects, and before her the flat yellow expanse of the field, which had been mowed and would soon have to be hayed, a job she hated.

Isabel had said coming to Rome was like coming home, and Edith had to take her word for it, because she had not ever had that sensation in her life and she doubted that she ever would. It was too late now to find a home to go back to. She pictured herself lying flat on her back on the floor of a leaky rowboat, above her face the blue sky, and all around water, water, to the end of the world. In the distance she heard a door open, which she registered unconsciously as the door of the lecture room. Then there was the sound of rapid footsteps coming toward her. The lizard heard it too, scurried across the sill, disappeared into the vine. Edith abandoned her reverie and turned from the window to see Isabel approaching, moving swiftly with the dancer's powerful, slightly duck-footed gait. She was exhausted, Edith observed. Her eyelids were still swollen from last night's tears, and there were dark circles beneath them. She'd pulled her hair back tightly and made a schoolmarmish bun at the nape. She hadn't neglected the lipstick, which was bright red, but it served only to outline the downward cast of her mouth.

The ugly business at the college had shaken Isabel, Edith understood. She was wounded by it in some vital center of her confidence. It was her way to dismiss what she couldn't control, and put the best possible face on every failure, and that was what she was doing now, but it was hard, she was having a hard time of it. She came to the doorway and leaned against the frame, giving Edith the wan smile of a comrade in arms. "Are you ready?" she asked.

METAMORPHOSES

THE CHANGE

Gina had all the symptoms: sleep disturbances, hot flashes, irritability, weight gain, loss of libido, aching joints, and heart palpitations. The one she complained of most was hot flashes, which she dealt with by throwing off her clothes and cursing. As far as Evan was concerned, her irritability was the worst symptom; she was increasingly difficult to get along with. Churlish, he told her. Her lack of interest in sex was possibly more frustrating, though he admitted to himself that he found her less desirable because she was so uncivil, so he didn't suffer unduly from wanting her and being rejected. When they did make love, it was a wrestling match, which Evan enjoyed well enough. They had never been much for tender embraces.

Her work was changing, too; it was getting darker. As he stood looking at an engraving of trees, of a dark forest, he wondered how it could all seem so clear when it was almost entirely black. She was working all the time, well into the nights, because she couldn't sleep. Often enough he found her in the mornings curled up under a lap rug on the cot in her cluttered, inky little studio with the windows open and the chill early morning light pouring in.

She wasn't taking care of herself properly, not eating enough, not washing enough; she hardly took any exercise at all. Sometimes she lay around the living room all day, napping or reading magazines, getting up now and then to rummage around in her studio, then back to the couch, where she left ink stains on the upholstery. There were dust balls under the beds and in the corners of the rooms, dishes always stacked in the sink.

"It's driving me crazy," Evan complained. "Can't we get someone in to clean this place, since you can't keep up with it?"

She gave him a cold, reproachful glare over her magazine. "I can keep up with it," she said. "I just don't keep up with it."

"Well, then, hire someone who will."

"You hire someone," she replied. "Since it bothers you so much."

Evan turned away. He did all the cooking as it was. How could he possibly take on the cleaning as well? And he had no idea how to hire someone. He went to the kitchen and threw open the refrigerator. "And what are we going to eat for dinner?" he shouted to her. "This refrigerator is practically empty."

"We'll go out," she shouted back.

They went out. She was in a good mood for a change. They laughed, drank too much wine, walked back through the city streets with their arms locked around each other, made love on the living room floor. Evan went to bed, but she wouldn't go with him. She went to her studio, and twice when he woke in the night, he saw that the light was still on.

The next day she was a harridan again, peevish and distracted. His own work was going poorly; he had taken on too much and had two deadlines he didn't think he could make. When he complained to her, she shrugged. "Then don't make them," she said. "Tell the editor you can't do it."

"Right," he said. "And then she never calls on me again. I need the work."

"You always say that," she snapped. "And you always have more work than you can do. So obviously you don't need it."

Evan followed her out of the room into her studio. "I don't always have more than I can do. Sometimes I don't have any. It's feast or famine in this business, as you well know."

Gina yawned, put her hands on her hips, and stretched, making an agonized face at him. "Jesus, my back hurts," she said.

"It's freezing in here," he said, moving toward the open window. "Why don't you close this?"

But before he could reach it she blocked his path. "Don't close the window," she said angrily.

"Ugh," Evan said. "What is that?" For on the windowsill were the remains of some animal. Evan pushed past his wife to get a closer look. It was the back half of a mouse, tail, feet, gory innards.

"Where did this come from?" he said.

"The cat must have left it." She turned away, bending over a partially engraved plate.

"We don't have a cat."

All at once she was angry, as if he'd done something annoying. "The neighbor's cat," she sputtered. "Would you just leave it? I'll take care of it."

"It's disgusting," he said. He looked around the room at the half-empty coffee cups, the dishes with crumbs and bits of old sandwiches or dried cottage cheese stuck to them, the confusion of ink and paper, copper plates, presses, the disorder of the bottles of acids and resins, the writing desk overflowing with unanswered mail, bills, and photographs. "This whole room is disgusting," he concluded. "How can you find anything in here?"

To which she replied, "Who asked you to come in here? Will you get out of here?" And she pushed him out the door.

They were invited to a dinner party. Gina was in her studio until it was almost time to leave. Then she came out, washed her hands, combed her hair, threw on a skirt, and said she was ready. Evan had showered, shaved, dressed carefully, even polished his shoes. He looked at her skeptically. "That's it?" he said. "You're ready?"

"Why not?" she said.

No jewelry, he thought. No makeup, no perfume. There had been a time when it took her at least an hour to dress for a party.

The party went well, it was easy conversation, good wine, old friends, until a couple Gina and Evan had not seen for some time arrived. Evan spotted the woman, Vicky, first, smiled and waved as he caught her eye. Something was different about her, he thought, but he couldn't be sure. She looked great, very bright, very intense. Her blouse had flecks of gold in it; she was sparkling. Gina, standing next to him, laughing at something their host was saying, turned and saw the woman too. "Oh my God," she said softly. Vicky moved slowly toward them, smiling.

Seeing Gina's drop-jawed amazement, the host said confidentially, "She's been done." Evan sent him an inquiring look, to which he responded by tapping his lower jaw with the backs of his fingers.

Vicky had stopped to speak to someone else. Evan watched her, though he tried not to stare. In a distant, agreeable way he had always admired her. The last time he had seen her, several months ago, he had observed that her delicate beauty was fading. Now she looked good, he thought. She'd changed her hair too, probably to disguise the more surprising change in her face. They'd done a good job on her. Perhaps her mouth was a little stretched at the corners, and of course the flesh around her chin looked tight. She broke away from her conversation and continued toward Gina and Evan.

"Vicky, how are you?" Evan said, catching her outstretched hand in his own, as if he were retrieving her, he thought, or pulling her out of a fish tank. "It's good to see you."

He was aware of Gina at his side, of her steady, even breathing, but he didn't see her face until it was too late. "Have you lost your mind?" she said sharply to Vicky. "Why would you do something like that? You look awful."

Vicky missed a beat to astonishment and another to dismay, but that was all. "I may have lost my mind," she said, "but you seem to have lost your manners."

Evan turned on his wife. He was so angry he wanted to slap her. "For God's sake, Gina," he said. "Are you drunk?"

Gina blinked her eyes rapidly, ignoring him. She was concentrated on Vicky, who was easing herself away. "So you count on people not to say anything. Do you tell yourself they don't notice?"

"Excuse me," Vicky said, disappearing into the crowd.

"It's ridiculous," Gina continued. "She looked perfectly fine before. Now she looks like something from television, like a talk show host."

"I think we'd better go," Evan said, trying to take her arm, but she shook him off.

"Will you calm down," she said.

So they stayed and the rest of the evening passed uneventfully, but Evan was miserable and felt humiliated. At dinner they were seated as far from Vicky and her husband as possible, probably at her request, Evan thought. Vicky was the center of attention; Evan could hear her tinkling laugh but couldn't bring himself to look her way. Gina leaned out past him now and then to shoot a disapproving look toward the offending jawline, but she said nothing more about it, and once she got into a conversation with her neighbor, which Evan joined, she seemed to forget the unpleasant incident. They talked about publishing—the neighbor was also a journalist—and then about travel. Gina told a funny story about a hotel they had stayed in on a Greek island, and Evan, though he had heard this story before, though he had actually been there when the porter threw Gina's suitcase out the window, found himself laughing as heartily as their friend. He applied himself to his wine and resolved to forgive his wife.

○

Evan noticed the book a few times before he actually picked it up to look at it. He'd seen it on the table in the living room, half buried in a pile of magazines, and on the kitchen table, and once on the nightstand next to their bed. A woman's book about women, he thought, about all the trials of their biology

and psychology, the special wonderfulness of it all and the failure of men to comprehend any of it, though it was going on
right under their noses. Women lapped this stuff up like cream,
even intelligent women like Gina, which was what really made
it annoying. Here was the book again, jammed between the
cushions of the couch with a pencil stuck in it to mark the page.
He pulled it out and opened it to the page with the pencil. The
chapter was titled "No Longer a Woman," and it told all about
the biological changes attendant on menopause: the shrinking
of the uterus, the drying out of vaginal tissue, the atrophy of the
ovaries, the steady depletion of estrogen.

Pretty dry reading, Evan thought with a sardonic chuckle.
He put the book back where he had found it and wandered off
to his desk, where his article was not taking shape. No longer a woman, he thought. But if not a woman, then what? It
was ridiculous. When was a woman ever not a woman? All the
symptoms Gina complained of only proved she was a woman,
and a susceptible one at that, which was part of being a woman
too. An old woman was still a woman, still behaved as she always
had, only more so. Evan thought of his grandmother. Not an
old woman but an old lady. She wore violet perfume—he could
still remember it—and was fond of a certain candy, a puffy,
spongy, fruit-flavored ball that came in tins; he hadn't seen any
in years. She was small, bent, arthritic, but industrious to the
end. She did a little gardening on the last day of her life. She
had survived her husband by twenty years. Perfectly nice, perfectly sexless. Serene, agreeable. Everyone loved her.

Though he remembered that once, when he was praising
this wonderful woman to his mother, she had commented drily,
"Yes, she's very nice now. But she wasn't always."

○

Their son, Edward, called. Gina answered the phone. Evan stood by waiting for his turn; he was fond of his son and looked forward to these weekly calls. Gina was smiling. She laughed at some witticism and said, "Watch out for that." Then for several minutes she fell silent. Her eyes wandered around the room, never settling, and she shifted her weight from foot to foot restlessly. At last she said, distantly, "That's really great, dear. Here's your father. I'll talk to you next week," and held out the phone to Evan.

While he stood talking to Edward, Gina sat down at the table and pulled off her sweater. Then, as Edward went on about his psychology class, she stripped off her shirt and bra. She stretched her arms out across the table and rested her head upon them. Evan turned away from her and tried to concentrate on his son's description of his daily life. When he hung up the phone she was sitting up, blotting her forehead with her sweater.

"You were a little abrupt with him," Evan said. "He asked if you were okay."

"Of course I'm okay," she said.

Evan took a seat next to her and watched as she pulled her shirt back over her head. "Did he tell you about his psychology professor?"

"Yes," she said. "He talks too much."

Evan ran his hand through his thinning hair, trying to stroke down his impatience. "You're not the only one who's getting older, you know."

She pushed back her chair, dismissing him. She was on her

way to her studio. "It's not the same," she said in parting. "It's different."

It was always different, he thought. They wanted to be treated the same, but only with the understanding that they deserved special treatment because they were different. It was true that they had been treated as if they were different for a long time, but they had been treated as different in the wrong way, they were not different in that way. What was different was the deal they got, the way they were treated, which was never fair. He loosened his collar; his face felt hot. But oh no, it wasn't anything that wasn't his fault. It wasn't hormones surging uncontrollably like guerrilla fighters, it was just his lousy blood pressure, which was elevated by his annoyance with his wife's suffering, and if he was uncomfortable, if he felt a little snappish, well, it was all his fault, because her bad temper was a symptom, and his was just plain old garden-variety bad temper, typical in the male. He got up and staggered into his study, where his article accosted him, demanding what he could not, because of Gina, seem to give it: his undivided attention. He turned away and went into the kitchen to make coffee.

○

Gina had gone out to have lunch with a friend. Evan was alone in the apartment with his article. He sat at his desk reading over his notes, listening to the taped interview he had done with a teenage girl who, he recalled, had been dressed in something that resembled two pieces of bicycle tubing. It depressed him to listen to her agitated, rage-filled monologue. She had a vocabulary of twenty-five words or so, insufficient to express any but the most basic threats and complaints. She was the current girlfriend of a gang member named Smak; Evan's article was about these girls, the attendants of brutal young men, about their precarious, angry, voluptuous, and mindless daily lives. On the tape she was trying to explain to Evan that she did not get up at the same time every day, which was why school was not a possibility for her.

He switched off the tape machine and stared at his bright computer screen for several minutes, but nothing came to him so he switched that off too. Then he got up and wandered through the apartment to Gina's studio.

The lunch was a kind of celebration; she'd finished all the work scheduled for a show next month. There were two new engravings on the drying rack; the rest were stacked away in two big portfolios, ready to go. As Evan stood looking at one on the rack, a line from one of her catalogs ran through his head: "She is a woman who has never stopped loving the forest." They had a joke about it, a follow-up line: "And she is a woman who has never stopped living in Brooklyn."

For twenty years her subject had been the same, but this didn't mean her work had not changed. In Evan's opinion the change had been gradual and persistent. She was more patient, saw more clearly, though the prints were progressively darker. That was the odd, wonderful thing about the newer prints; though they seemed to be covered with ink, they were full of an odd kind of light, an almost subterranean glow. In this one, for instance, he could see through a tangle of vegetation to the ground beneath, and on that dark ground he could make out the tracks of some small animal, a mouse or a chipmunk. In both prints on the rack, the viewpoint was high, as if the viewer were above it all, in a tree perhaps, looking down. Evan studied the second one. He seemed to be falling into it; it was truly an exhilarating angle. There, as he looked deeper and deeper through the accumulation of lines, he made out something extraordinary. He crouched down, close to the paper. It was the small hind foot of a rabbit, no bigger than his fingernail, but perfectly clear. In the next second, he knew, it would be gone.

He went to the portfolio, opened it, lifted the first print. Again the odd feeling of vertigo seized him as he looked down upon the teeming world of branches and vines. He could almost hear the dull buzz of insect life, breathe the oxygen-laden air. "These are terrific," he said aloud. No wonder she had been so absorbed, so distracted, so uninterested in the daily course of her life. He felt a little stab of jealousy. His own work did not claim him; he had to drag himself to it. But that feeling passed quickly. He sat down on her cot, flushing with excitement, imagining how the room would look filled with his wife's strange vision. He heard her key in the door, her footsteps in the hall, then she was standing in the doorway looking in at him.

"What are you doing in here?" she said, just an edge of territorial challenge in her tone.

"I was looking at the new work," he said.

She leaned against the doorframe, pushed her hair off her forehead. She'd had a few drinks at lunch, celebrating. "Well, what do you think?" she said.

"I think it's just amazing," he said. "It's so good I had to sit down here and mull it over."

She sagged a little more in the doorway, smiling now but anxious. "Do you really think so? I've been almost afraid for you to see it."

"Oh, my dear," he said.

Tears filled her eyes. She brushed them away with the back of one hand. "I'm so happy," she said. She came into the room and sat beside him, still wiping away tears. "These stupid tears," she said impatiently.

Evan put his arm around her, muttered into her shoulder, "I'm so proud of you." There they sat for some time, contented, holding on to each other as if they were actually in the forest of her dreams.

○

There was always a letdown after she'd finished a block of work, Evan told himself in the difficult days that followed. She was petulant and weepy, angry with the gallery owner, who had been her friend and supporter for years, complaining about every detail of the installation. She hardly slept at night, though what she did in her studio Evan couldn't figure out. She wasn't working, and she hadn't, as she usually did between showings, cleaned the place up. But night after night he woke just long enough to watch her get up, pull on her robe, and go out, then he saw the light from her studio. During the day she lay about the apartment, napping or reading, getting nothing done and snapping at him if he so much as suggested a trip to the grocery. He tried to ignore her, spent his days struggling with his article, which resisted his efforts so stubbornly he sometimes sat at his desk for hours, literally pulling at what he called the remains of his hair. Finally he began to have trouble sleeping too. He lay on his back in the darkness, unable to move or to rest, while panic gripped his heart. When he did sleep, he had strange, unsettling dreams in which he was lost, pursued by something terrifying, powerful, something silent and brooding, something with wings.

One night, waking in terror from such a dream, he found himself, as he often did, alone in the bed. Once his heart slowed down and strength returned to his legs, he resolved to get up. His throat was parched; he felt dehydrated, as if he had been wandering in a desert. Pursued by what? he thought as he sat up and fumbled around for his slippers. Some desert creature? A creature with claws and wings and the face of a woman who would pose some unanswerable riddle before tearing him to bits? The idea amused him as he stumbled to the kitchen and switched on the lights, which made him recoil so violently he switched them back off. He poured himself a glass of water and stood, still sleep-shocked, gazing out the kitchen window at the back of the building across the alley. Above it he could see the milky luminescence of the half-moon. He finished his water, feeling quiet now, and friendly. The light from Gina's studio made a pool across the kitchen floor. He put his glass in the sink and followed this light to her room. The double doors had glass insets, but the glass was mottled so as not to be transparent. They were closed, but not tightly—in fact, one stood free of the latch and could be opened noiselessly with a push. He didn't want to startle her, but if she was asleep he didn't want to wake her, either. "Gina?" he said softly once, then again. Carefully he pushed the door open a few inches. He could see the cot from where he was; she wasn't in it. He opened the door a little further, then all the way. The window stood open, the room was bright and cold; Gina was not in it.

It took him a moment to apprehend this information. He

looked around anxiously, as if he could make her materialize by his determination to find her there. He went to the living room; perhaps she was sleeping on the couch. He looked in the bathroom and then the bedroom, though of course he knew she was not there. He glanced at the clock, 3:00 a.m. He went back to the studio.

What did it mean? How often in the past months when he had believed her to be here in this room had she been . . . wherever she was? His heart ached in his chest; he laid his hand upon it. She had a lover, there could be no doubt of it. That was why she was so tired all the time, why she slept all day, and why she was so cold and bitter.

Evan switched off the light and went to sit on the couch in the living room in the dark. He would wait for her; they would have it out. His rival was probably much younger than he was. When women Gina's age could, they often did. He thought of Colette and George Eliot. He would be a young man impressed by her because she was an artist and he was, surely, a nothing, a boy in need of a mother. It went like that; there were countless such stories. The minutes ticked by. He waited in a fog of anxiety and weariness. He wasn't up to the scene to come. Perhaps he should get back in bed and pretend he didn't know. Maybe then the affair would run its course, she would tire of the young man, or he of her, and things would get back to normal.

He was awakened by a clatter coming from Gina's studio. It sounded like someone was smashing china. He leaped to his feet, crossed the narrow hall, and threw open the doors. The early-morning light was soft and pale, bathing the scene before him in a wash of pink and gray. Gina was on her hands and knees on the floor just inside the window. Next to her was a broken plate. A few crusts had flown from it and landed near her foot. One was lodged in the cuff of her pants.

"What on earth are you doing?" he cried.

She sat up, rubbing her ankle, picking out the bit of bread. "What does it look like I'm doing?" she said crossly. "I'm trying to get up off the floor."

"But where have you been? You weren't here."

She lifted her head toward the window. "I was on the fire escape."

She couldn't have come in the door, Evan reasoned. She would have had to walk through the living room, and he would have seen her. "What were you doing out there?" he complained. "Didn't you hear me call you?"

"No," she said. "I guess I fell asleep." She got to her feet, brushing herself off. Evan pushed past her and stuck his head out the window. "How could you sleep out here?" he called back to her. In the summer she kept plants on the landing, herbs and geraniums, and on hot nights she sometimes took a cushion and sat among the pots. But now there was nothing but the cold metal, the cold air, and the cold stars fading overhead in a pale sky. The stairs led down to a narrow alleyway, which opened into a school parking lot that was fenced and locked at night. She couldn't have gone down there. His eye was caught by something on the landing below. It was a long brown feather with a black bar across it. He turned from the window to his wife, who was sitting on the cot, her head in her hands.

"You don't expect me to believe that," he said.

She raised her head and gave him a brief, weary inspection, as if she were looking at an annoying insect. "I don't care what you believe," she said.

"Gina, what's happening to you?" he exclaimed. "You disappear in the middle of the night, you tell me an absurd lie nobody would believe, and then you give me your too-tired-to-care routine."

"I'm not tired," she said. "I just don't care."

"We can't go on like this," he said, in despair.

"I know it," she said.

○

But they did go on. What else, Evan thought, could they do? He accepted her story, partly because he couldn't come up with an alternative scenario—she had been coming in through the window, and the fire escape, as she pointed out, led nowhere—and partly because it didn't seem to matter. He didn't think she was having an affair, because she didn't act like someone who was in love; she was neither defensive nor elated, and she seemed completely uninterested in her own body. What he had often thought of as a brooding sensuality now became just brooding. He continued his struggle with his article, Gina battled it out with her gallery, and finally they were both finished and both were moderately successful. They had a little time to rest, to cast about for new projects. Usually when this happened they gave themselves over to the pleasure of having no deadlines, sleeping late, eating at odd hours, gorging on videos, food, and sex. But this time it was different. Gina was still sleeping very little at night, and she seemed so uninterested in sex that Evan made a resolution that he would not initiate it. In the past, he thought gloomily, he had never paid much attention to who started it. Now he was self-consciously aware that it was always him. She rejected him without speaking, with a shrug, or by walking away. And if she did accept his overtures, she hurried him along, as if she didn't really have the time and her mind was somewhere else. He grew sick of trying and sick of waiting. Winter was dragging on; the weather was rotten, cold and rainy.

Evan was drinking too much, and for the first time in his life he began to put on weight. One Sunday when the sun was shining for a change and there was a hint of warmth in the air, he ran into a neighbor at the farmers' market. During their conversation Evan jokingly mentioned the latter problem; the drinking was a secret he was keeping even from himself.

"It happens to the best of us," his neighbor said. "Especially at our age. I've joined a gym; it's not far from here. It's made a big difference in how I feel."

Evan had to admit that his neighbor looked fit and energetic. "Give me a call," the neighbor concluded. "I go two or three times a week. I'll take you over and show you around. Bring Gina, if she's interested."

But of course she wasn't interested. "It's ridiculous," she said, throwing one magazine on the floor and taking up another. "I'm not going to spend my time running on a treadmill like a laboratory rat."

So Evan went alone. He met his friend at the reception desk and received a pass, then a tour of the facility. He was impressed with the size of the place, the up-to-date equipment, swimming pool, racquetball courts—he hadn't played in years, but he remembered enjoying the game. There was even a juice and salad bar. It was in this bar, as he was leaving, that he found Vicky and her husband, who waved him over to their table with soft cries of enthusiasm and surprise. As he walked to join them, Evan experienced a mild pang of discomfort; he hadn't seen either of them since Gina had behaved so rudely at the party. But Vicky seemed not to remember, or not to care. Her hand pressed his warmly in greeting and she patted the chair next to her, inviting him to sit.

"So you're thinking of joining up?" her husband, Victor, inquired.

Evan smiled at him and nodded, looking around the pleasant, busy room. He was thinking, as he always did when he saw them together, Vicky and Victor, such silly names. "It's much bigger than I thought it would be," he said.

Vicky drained her carrot juice. "We've been coming for a year now. It's a lifesaver."

"You look great," Evan said. She really did. She was wearing a sleeveless scoop-neck leotard and leggings, so he could see exactly how good she looked. There was just a hint of cleavage visible at the neckline, enough to show that her breasts were still firm, not sallow-looking or wrinkled. Her arms looked firm and strong too, though the thick cords and darkened skin on the backs of her hands gave some hint of her age. She had a scarf tied around her waist—not the best idea, Evan thought, because it called attention to the small but distinctly round belly just below. He couldn't see her hips. She pushed her hair back from her face, giving Evan a quick, complex look made up in parts of gratitude, flirtation, and suspicion. "Thanks," she said. "I feel great."

Victor patted her shoulder proprietarily. "She's fantastic," he said. Vicky laughed, childishly pleased to be the object of her husband's praise. Evan looked down at himself with fake dismay. "I'll need a lot of work," he said. "It may be too late for me."

"Never too late," Victor assured him. "You're as young as you feel."

Evan wished they could talk about something else, but there was no way to change the subject. This was a gym, after all. The subject was bodies. Victor told Evan about his routine. He liked the stair-step machine; Vicky preferred the treadmill. The aerobics classes were excellent. Vicky even did yoga. The free-weights room was sometimes a little crowded; the young jocks did not always leave the racks in perfect order, that was the only drawback. At last there was a lull long enough for Evan to make an excuse. He had to get back to work, he said. As always, he had a deadline.

"Time for us to hit the showers," Victor said, getting up. He popped Vicky playfully across the shoulders with his towel. "Great to see you," he said, grasping Evan's hand. "Give Gina our best."

Evan noted the brief flash of distress that crossed Vicky's face at the mention of his wife. She remembers perfectly well, he thought. She's just being nice about it. Then he was angry at Gina all over again. What right had she to criticize this nice woman because she cared enough about her appearance to have her face lifted? What was wrong with staying fit and wanting to look good for each other, as Vicky and Victor obviously did?

Evan left the gym with a printed sheet of membership privileges and prices gripped tightly in his hand. Filled with resolution and optimism, he stopped in the chilly parking lot to look it over. This was a good thing to do, he told himself. He wanted to be like Vicky and Victor. Gina would ridicule him, but he didn't care. He wanted to feel good about himself, he wanted to change his life. Carefully he folded his informational paper and put it deep in his coat pocket.

That night Gina was particularly restless and distracted. Evan made pasta and a salad for dinner, but she hardly touched it. She complained that her neck and shoulders were stiff, shrugging repeatedly, trying to loosen up the muscles. Evan told her about the gym, expecting a tirade, or simply a dismissive remark, but to his surprise she listened attentively. In fact, as he explained why he thought it would be a good investment for him, how he feared that his sedentary ways resulted in fatigue and depression, she seemed to focus on him with a distant but sincere interest. "It can't be good for you to be closed up in here with me all the time," she said.

"It's not that," he protested.

She said nothing. Evan chewed a piece of lettuce. He could feel her eyes on his face. At last he looked up at her, expecting to find contempt, or anger, or indifference, but she was studying him with a look of complete sympathy, devoid of pity or self-interest, as if, he thought, she were looking right into his soul and finding it blameless, but also infinitely sad. He felt a hot flush rising to his cheeks, and he looked away, at his fork resting among the salad greens, at his half-full glass of wine.

"I think it's a good idea," she said.

○

They sat together on the couch watching a video. It was a complicated story of intrigue on a Greek island. Evan had chosen it because the cover showed a man standing in front of a white building set against a sky so blue and so clearly warm he wished he was in the picture. The scenery in the film was terrific; the television screen seemed to pour warmth and color into their drab living room. When it was over Evan talked a little about how much he wanted to travel, to go to Greece again, and also to Italy and Spain, warm, sunny countries where the people were relaxed and friendly and the food was fresh, healthful, and prepared with care and enthusiasm. Now that their son was grown they could think about going off-season, when there were no tourists. Gina listened, inserting qualifiers here and there—the food in Spain was notoriously filthy, the Italians were far from relaxed—but she seemed more amused than irritated by his aimless fantasies. "You're full of desires today," she said.

"It's true," he admitted. "I am." He rubbed his hand along her thigh, nuzzled his face against her shoulder. She neither responded nor pushed him away. He brought his hand up to her breast, took her earlobe gently between his teeth. "Please don't," she said softly.

He dropped back on the couch, letting out a sigh of frustration.

"I'm sorry," she said, getting up.

"Don't worry about it," he said.

She went into her studio and began gathering up dishes, wadding up pieces of paper. She left the doors open and Evan could see her from where he sat. She went into the kitchen carrying plates, came back with a garbage bag. Evan looked at the clock; it was after midnight. A great time for a little light cleaning, he thought. "A little night cleaning," he called to her.

"I can't stand it anymore," she said, amiably.

"Me neither," Evan said, but softly, to himself. She didn't hear it. After a few minutes he realized he was falling asleep. He got up, pulling off his clothes as he went to bed.

○

The dream ended, as he had known it must, with his missing the plane. Evan woke feeling breathless. He had been running, but they kept the planes across a busy six-lane highway from the check-in. There was a fence too, he recalled, chain-link, tall, over six feet. He rolled onto his side and looked at the clock. It was 5:00 a.m. Gina had still not come to bed. He sat up, rubbing his head, disoriented and strangely apprehensive. After a few moments he got up and made his way to the kitchen. While he stood at the sink drinking water, it dawned on him that the lights in Gina's studio were off. She must have decided to sleep in there. Usually when he found her asleep, the lights were on, the book she had been reading had slipped to the floor or lay, still open, beneath her hand. He stepped out into the hall.

The day was just beginning to dawn, and there was enough gray light for him to see his way. It was, he thought, the most beautiful time of day. The air was still, the building all around him wrapped in a nearly palpable silence, yet alive with the impending and inevitable intensification of light. It was warm in the hall; the apartment was overheated and there was no way to adjust it. A blast of cool air greeted him as he reached Gina's studio. There he stood absorbing one shock after the other.

She had left both the doors and windows wide open. The room was in perfect order, down to the pencils. Some of the habitual clutter had even been stored away in boxes, which were stacked against one wall. The cot was made up neatly: Gina was not in it. Nor was she anywhere else in the room. He said her name once, turned and looked out into the living room, but of course she wasn't there either. He crossed the orderly studio—it seemed alien yet familiar to him, like a room in a dream—to look out on the fire escape, which he found, as he expected, unoccupied. Why was this happening? he thought. Why couldn't everything just go on as it always had? He gazed up at the pale sky, down at the iron clutter of the fire escape, across the narrow, ugly yard at the opposite building. He felt an ineffable sadness curling up into his consciousness like a twining plume of smoke. The building was mostly dark; no one was up yet. One narrow window had a light on, probably a bathroom light left on all night.

He had the uncanny feeling that he was being watched. An abrupt snapping sound drew his eyes to the ledge at the top, just one story above his own.

That was when he saw the owl.

His sadness was dissipated by this wondrous sight. He leaned out the window, craning his neck to see more clearly. "Wow," he said. "An owl in Brooklyn."

A big owl too, or so it seemed to him. He reflected that he had never actually seen an owl before, at least not at such close range. The bird was perfectly still, but its head was inclined forward, its golden eyes focused on Evan. Then, to his astonishment, with a sudden convulsion of motion that was as soundless as it was alarming, the owl opened its wings and flew directly at him. The distance between them, some thirty yards, disappeared in a second. Evan reeled away from the window, aware only of fierce talons extended in his direction. In the next moment he stood clutching the edge of Gina's drawing table, and the owl was perched comfortably on the window ledge, not ten feet away.

His momentary terror faded, replaced by fascination and wonder. The bird was evidently not going to attack him. There was a raised metal bar along the sill, part of the fire escape, and the owl had wrapped its feet around this. He could see the talons sticking out beneath the thick brown fluff of the legs, black and long and sharp as a cat's claws. The bill too looked sharp and dangerous, like a hard black finger pointing down between the large golden eyes. These eyes were fixed on Evan's face with unblinking, unnerving directness. They seemed to be looking right through him, possibly at something behind him. He shifted uneasily from one foot to the other. "I'd ask you to stay," he said, "but we're fresh out of mice."

The bird opened its beak, as if to speak, then spun its head around to face the courtyard, where some tiny motion or sound, invisible or inaudible to Evan, attracted its attention. The whole maneuver was so sudden he had only an impression of having seen it, but it seemed to him the bird's head went all the way around. The eyes drilled through him again. What a disturbing thing it was to be scrutinized in this way by a creature who had, he knew, no sympathy with him. Again the owl opened its beak, but this time a sound issued forth, a high-pitched, startling scream, such as a frightened woman might make. It was so loud and sudden it made Evan step back. Then, as suddenly, the bird was silent again. "Please," Evan said. "You'll wake the neighbors." The owl, unconcerned, fell to picking at its chest feathers. Evan stepped closer, quietly, stealthily, as if the bird didn't know with each second exactly where he was. He was so close he could have reached out to touch the beautiful mottled wings, though he knew he would not dare. The owl raised its strange, otherworldly face, made a calm sidestep on the bar, dipped its head, then refocused on his face.

"Why have you come here?" Evan asked.

But the owl only stared at him, and he felt foolish for speaking. With the intrusion of this portentous creature, all the tedium and anxiety of his life had fallen away. A thrill, as of discovery, passed through him, but he did not move. It was best to be still in such a presence, which surely would not stay long or ever come again.

SEA LOVERS

On moonless nights the sea is black. Ships sail upon it and shine their lights through the double blackness of water and air. The darkness swallows up light like a great yawning snake. On the beach people walk, looking out to sea, but there is no sign of the ships, no sign of the drowning sailors, no sign of anything living or dead, only the continual rushing and ebbing of water sucking and sucking at the shoreline, drawing the innocent, foolish lovers out a little farther. They are unafraid, showing each other their courage. They laugh, pointing to the water. No one can see them. They slip off their clothes and wade in. The waves draw them out, tease them, lick upward slowly about her pale thighs, slap him playfully, dashing a little salt spray into his eyes. He turns to her, she to him; they can scarcely see each other, but they are strong swimmers and they link hands as they go out a little farther, a little deeper. Now the waves swell about them and they embrace. She is losing her footing, so she leans against him, allows the rising water to lift her right off her feet as she is pressed against him. He pulls her in tightly, laughing into her mouth as he kisses her.

They can't be seen; they can't be heard. The people on the shore will find their clothes, but they will never find the lovers. A solitary mermaid passing nearby hears their laughter and pauses. She watches them, but even her strange fish-pale eyes can barely see them; the night is so black, so moonless. She could sing to them, as she has sung to other drowning mortals, but she is weary tonight and her heart is heavy from too much solitude. She has not seen another of her kind for many months. She was nearly killed a few days ago, swimming near a steamship. Her head is full of the giant engine blades, of that moment when she looked up and saw that she was a hair's-breadth from death. That was when she turned toward shore. She is swimming in with the tide, even as the lovers are sucked out and down. When she drops beneath the surface of the water, the mermaid can just see the woman's long hair billowing out around her face. Her mouth is open wide in a silent scream. Oh yes, the mermaid thinks, if she could be heard it would be quite a racket. People would come running for miles. But the sea filled her mouth before the sound could get out and no one will ever hear her now. She clings to the man, and he, in his panic, pushes her away. This started out as such a lark. It was a calm, hot, black night and the white sands of the beach made all the light there was. They had wandered along, stopping to kiss and tease, laughing, so happy, so safe, and now this: She was drowning and he could not save her. Worse, worse, she would pull him under.

The mermaid rises above the crest of a wave and looks back at them. She sees only one pale hand reaching up, the fingers splayed and tense, as if reaching for something to hold; then the water closes over that too.

The sea is full of death, now more than ever. Twice in her short life the mermaid has found herself swimming in a sea red with blood: once from a whale struck by a steamship, once from men drowning during a war. Their ship had been torpedoed and most of them were bleeding when they hit the water. The sharks had done the rest. That time she had dived beneath the battle, for the noise was deafening and the light from the explosions dazzled her so that she could scarcely see. One of the drowning men clutched at her as she swam away, but she shook him off. She disliked being seen by men, even when they were about to die. She could amuse herself singing to them when they couldn't see her; when they were wild-eyed and desperate, clinging to a broken spar from a boat shattered by a storm, or treading water in that ridiculous way they had, with those pathetic, useless legs; then she would hide among the waves and sing to them. Sometimes it made them more frantic, but a few times she had seen a strange calm overtake a drowning man, so that his struggles became more mechanical, less frantic, and he simply stayed afloat as long as he could and went under at last quietly, without that panicked gagging and struggling that was so disgusting to see. Once a man had died like that very near her, and she had felt so curious about him that she drifted too close to him, and in the last moment of his life he saw her. His eyes were wide open and startled already from his long, bitter struggle with death; he knew he was beaten yet could not give up. He saw her and he reached out to her, his mouth opened as if he would speak, but it was blood and not words that poured over his lips and she knew even as he did that he was gone. She had, by her nature, no sympathy for men, but this one interested her.

The man was so far from land that it would be days before his body was tossed up, bloated, unrecognizable, on some shore. He had been sailing alone in a small boat, far out to sea; she had, in fact, been watching his progress for days. The storm that had wrecked his little craft was intense but quickly over, and he had survived it somehow, holding on to pieces of the wreckage. Then it was a few days of hopeless drifting for him. She watched from a distance, listened to him when he began to babble to himself. Near the end he stunned her by bursting into song, singing as loud as he could, though he had little strength left, a lively song that she couldn't understand. When he was dead she did something she had never done: She touched him. He was already stiffening, and his skin was strange; she was fascinated by the smooth, dense feel of it. She held him by his shoulders and brought him down with her, down where the water was still and clear, and there she looked at him carefully. His eyes fascinated her, so different from her own. She discovered the hard nails on his fingers and toes. She examined his mouth, which she thought incredibly ugly, and his genitals, which confused her. Gradually a feeling of revulsion overtook her and she swam away from him abruptly, leaving him wedged in a bed of coral and kelp, food for the bigger fish that might pass his way.

Now she remembers him as she swims toward shore, and her thin upper lip curls back at the thought of him. She is being driven toward land by a force stronger than her own will, and she hates that force even as she gives in to it, just as she hated the dead man.

It is dark and the air is still. Though the sea is never still, she has the illusion of calm. She swims effortlessly just beneath the surface of the waves. She is getting close to shore, dangerously close, but she neither slows nor alters her course.

She is acquainted with many stories that tell of the perils of the land, stories similar to the ones men tell about the sea, full of terror, wonder, magic, and romance. The moral of these tales (that she can no more live on land than men can live in the sea) has not escaped her. She has seen the land; she knows about its edges and she has seen mountains rising above the surface of the water. Sometimes there are people on these mountains, walking about or driving in their cars. This coast, which she must have chosen, is flat and long. There is white sand along it for miles and behind the sand a line of green, though in the darkness its vivid colors are only black before white before gray. The mermaid can scarcely look at it. She is caught up in the surf that moves relentlessly toward land. For a while she can drop beneath the waves, but soon the water is too shallow, and when her tail and side scrape against the hard sand at the bottom, she shudders as if death had reached up suddenly and touched her. The waves smash her down and roll her over. Her tail wedges into the sand and sends a cloud over her; she feels the grit working in under her scales. She raises her webbed hands to wipe it away. It is different from the sand in the deep water; it feels sharp, irritating, and it smells of land.

It's useless to fight the waves. She lets her body rise and fall with them, rolling in with the surf as heavy and unresisting as a broken ship or a dead man. Soon there is nothing but sand beneath her, and the water ebbs away, leaving her helpless, exposed to the warm and alien air. The pounding she has taken has left her barely conscious. She lies on her belly in the sand, her arms stretched out over her head, her face turned to one side so that what little water there is can flow over it. Her long silvery body writhes in the shallows and she is aghast with pain. From the waist down she is numb, and she lifts her head as best she can to look back at herself. She can hardly feel her tail, rising and falling in the sand, working her in deeper and deeper, against her will. It is horrible, and she is so helpless that she falls back down with a groan. Something is seeping out of her, spilling out into the sand. It is slippery and viscous; at first she thinks she is bleeding, then she imagines it is her life. She moans again and struggles to lift herself, pushing her hands against the sand. She opens and closes her mouth, gasping for water. Her skin is drying out; it burns along her back, her shoulders, her neck. She presses her face down as a little trickle of water rushes up near her, but it is not enough and she manages only to get more damp sand in her mouth. She lifts her head and shoulders once more against the unexpected weight of the air, and as she does, she sees the man.

He is running toward her. He has left his fishing gear to the whims of the sea and he is running toward her as fast as he can. Her heart sinks. He is in his element and she is at his mercy. But in the next heartbeat she is struck with cunning and a certainty that flashes up in her consciousness with the force of memory. In the same moment she knows that her lower body is now her own, and strength surges through her like an electric current. He must not see her face; she knows this. She spreads her hair out over her shoulders and hides her face in the sand. Her body is still; her strong tail lies flat in the shallows, as shiny and inert as a sheet of steel.

She listens to the slap of his bare feet against the hard wet sand as he comes closer. Soon she can hear his labored breathing and his mumbled exclamations, though his words are meaningless to her. This is a big catch, but it will be a while before he understands what he has caught. In the darkness he takes her for a woman, and it is not until he is bending over her that he sees the peculiar unwomanly shape of her lower body. For a moment he thinks she is a woman who has been half devoured by an enormous fish. He looks back at the shore, as if help might come from it, but there is no help for him now. His hands move over her shoulders. He is determined to pull her out of the water, not for any reason but that she has washed up on the shore and that is what men do with creatures that wash up on the shore. "My God," he says, and the pitch of his voice makes the mermaid clench her jaw, "are you still alive?"

She doesn't move. His hands are communicating all sorts of useless information to him: This creature is very like a woman, and though her smooth skin is extraordinarily cold, it is soft, supple, alive. His fingers dig in under her arms and lift her a little. She is careful to keep her face down, hidden in the stream of her long hair. This hair, he can see even in the darkness, is white, thick, unnaturally long; it falls voluptuously over her shoulders. He is losing his grip; she is heavier than he imagined, and he releases her for a moment while he changes his position. He straddles her back. She hears the squish of his feet as he steps over her head and positions himself behind her. As he does he takes a closer look at her long back and sees the line where the pale skin turns to silver. "What are you?" he says, but he doesn't pause to find out. His hands are under her arms again; one of them strays lightly over her breasts as he lifts her.

Her heart is beating so furiously now she can hear nothing else. For one moment she hangs limp in his arms and in the next she comes alive.

She brings her arms quickly under her and pushes up so suddenly and with such force that the man loses his balance and collapses over her. She is, thanks to the sea, several times as strong as he is, and she has no difficulty now in turning over beneath him. He struggles, astounded at the sudden powerful fury of the creature he had intended to save, but he struggles in vain. They are entwined together in the sand, rising and falling like lovers, but the man, at least, is aware that this is not love. Her strong arms close around him and he can feel her cold, clawed hands in his hair. His face is wedged against her shoulder, and as he breathes in the peculiar odor of her skin, he is filled with terror. She takes a handful of his hair and pulls his head up so that she can look at him and he at her. What he sees paralyzes him, as surely as if he had looked at Medusa, though it is so dark he can make out only the glitter of her cold, flat, lidless eyes, the thin hard line of her mouth, which opens and closes beneath his own. He can hear the desperate sucking sound fish make when they are pulled from the sea. She rolls him under her as easily as if he were a woman and she a man. With one hand she holds his throat while with the other she tears away the flimsy swimming trunks, all the protection he had against her. Her big tail is moving rapidly now, pushing her body up over his. Her hand loosens at his throat and he gasps for air, groaning, pushing against her with all his strength, trying to push her away. She raises herself on her arms, looking down at him curiously, and he sees the sharp fish teeth, the dry black tongue. Her tail is powerful and sinuous; it has curled up between his legs like an eel and now the sharp edge of it grazes the inside of his thighs. It cuts him; he can feel the blood gathering at the cuts, again and again, each time a little closer to the groin. He cries out, but no one hears him. The mermaid doesn't even bother to look at him as her tail comes up hard against his testicles and slices through the unresisting flesh. His fingers have torn the skin on her back and he has bitten into her breast so that she is bleeding, but she can't feel anything as pain now. She drops back over him and clasps his throat between her hands, pressing hard and for a long time, until he ceases to struggle.

Then she is quiet but not still. Carefully she takes up the bleeding pocket of flesh from between his legs; carefully cradling it in her hands, she transfers it into the impression she left in the sand before this struggle began. The sea will wash it all away in a minute or two, for the tide is coming in, but that's all the time she needs. She pushes the sand up around this bloody treasure; then, exhausted and strangely peaceful, she rolls away into the shallows. The cool water revives her and she summons her strength to swim out past the breakers. Now she can feel the pain in her back and her breast, but she can't stop to attend to it. As soon as the water is deep enough she dives beneath the waves, and as she does her tail flashes silver in the dark night air; like great metal wings, the caudal fin slices first the air, then the water.

On the shore everything is still. The waves are creeping up around the man, prying him loose from the sand. Little water fingers rush in around his legs, his arms, his face. Already the water has washed his blood away. Farther down the beach his fishing gear floats in the rising water. His tackle box has spilled its insides; all his lures and hooks, all the wiles he used to harvest the sea, bob gaily on the waves.

Farther still I am walking on the shore with my lover. We have been dancing at a party. The beach house is behind us, throwing its white light and music out into the night air as if it could fill the void. Inside, it was hot, bright; we couldn't hear the waves or smell the salt air, and so we are feeling lightheaded and pleased with ourselves for having had the good sense to take a walk. We are walking away from the house and away from the dead man, but not away from the sea. I've taken my shoes off so that I can let the water cool my tired feet. My lover follows my example; he sheds his shoes and stops to roll up his pants legs. As I stand looking out into the black water and the blacker sky, it seems to me that I can see tiny lights, like stars, flashing in the waves. When he joins me I ask him, "What are those lights?" and he looks but says he doesn't see any lights.

"Mermaids," I say. I could almost believe it. I raise my hand and wave at them. "Be careful," I say. "Stay away from the shore." My lover is very close to me. His arms encircle me; he draws me close to him. The steady pounding of the waves and the blackness of the night excite us. We would like to make love in the sand at the water's edge.

THE INCIDENT AT VILLEDEAU

"I am a man upon the land."
CHILD BALLAD NO. 113

Before Felix Kelly's death, my uncle Leonce informed me, there hadn't been a murder in Villedeau in fifteen years. At first the homicide appeared to be little more than a hunting accident; in truth, the grand jury wasn't convinced the affair need go to trial at all. Because the accused, Octave Favrot, was a gentleman of both reputation and wealth, and the victim, Felix Kelly, was an outsider, many of us believed that even if there were a trial, Octave would be speedily acquitted.

At that time I was a student of the law, and the prospect of a trial, and a murder trial at that, going forward in our obscure corner of the great world was a circumstance I considered propitious, though of course for the poor victims—there were two, a grown man and his infant son—it could be understood only as a tragedy.

Octave Favrot didn't deny that he had killed Felix Kelly, but he claimed he had acted in self-defense. While hunting near Baie d'en Haut he spied through the foliage a fierce creature as big as a man, which he took to be a bear. When this apparition charged him, in his terror he fired a single shot. Then he heard a cry and understood that the crazed animal was of the human variety. Not until Octave bent over Felix Kelly's corpse did he discover the child, a babe of perhaps two years, fastened to his father's chest by a rope harness. A sluggish ooze of blood gathered at the hole between his startled dark eyes.

Horrified by what he had done, Octave walked out of the forest and straight to the police office at Villedeau, where he reported the accident.

Felix Kelly had arrived in our parish four years earlier under the most extraordinary circumstances. The steamship *Decla*, having taken on passengers and cargo at New Orleans, was navigating the river channel just west of Reserve, when a shout went up on the upper deck that a passenger had fallen overboard. From his station in the wheelhouse, the captain verified that there was indeed a man in the water. The deck hands, equally vigilant, were quick to throw out a rope, which the swimmer grasped and hung on to while the steam engine groaned and the great paddle wheel slowed. The hands hauled in the rope, drawing him closer and closer until he was able to cling to the rail of the lower deck. The crowd gathered at the upper rail to cheer him on, and the mate stretched his arm out over the water to help him aboard, but the man made no effort to avail himself of assistance. By this time the captain had made his way to the scene. He was so outraged by the stolid resistance of this foolish passenger he had halted his great ship to rescue that he spoke harshly. "For God's sake, sir," he exclaimed, "put out your hand, or I shall leave you to the fishes."

The swimmer gazed up, and it was remarked that his eyes were strangely round, black, and placid beneath a thick overhang of brow. "I can't come on board," he said in a voice not defensive but rather confidential. "I've not a stitch of clothes on and there are ladies present. My dear captain, consider my predicament."

This protestation was quickly passed among the passengers, who found much to marvel at in both its import and its tenor. Clearly the man had not lost his clothes in a fall from the ship; therefore, it was deduced, he had entered the water in some other manner, either swimming out from the shore or capsized in some lesser craft. His calm delivery, his reluctance to give offense even in direst circumstance, bespoke the courtesy of a gentleman, as well as a certain bravado which could not fail to engage the admiration of both the fair and the forceful sex. It was also noted that he spoke in a lilting accent, not of the region and not easily assigned to any other. From how far had he come to turn up without his clothes in the treacherous currents of the mighty Mississippi? The gentlemen urged the ladies away from the rails as the captain tossed down a bed sheet the bursar had snatched from a drying line. Taking one corner in his teeth, the swimmer managed to wrap it around his torso. Then, bracing his feet against the ship's side and reaching up to the outstretched hands of the mate, he rose from the turbid waters, trailing the sheet like a king's mantle behind him.

Thus it was that Felix Kelly came among us, naked as a babe thrust from the womb. The crew whisked him away and he appeared some hours later in borrowed trousers and a shirt.

He explained that he had been camping in the woods near the shore, living on what he could shoot or pull from the river, and having gone down to the water for his morning ablutions, was caught by a treacherous current, of which there are sundry in our great Father of Waters, and couldn't fight his way back to the shore. He promised to leave the ship at the next docking and, as soon as he found employment, to repay the kind sailor who had provided him with clothing as well as the captain who had generously invited him to dine at his own table.

The next docking was Villedeau.

Felix, we soon learned, was a man of many parts. A blacksmith by trade, he was a good builder as well, and he manufactured ingenious first-rate traps such as had never been seen in these parts for birds and small mammals, crabs and shrimp; he even had a unique system for waylaying crayfish in their nightly perambulations. His manner was quiet and polite; he had a wry sense of humor much appreciated by those who were not the butt of his jokes, and much resented by those who were. He rented a room from the blacksmith for a few months, and then, having saved enough to lease a small storefront on the main street with a room and a stove behind it, he set himself up there, selling his traps and various pieces of furniture cobbled together from scraps he bought from the lumberyard. Occasionally he assisted the blacksmith when he had more hooves than ready shoes in his establishment.

Felix was solitary and—some said—a little strange, a bit deep, but that might have been suggested by his wide dark eyes, in which the oversized irises crowded out the white at the edges, so that he seemed always to be looking straight ahead.

He had been among us a little over a year when the rumor that he had attracted the attention and even the affection of Odile Chopin began to surface in the repartee at the dance hall and in more pointed conversations at the Ladies' Society meetings. Odile was a beauty, the daughter of a recently deceased rich man and a prize beyond reckoning to the lucky husband who might someday win her hand. The local swains danced her ragged every Saturday night, and the bouquets that appeared at her door on Sunday morning attested to the charm of her company. She had graces and airs taught to her by the nuns of Mount Carmel, she could play the piano and sing like a lark, her spine was straight and her gaze without guile. That she would so much as glance at a dark-eyed stranger with little money and naught but his wit to recommend him was a thing past understanding. Felix Kelly didn't even dance.

Some claimed he'd cast a spell upon Odile or that he had some magnetic apparatus in his clothing, something he'd fashioned from iron with his cunning for laying traps. But this was jealous talk, and it was probably only Felix's attentive eyes and distant, courteous manner that interested Odile. It seemed nearly every day she found some reason to pass down the street and stop on the banquette in front of his shop, engaging in what she described to her unsuspecting mother as harmless conversation. When the weather turned cold, he invited her inside to warm herself by the stove.

Before long, naturally enough, Odile revealed that she was with child, and Felix Kelly freely acknowledged himself to be the father. The town braced for an unsuitable marriage, but Felix then committed the outrage against all decency that made him a pariah among his previously well-disposed neighbors: He refused to marry Odile and would not agree to provide for her baby.

To the great relief of her family, only a little time passed before Octave Favrot, who was Odile's second cousin, offered to marry her and to adopt the yet unborn child as his own. Sadly, at his birth this infant proved more likely to be a burden to his parents than a joy, for, though healthy and good-natured, Michel, as his unfortunate mother named him, was born blind.

So what we had was the story of an outsider, Felix Kelly, who comes to a civilized place, abuses the trust of a virtuous young woman of a good family, and is subsequently murdered by her rescuer, her husband, and her relative, all three in one man, Octave Favrot. Such a sequence may not be that uncommon in the annals of human affairs but for the detail that Felix Kelly died with his unwanted son wrapped in a fur and strapped to his chest. He was not far from the place where he had first appeared, naked and without resources, flagging down a steamship.

No sooner had Octave confessed to the accident than Odile, wild-eyed and breathless, came clattering down the street on her bay mare to report that her son was missing. In the vestibule of the sheriff's office she saw her husband's rifle propped against a chair, and a fresh terror gripped her heart, for she didn't expect his return for two or three days. She threw open the door to the inner office, where Octave sat, head in hands at the desk, soberly dictating his statement to the secretary, Marie Barrois. Odile cried out, "Octave, Michel is gone." When her husband lifted his eyes, which were heavy with the death he had administered, she moaned wordlessly and collapsed in a faint on the floor.

The sheriff dispatched a party of deputies to bring in the bodies of the victims. Octave's cooperation was so assured that he was allowed to lead the way without restraint. He knew the terrain, having hunted there for many years, supplying from the bounteous wildlife that teemed in the swampy inlets fish, crustaceans, meat, birds, furs, and hides for his family and friends. Though he was prosperous enough to buy what he needed, his wealth also provided him with ample leisure. Hunting, fishing, stalking by day, camping by night in a canvas tent with a fire and sometimes a dog or two for company, soothed and refreshed his spirit. He was a creature of the place, as at home in the bayou as any nutria, fox, or squirrel.

The bodies of Felix and his son, Michel, were transported back to Villedeau, and the coroner from Edgard, to which news of the accident had quickly spread, arrived in the afternoon to take custody of them. He spent the night absorbed in his grisly work and in the morning filed his report with the proper authorities. The victims' bodies were then transferred to the Dupuy funeral home. It was agreed that the sale of Felix's property would defray the cost of his burial. He had left no will and no next of kin could be located, though the town clerk made some superficial effort. Felix had died, as he had lived, undocumented, a man who came out of a river.

Odile requested that Michel's small corpse be delivered to her house, where he was laid in a child's white casket, loaded into a cart, and interred, after a heartbreaking journey, in her family's cemetery plot. Felix Kelly was buried in the town cemetery, in a far, shady corner reserved for those few with neither money nor family to see to their remains. A flat stone with only his name marked the location of his grave.

The coroner's report was not made public, but rumors about its contents spread like a grass fire, and it wasn't long before everyone knew the details. One bullet, fired at a distance of no more than thirty feet, had pierced both the brain of the child and the heart of the man. Felix's body bore an old scar from his left hip to his knee. The child's blind eyes had a filmy silvery lining behind the retinas, an anomaly never before observed by the attending physician. An interesting detail, not unheard of and clearly the result of inherited tendencies, was that both father and son had thin, translucent webbing between their toes.

"Always knew there was something fishy about Felix," the town wit remarked on this last revelation. He was corrected at once by his more literal friend: "Something froggy you mean, don't you?"

No weapon was found in the vicinity, nor anything suggesting the intentions of the victim. Felix Kelly had lifted his son from his crib, wrapped him in a soft monk-seal skin, fastened him to his chest with a rope halter, and headed into the forest. The coroner printed his conclusion in square letters on the line indicating cause of death: HOMICIDE.

The trial would be held in Edgard, the parish seat. While the charges were being prepared, Octave was lodged in Villedeau's prison, which was a simple room furnished with a bed, a washstand, and a chamber pot, with bars on the window and a grate in the door. Our sheriff, the portly and self-important Cyrus Petit, called it his hotel, and its guests were usually drunks who had outraged public decency in some way, by fighting or breaking furniture or raving in the street. They slept it off, and in the morning, when they had recovered their senses, they were released to their unwelcoming families. Octave's residence there, which was of some duration, was eased by the sheriff's familiarity with and respect for his prisoner's character and wealth. Odile arrived daily with her husband's dinner, and the sheriff allowed the couple to dine at his desk while he retreated to a rocking chair on the porch, his rifle resting across his paunch. At the window he could hear the conversation between the couple, which, he reported to his wife, was laconic at best.

"Perhaps that's because Odile knows you're out there listening," this matron remarked.

"I don't know," her husband replied. "Odile is different now. This business has broken her spirit. She's got a ghostly way about her. It's like she can't hear, or don't understand what she does hear. She can't look him in the eye, or anyone else for that matter."

"Well," concluded his wife, "he killed her poor baby, and she may never have another."

Lyle Sanchez, the defendant's lawyer, maintained that the prosecutor, Cesar Denis, was an ambitious, hotheaded, coldhearted upstart too young for the job. He had no connection to the Favrot clan, no interests in Villedeau, and he'd married a Bohemian girl from Pointe à la Hache. I had met Cesar during my law studies and admired his skill as an orator. Quick-witted and unfailingly lucid, he led a jury along to his inevitable conclusions like a good shepherd dog, his quick eyes alert to any stragglers, his bark sharp and clear, persuasive rather than threatening; he made you want to see things his way.

His way in this case was a charge of first-degree murder, which no one believed he could make stick, considering who Octave was, the general antipathy toward Felix Kelly, and the lack of witnesses to the incident. But Cesar had investigated the scene of the shooting, interviewed various parties, and was convinced that Octave had a motive, and that the confrontation in the forest was not an accident, or even an impulsive act of violence, but a premeditated crime.

It struck Cesar as odd that Felix Kelly, who had lived and worked in a small town for several years and was by all accounts a frugal and industrious craftsman with no expensive habits and no one to support but himself, should leave so small an estate. There should have been, he reasoned, more money. Accordingly he requested an interview with Silas Bunkie, the head of the Savings Bank in Vacherie, the closest such institution to Ville-deau. Silas revealed that Felix Kelly had indeed been a regular depositor, having opened an account shortly after he leased his shop, and over the years had amassed a considerable savings, a little over a thousand dollars, which amount he had withdrawn in its entirety one week before his fatal encounter with Octave Favrot.

Where was the money? Felix didn't have a cent on him when he died. His home and possessions had been thoroughly searched and dispersed. Why would he have taken out his entire savings and left town without it? It made no sense.

When the court official arrived with an order to search the house of Octave Favrot, Sheriff Petit expressed his outrage with some vehemence. His first impulse was to warn Odile that he would be obliged to carry out the order, but the official, calm in the face of resistance and sure of his duty to the court, insisted that the action must be performed without delay, and that he would accompany the search party and report the results to the prosecutor.

"What in God's name are we looking for?" exclaimed the indignant sheriff. "Are we to go through that poor lady's armoire, are we to rifle her linens and her dresses and her undergarments?"

"You are looking for one thousand dollars in gold coin," retorted the messenger. "So I would think the armoire might be a very likely place to begin."

Sheriff Petit rose ponderously from his desk, lumbered to the door of the prison room, and threw it open with more than necessary force. "Octave," he shouted into the dim room beyond, "have you got a thousand dollars in gold at your place?"

"I do not," came the offended reply.

The sheriff turned a glacial eye upon the court official. "There you are," he said. "He don't have it."

The official was not amused by the sheriff's complacency. A boy was sent out to call in three men to be deputized, and in the afternoon, accompanied by the court official, they set out for the Favrot house.

Though not grand, this was a comfortable, spacious cottage, with wide porches across the front and the back, the front giving on to a lane of old oaks, the back upon a wide green lawn ending at the sparkling blue of the bayou. A fanciful screened gazebo, with a domed roof and classical columns, appeared to float upon a cloud of pink azaleas near the water's edge. Odile's mother, a dignified lady in whose features the original stamp of her daughter's loveliness was still evident, greeted her visitors without suspicion, for she knew the deputies by their first names. The court official stepped forward, proffering the order to search the premises, while the townsmen hung back sheepishly, embarrassed by their mission. Madame Chopin studied the document, clearly mystified. "What does it mean?" she asked calmly.

"It means these men must come in now and search your house."

"My daughter is ill," she said coldly. "Surely this can wait until she has recovered."

At this the deputies literally hung their heads, but the court official was firm. "I'm afraid not, ma'am," he said. "The warrant must be carried out without notice."

Madame Chopin gave the official, who was young enough to be her son, a long, searching look. Something she saw, perhaps his inherent obstinacy, piqued her interest. "Because you think we might take the opportunity to hide whatever it is you're looking for," she observed.

"That's not for me to say, ma'am," he replied. "The court is very clear on the procedure, and it's my duty to carry out the wishes of the court."

"The wishes," she repeated.

"The orders," he corrected. "It's a court order you're holding."

As she folded the paper and handed it back to the young man, the faintest of smiles played at the corners of her mouth. "I see," she said. "My daughter is resting in the parlor. I don't want her needlessly disturbed. I'll bring her out and sit with her in the gazebo while you gentlemen"—she nodded at the miserable trio skulking on the steps—"go about your business here."

As she turned to reenter her daughter's house, the young

man stepped forward, his hand raised as if to make a salient point. "Excuse me, ma'am," he said. "I'll have to accompany you."

Her only reaction was a visible drawing up of the spine, a slight tilt of her chin in the direction of her unwelcome visitor. "Very well," she said. "Come along."

The three deputies retreated to the shade of an oak tree, scarcely speaking as they waited, each of them feeling in his own conscience the burden of this unsolicited employment. Rifling the personal possessions of a wealthy man upon whom adversity had fallen as surely as it falls on the indigent and the poor was not an honorable activity. If Octave had been a skinflint or a brute, there might be some pleasure in seeing him brought low, but he was a gentleman, a fair employer, a man whose sense of duty to his family had been sorely tested and proved sufficient to the test.

At last the screen door opened and Odile Favrot, supported by her mother and followed with ecclesiastical solemnity by the court official, stepped out. Odile was dressed in black, her pale face partially obscured by her dark hair, which fell loosely over her shoulders. She kept her eyes down, inclining her head toward her mother's ear and mumbling something the men couldn't make out. She was spectrally thin; the forearm that showed beyond the sleeve of her dress was nearly fleshless. Nervously she tapped her long, skeletal fingers against her mother's shoulder. The two women descended the steps and turned from the walk onto the worn path to the gazebo. It was a bright, clear, fresh fall day, but to the men following the melancholy passage of this wraith, whose beauty and vivacity had once entranced the town in a blissful spell, it was as if a cold, dark wave rose in her wake and smote the bright shore on which they wonderingly stood.

The official summoned the men to the house and directed them into various rooms, reminding them that the gold might not be all in one place, that they were to open every drawer and search under and behind all furniture, inside all sacks and casks in the kitchen. They glared at him as a group, but once separated, each set to work resolutely. Odile's arrangements were tidy, which made their job easier and inclined them to leave everything as they had found it. The official himself examined the baby's room, noting that to take the babe without alarming the household, the thief would have had to climb to the porch roof and slip in through the window. He knew it was the prosecutor's theory that Felix Kelly had never entered the house and that Octave had sold the child to him for a bag of gold. As he opened the chest of drawers, which was a fine oak piece with drawer pulls carved in the shape of leaves and an ebony inlay on the top, he wondered why a man so obviously as wealthy as Octave Favrot would take money from a man he must have despised.

In the chest he found folded linens scented by a lavender sachet, a drawer of neatly pressed baby clothes, and another containing soft toys, stuffed animals, and a smooth satin ball. The poor child, blind as he was, couldn't see the button eyes and sewed-on smile of the plush bear, but he could probably feel the shape and make some image in his mind. He was said to be a bright little boy, in spite of his affliction, who learned to speak early, loved music, and walked boldly with his hands out before him, unruffled when he fell, as he frequently did. His mother adored him.

The official turned to the child's bed. Surely there was nothing to be found there. Absently he lifted the pillow and stood looking down in surprise at a shiny coin. He picked it up. A five-dollar gold piece.

Perhaps the money was hidden coin by coin, throughout the house. He carried his find to the parlor, where a deputy was carefully returning a vase to the sideboard. "Did you look inside the vase?" asked the official.

"'Course I did," replied the man.

"I found a gold piece," the official said, holding out the coin. "Under the pillow in the child's bed."

His colleague took the piece and turned it over in his hand. "What in this world was it doing there?" he said.

"There must be others," the official insisted. "They must be hidden all over the house."

But three hours later, when it was agreed that the search was ended, they had not found another coin of any kind.

○

Because of her illness, Odile had stopped visiting her husband, and it was now Madame Chopin who brought the daily meal to the sheriff's office. The day after the fruitless search she arrived in high dudgeon and made a fuss about the men searching through her daughter's possessions. Her son-in-law had admitted his offense, she reminded the sheriff. Why should his family be subjected to this indignity? "How dare those fools come lounging around the door and then drive us straight out of the house!" she exclaimed. Her daughter was so ill the doctor feared for her life; was the law not tempered by such mercy as you would show a wounded animal?

Sheriff Petit had the thought that the mercy she referred to generally came in the form of a bullet, but he kept that observation to himself. Madame Chopin was notoriously full of herself and indifferent to others. She was always willing and eager to express her low opinion of the town officials, whom she compared unfavorably to those in Vacherie, where she was from. Still, everyone knew she was devoted to her daughter, and doubtless she had suffered mightily of late, so he counseled himself to be charitable. "Seems Felix took a lot of money out of the bank right before he died," he replied calmly. "Gold coin. And it disappeared. So they have to look for it."

"Why would Octave Favrot have money belonging to that scoundrel, I ask you?" said Madame Chopin, raising her voice, as if, thought the sheriff, he was hard of hearing.

"I can't think of a reason," agreed the sheriff. "But when money goes missing, it constitutes a motive."

She narrowed her eyes. "A motive for what?"

"Well . . ." The sheriff paused. His sympathy for his interlocutress faded. She had called his men fools for doing their duty, and the dead man a scoundrel, which might have been true, the sheriff couldn't say, but Felix was dead and couldn't defend himself. So he decided to set Madame Chopin straight. "Murder," he said.

○

Cesar Denis had worked out various scenarios that might account for the disappearance of the gold, but the one he kept returning to was this: Felix Kelly had offered to buy his blind son from Octave for a thousand dollars, and Octave had agreed. The exchange was made, but somehow Odile found out and sent Octave after her seducer to demand the return of her son. By that time Octave had hidden the money somewhere. He took up his rifle and pursued Felix and the baby into the woods, where he shot them in cold blood. Now he was free of both the man he despised and the usurping son who was a burden to him. The money was secure and he had no immediate need for it. The perfect crime.

But without the gold, without any witnesses to the crime or to any social exchange, no matter how fleeting, between Felix and Octave, with Odile too sick to attend the trial, the public's natural sympathy for her and for her husband, and the universal antipathy of the town toward the outsider, Felix Kelly, Cesar despaired of making a case that would persuade even a disinterested jury—which he was not likely to find in Edgard, where the Favrot clan numbered both relatives and investments—that Octave was guilty of anything more serious than involuntary manslaughter. And in fact, when his investigations were complete and the matter was finally brought before a jury, this was the charge.

The trial lasted two chilly, rainy days in November. The accused, seated next to his lawyer, who exuded confidence, followed the proceedings intently. Octave had never denied that he killed Felix Kelly, and this made his situation before the court less a matter of finding guilt than of assessing its gravity. Cesar presented his findings, speculated upon the possible motives, but with no witnesses and much of his conjecture objected to or prohibited by the laws governing admissible evidence, his argument had a quality of desperation that caused the jurors to study their hands politely. When it was over, these gentlemen deliberated for under two hours, during which time they were served several pots of coffee and some excellent cakes sent over from the baker in Villedeau. When they returned to their box, Cesar noted that several of them gazed directly at the accused with expressions of benignity and that when the foreman stood up to read the verdict, an elderly juror drew two cigars from his breast pocket and offered one to his neighbor.

So it was with no surprise that he learned the jury had found Octave Favrot not guilty. Not guilty of anything any respectable gentleman wouldn't have done in the circumstances.

Octave listened to the verdict; rose from his seat, solemnly shook his lawyer's outstretched hand, and, without comment, walked calmly and with great dignity out of the court.

"Some kind of justice was done," opined my uncle. "And it's just as well that poor Odile doesn't have to suffer more than she already has."

I tended to agree with him, but as events unfolded, our assumption that justice had been well and properly served and that now our neighbors might return to their ordinary lives proved too sanguine.

Within a month of the trial, Odile, not in perfect health but having recovered enough of her strength and her wits to make a choice, determined to move to her mother's house. A flimsy explanation was offered to the curious—and the entire town was curious—that the Chopin house was closer to town, making the care of the patient easier for her principal nurse. Octave professed himself to be of the opinion that this move was the best option for all concerned. The rumor that swirled in the dust the Favrots' maid Marie swept out the front door was that Odile couldn't bear the sight of her husband and refused absolutely to speak one word to him.

Octave occupied himself with his business interests, which thrived so exuberantly that he was soon exporting his rice as far away as Atlanta. Between the trips he made to expand his market and his frequent hunting or fishing expeditions, he was not much among us. When he was, he seemed unchanged: confident, courteous, generous. He employed many of the local carpenters and tradesmen. He enlarged the gardens at his house, bought new furniture for the parlor, had a fishing boat constructed from his own design, and ordered an expensive rifle from a catalog at Mat Girot's store. Many a young lady gazed upon him as he passed along the main street on his piebald gelding and thought to herself, *It's a shame, such a man, and no wife waiting for him at home with his supper, no pretty child rushing out to greet him on his return.*

Two years passed, during which time I completed my law studies and moved to New Orleans, where I was employed as a clerk in the chambers of Judge Antoine Dubonnet, whose reputation for fairness and exactitude was borne out by my own observation. In the second summer an outbreak of yellow fever sent everyone who could leave as far as they could get from the pestilential streets of the city. Judge Dubonnet closed his offices for a fortnight, and with the encouragement of my dear uncle, I resolved to spend the break in Villedeau.

I arrived on a torrid afternoon and settled myself in my

accustomed lodgings. Villedeau was a welcome and salubrious refuge, and it struck me as unvarying, like a storybook village lost in time. But that evening, over glasses of his excellent cognac, my uncle apprised me that much had changed in the town, most glaringly in the fortunes of Octave Favrot.

It was as if the fates had turned against him and in three strokes reduced him to dust. The first blow came in the spring, bearing an unprosaic name: sheath blight. This plague transformed his rice fields from ranks of healthy green shoots to scattered patches of blotchy red and tan sticks, each gradually sealed inside what looked like a snake's skin. When the breeze rustled through them, they made a rattling sound, so that they were as horrid to the ear as to the eye.

The second stroke, in August, was the stock market panic, which wiped out several of our richest families that year, as many were invested in railroad stock, or in the banks that folded hard upon the revelations of chicanery in the management of those enterprises. Octave, it was said, lost more than most.

The third stroke was fire. Octave was away on one of his hunting trips, or perhaps he was in New Orleans trying to save his fortune, when lightning struck an oak that shaded the porch of his house. A heavy branch fell onto the roof and smoldered until the dry wood shingles ignited, and because there was no one there to stop them, the flames spread, consuming the house all through the night. It was not until the morning, when Mat Girot, riding from his mother's house to his dry goods store in town, spotted a thick column of smoke rising over the treetops, that the alarm was raised and the fire brigade set out. By the time they arrived, the house was a mass of charred lumber. Flames flickered in the ruins, consuming the last hard bits of the furniture.

Octave responded to this thorough reversal of his fortunes with admirable fortitude. He didn't rave against the gods, as some men might have, or take to drink and appear sullen and sodden in the streets. He sold most of the land adjoining the house and, with the assistance of the neighbor who bought it, constructed a small three-room cabin on the original site. He planted a garden plot, bought a few sticks of furniture, and moved in. No young ladies smiled upon him in the town, where he walked now, having sold his horses. He appeared to embrace a stoical solitude that was part of his nature. He spent more and more time hunting, fishing, trapping. He still had his boat, which he lived on, sometimes for days on end. On his return he sold his plunder—all manner of fish and birds; nutria, raccoon, and squirrel skins; crabs and crayfish; the occasional alligator—to his neighbors, who, recalling his largesse in better days, were willing to pay more than he asked. Octave's fall from grace, my uncle concluded, was a cautionary tale. A lesser man would have been broken by it.

And what of Odile? I asked my relative. Had she recovered her health? Did her husband's nobility and suffering reconcile her to him? Did she not, perhaps, send him some message or token of reconciliation?

"Ah, there," said Uncle Leonce, taking up the cognac bottle and refilling our glasses, "is the saddest and strangest part of the whole strange and sad affair."

Odile had indeed improved in health and was well enough

to appear in public, always dressed in black, at Mass and occasionally at her mother's side in the market. She was now a tragic beauty, enveloped in a nearly palpable cloud of melancholy. One gazed upon her, as she told her beads in the family pew or idly examined a mountain of cooking pears at the fruit stall, and sighed. She wasn't a widow or entirely a wife. No swain could come forward to court her; her life was closed. Yet she was still young; blood coursed in her veins; the will to flourish might reemerge, and so the town watched her with tender concern.

But, to her well-wishers' chagrin, she stubbornly refused to thrive and kept her thoughts on death. She was seen repeatedly, late in the evening, when, as my uncle put it, decent women were in bed with their husbands, gliding through the cemetery in her black mourning clothes, past all the monuments and markers designating the final addresses of the former respectable and much-lamented citizens of our village, to stand in the gloomiest corner at the grave of Felix Kelly. She brought no flowers; she didn't kneel to offer a prayer or clear the weeds that obscured the stone. She just stood there. The gravedigger, from his shed near the gate, observed her, and Father Paul, returning one night from administering the last rites to a communicant who lived at the edge of town, happened to cross the cemetery and saw her there. He stopped to remonstrate with her, but at his approach she fled, frantic, he reported, as if she had seen a ghost.

No effort to dissuade her from these nocturnal visits was successful. If her mother locked the door, she went out the window. If left undisturbed, she stood at her dead lover's grave until the first rays of sunlight filtered through the leafy canopy of the graveyard corner. The concern of her neighbors turned to consternation, and at length her mother decided to leave Villedeau and all the suffering her family had endured there. She sold the house in which Odile had been born and moved to New Orleans, where her sister had found for her a comfortable, light-filled cottage in the Faubourg Marigny, only steps from her own, larger residence.

"Odile is in the city," I said, in some amazement. I had so long associated her with Villedeau—as one of its prime attractions, in fact—that the thought of her shopping among the stalls at the great market near the levee or popping open a parasol for a stroll across the Place d'Armes unnerved me.

"She is," my uncle averred, nodding his head at my wonder. "I arranged the sale of Madame Chopin's house. I have the address here somewhere. You should pay her a visit when you go back to the city."

I never visited Odile, first from some irrational timidity, or perhaps it was because I preferred to preserve a particular memory I had of her as I had once seen her, dancing under the stars in the arms of a callow admirer to the lilting strains of an Acadian waltz, untouched by sorrow and loss. Later I didn't visit her because I had completed my clerkship with Judge Dubonnet, passed the bar, and moved to the state capital at Baton Rouge, where I have practiced law now for a decade, largely occupying myself with trusts and real estate transfers.

In that time the principal characters of my story have left this life. About six years ago, Octave Favrot drowned in a storm that came out of the Gulf of Mexico with such fury that much of the fishing fleet and two entire towns were washed away from the shores of Barataria Bay. Odile survived her husband by two years, living quietly with her mother in the Faubourg and reportedly taking a lively interest in her cousin's two young children. She succumbed, as did many of her neighbors, including one of the children she had cared for, to an epidemic of yellow fever, that plague of our climate that has sent so many to an early grave.

A few days ago I received a letter from my uncle, which contains a most curious postscript to this unhappy tale. I offer it here as proof, if proof be needed, that the fathomless sea conceals no mystery more recondite than that which may flicker beneath the surface of a neighbor's distracted greeting on a summer's day.

"I must tell you," my uncle wrote, "of a remarkable circumstance lately developed in the case of Octave Favrot, which I know has been of longstanding interest to you. M. Charles Charpentier, the owner of Madame Chopin's former residence, recently decided to expand his front veranda around the side of the house. His plans necessitated the removal of several overgrown azaleas and a venerable crape myrtle that I, for one, thought it a shame to destroy, but no, it stood between the Charpentiers and their pressing need for space, so down it came. In the process of their excavations, the workers' shovel blades struck something hard, and, with a little effort, they exhumed a pine box. It was about the size of a small orange crate, wrapped round with hemp cord, much decayed, and fastened by a metal latch with a rust-encrusted lock. At the request of M. Charpentier, a shovel blow broke the lock and the lid was easily removed. The contents, which I think you will find both strange and wonderful, were the following: a canvas drawstring bag containing one thousand dollars in gold pieces, a sealskin blanket, made of what must have been a dozen skins sewed together so skillfully that, I'm told, one cannot find the seams, a baby's hat, knitted of pale blue wool, and finally, a folded square of paper upon which, in a florid script, are written two words: *Forgive me.*"

ET IN ACADIANA EGO

In memory of Lyle Saxon

NIKOS

When Father Desmond excommunicated Mathilde Benoit, denying her the benefit of the sacraments, he wrote an account of his complaint against her. He described her as haughty, headstrong, known for her quick temper and her indifference to decorum. Was she beautiful? He didn't say. But she was young, she was an heiress, and she was an impressive horsewoman who kept a stable of horses as high-strung and temperamental as their mistress. She lived on a rice plantation near Hauteville, a small bayou town west of New Orleans. Hauteville was five miles long, one house deep on both sides of the water, laced together by a fantastical web of crossings: flat boats pulled across by ropes, wooden footbridges, bridges wide enough for carts, bridges made of bamboo, iron bridges with decorative trim, but not one stone bridge, because there is no natural deposit of stone in a hundred miles.

One of the finest bridges, of iron decorated with a filigree of fleur-de-lis, stretched across the water from the road that served the cane farmers to the door of the bank owned by Mathilde's father, Pascal Benoit. If you kept your money in the bank, you crossed the bridge for free; otherwise, you paid a toll.

When Mathilde was six, her mother, Marie Beauclair Benoit, died trying to bring a son into the world. The son died too. An aunt was brought in to supervise the girl's education, but she passed away in a fever epidemic the following year. Pascal did what he could to care for his daughter, which was largely a matter of giving in to her whimsical decrees: that she should have a pony, that she should wear white gowns and diadems woven from clover, that she should be allowed onto the levee at dawn to collect crayfish on their daily march from one side of the footpath to the other. At ten she was sent to the Ursuline nuns in the city to prepare for her debut into society. She was an apt student and she loved music. She learned to play the piano, to sing charming ballads, and, of course, she learned to dance. As a child she had stomped with the locals to the wild Acadian bands, but now she waltzed, her back straight, her feet barely touching the floor, whirling in the arms of her partner, a girl her own age in a room full of girls, all moving gracefully in interlocking circles, while the nuns sat on straight-backed chairs along the walls, tapping out the time with their high-laced boots. Twice a month her father came to visit her. He took her to the two entertainments for which she lived and breathed: the opera and the racetrack. In the summers, when all who could afford to escape the heat of the city did, she returned to her bayou town. She spent her days on her pony and her nights by candlelight, turning the pages of fantastic tales, imagining herself a princess on a mountain of glass or dancing in an undersea ballroom with sea horses peering in the windows.

When she was sixteen, her father died. She returned to the nuns for a year and then came home to another imported aunt who lived not long, and then, because the Napoleonic Code allowed it, her money was her own.

There were suitors, there were rumors, there was resistance to the very idea of a young woman of means doing as she pleased, but not even the priest could force Mathilde to marry, so she did not. She set up a charity school for orphans and turned over the management of the bank to her father's partner, thereby satisfying the nuns who had educated her and the investors who relied upon her. She occupied herself with her horses in the country and with music in the city. She was free.

One broiling summer afternoon in her eighteenth year, as the sun was dissolving redly into the bayou, Mathilde was riding home on her favorite filly, Chou-fleur, along the gentle curve of the levee. In Acadiana, nature runs riot and even a split-rail fence becomes an impenetrable wall of green. Along such a wall Mathilde was passing, drowsy from the *clop-clop* of her horse's hooves against the damp earth, when she observed, approaching from the opposite direction on the other side of the greenery, a fellow rider, so screened that his head and chest seemed to float disembodied toward her.

He was dark, handsome; his hair flowed from his temples like waves drawn by the moon from the shore, and his eyes were as limpid as the shallow pools at the water's edge. He was dressed in a loose linen shirt, such as the farmers in the area wore, but he had none of the red-boned rudeness of the local swains. His smile was sudden as a lightning bolt, the light springing disturbingly from his sizable white teeth. Mathilde found herself smiling back, which was not her habit upon encountering strangers. His attention was not arrested by her smile; he was admiring her horse, and his first words were, disappointingly, "What a powerful filly."

"She is, she is," Mathilde agreed. "She's the fastest in the parish. She has twice the spirit of the best stallion and three times the sense."

"Why three times the sense?" he asked.

Mathilde laughed. "Why do you think?" she said.

"My name is Nikos," he said. "I'm new to these parts."

"I am Mathilde," she said, flashing her whip at the hand he extended over the wall. She touched her boot to Chou-fleur's right side and left him there. He brought the rejected hand to his temple, smoothing back his hair, his eyes wide with admiration. What a rider she was! And what a rump on that filly!

There were sightings: A groom reported finding a stranger peering through the window of Chou-fleur's stall, a farm worker spied a man plucking quinces in the bushes near the meadow; a rider was seen galloping through the rice field, destroying a swath of new shoots just topping the water. A bag of oats went missing from the storeroom. A horse blanket disappeared, and then, two days later, was discovered neatly folded on the wrong shelf in the tack room.

Mathilde was more curious than angry. She was certain it was the man she had met over the fence and she persuaded herself that he was teasing her with these mysterious doings because she had been so impulsively rude to him. She revisited the green fence on her evening rides, but she didn't see Nikos there again.

A MOONLIT NIGHT

Mathilde had a clear conscience and she slept soundly, but one hot and humid night in September she woke with the conviction that something was amiss in her house. She lay still, listening in the darkness to the myriad creaks, buzzes, and squawks of the night, picking out the ghostly *whoo-whoo* of an owl, the rustle of mice in the woodpile near the veranda. No, there was no sound she couldn't identify. She turned onto her side and hugged her pillow close. She'd had a miserable ride in the afternoon. Chou-fleur was agitated and downright hostile, refusing the bit, dancing away to avoid the saddle, and when Mathilde turned away to lead her out of the barn, the horse nipped at her owner's well-padded backside. Mathilde chose a familiar path, but the filly stamped and started as if she'd been thrust into a dangerous and alien territory. On the return she bolted, reined in only with utmost difficulty by her perplexed and exasperated rider. The groom opined that the horse was doubtless coming into her season, and Mathilde agreed that this must be the case.

Now, in her dark bedroom, Mathilde felt as restless as her horse. She twisted and turned beneath the sheet, unable to find a comfortable position. At length she sat up and lit the lamp on her bedside table. She was thirsty and hot, too hot even for the cotton chemise she was wearing, but the nuns had instilled in her the importance of sleeping with clothes on. "If you can't stand the heat," Sister Marie de la Croix had told her, "do what I do and pour the water pitcher over your gown."

Mathilde didn't avail herself of this radical solution, but she did pour a glass of lukewarm water from the pitcher and drank it, standing at the window and fanning herself with her painted silk fan. The moon was full, casting a milky sheen upon the open lawn and the worn track that led to the barn. The air was dazzlingly still, curiously quiet. Too quiet, she thought. A grating sound she recognized tore the air—the barn door sliding on its iron track. Without hesitation, Mathilde dropped the fan and ran through the house to the veranda. Lamplight flickered in the windows of the barn. "He's in the tack room," she whispered.

Out into the night she flew, her bare feet scarcely touching the grass, through the wisteria arbor, along the path to the barn door, which was, as she had known it would be, open just wide enough for a man on a horse to pass through. She glanced over her shoulder at her house gleaming like a white marble temple, then stepped from the yard into pandemonium.

A clatter of hooves, a clamor of snorts, a chorus of outraged neighing. She moved from stall to stall, dispensing calming solicitude, but the disturbance was universal, and even Baron, a normally placid gelding, startled her with a double-barreled kick at the wall of his stall. Chou-fleur was just ahead. As Mathilde approached, the filly thrust her dark head over the gate, her neck fully extended, nostrils flaring, teeth bared, eyes bulging with fury. "Chou-chou," Mathilde cried out. The filly responded with a high-pitched squeal that set her barn mates on a new round of stamping and snorting.

The moon was neatly framed in the window over the stall, shedding a pure white light upon the chaotic scene inside. Mathilde could see another horse, and that man, that Nikos, in the narrow space. The alien horse's rear legs were jammed into the corner, his forelegs raised, his hooves curled over Chou-fleur's trembling shoulders. Mathilde was an experienced horse-woman; she knew what she was seeing, but what vexed her eyes was the position of the man. Nikos had somehow gotten between the struggling animals. He clung to the filly's neck, his eyes wide and his lips curled back, grunting and wheezing like a pig stuck in the throat. Was he sitting on Chou-fleur's back?

"What are you doing?" Mathilde exclaimed, hastening to unlatch the gate.

"Get back," Nikos shouted. "Don't open that gate." But Mathilde ignored him, and as the wooden dowel slipped free, the door drifted open on its hinges, giving her a full view of the impossible coupling, which came apart as she staggered backward. Chou-fleur bolted madly past her, down the aisle and out the open door.

Nikos stepped into the aisle, gazing longingly after the departing filly, and Mathilde took him in, from his disheveled hair, his flushed face, his bare chest wet with sweat, his long torso ending in a V where the tan flesh gave way to a chestnut hide, down to his long forelegs, his knobby knees, his fringed fetlocks and dusty black hooves. As her legs buckled and a fog closed over her consciousness, he turned his light eyes upon her and she heard him say ruefully, "Now look what you've done."

When she opened her eyes she was resting on a pile of blankets on the tack room floor, the lamp was lit, and Nikos was bending over her, his brow furrowed with concern. "How do you feel?" he asked.

"So it's not a dream," she said.

He straightened to his full height, shifting his weight to his hind legs. His right front hoof rolled slightly under in an attitude Mathilde would come to recognize as thoughtful. "It's possible," he observed, "that everything is a dream."

Mathilde sat up, smoothing the front of her chemise, which was wet and streaked with dirt. "I've read about creatures like you," she said, "But I thought they were fantastical."

"Meaning?" he said.

"Made up. Long ago."

"It's true there aren't many of my kind left," he said. "I was trying to do something about that when you opened the gate."

"Chou-fleur," Mathilde said.

"She's outside," he said. "She won't come in while I'm here. She's not very bright."

Mathilde got to her feet. "Where did you come from?" she demanded. "How did you get here?"

He flattened the hoof, laid his exceedingly long fingers against his cheek. "It's a long story," he said. "But the short answer is from an island, on a boat."

Mathilde pictured him trying to keep his balance on a pitching shrimp boat. He'd go over the side at the first squall. "Don't tell me you can sail," she said.

"It was a big boat. I was in the hold. In the dark. A long time."

"You were a stowaway?"

He frowned. "You ask too many questions," he said.

A whinny at the window announced the impatience of

Chou-fleur to be back in her stall. "You stay here," Mathilde said. "I'll close the door and bring her in."

Nikos went to the window and looked out cautiously. "She's a beauty," he said. "And you were right, she's spirited. She tried to bite me."

"How could you do such a thing?" Mathilde scolded him. "You should be arrested."

He snorted, lifting his head as if to elude a bridle. Mathilde stood her ground, glowering at him. The top of her head came midway up his muscular breast. He rolled his eyes down at her. "I'm bad," he said seriously, and then he grinned.

It was an infectious grin. Mathilde lowered her eyes, nodding her head, hiding her smile.

His eyes softened. He took a step closer, reached out, and touched her cheek with his fingertips. "You're a beauty," he said.

"You said that about my horse."

"She is too, in her way, you in yours."

"And which do you prefer?"

His brow furrowed again and the front hoof rolled out slightly. "Which do I prefer?" he repeated.

Mathilde blew air between compressed lips. "Well, if it's a difficult question . . ."

Nikos turned to the window, then back to Mathilde. "What can I say?" he replied. "I'm divided."

For a moment neither spoke. Mathilde gazed up at him; his tail swished lightly at a horsefly hovering over his flank.

"You're divided," she agreed, and they both smiled.

AT THE OPERA

Though it was not in his nature, to preserve his life Nikos became a nocturnal creature. In the daylight hours Mathilde provided various refuges where he sheltered from the eyes of men: the cool shadows of a pine forest, posted round with placards warning trespassers they would be shot; a lean-to at the edge of a rice field; and a run-down barn used for grain storage, which served him both for rest and for food. In the evenings he made his way carefully along the lanes and across the lawn that ended in the French doors of Mathilde's drawing room.

Nikos was wild and defiant, but like many unruly children, he was tamed by an exciting story. Mathilde had these in good supply, tales of romance, revenge, and treachery from the operas she adored. Whenever a new score arrived from Paris or Milan, she read the libretto to him first, then sat down at the piano and played the various arias, singing along in her clear, high voice. During these concerts Nikos positioned himself near the soundboard, his head bowed, his eyes closed, like a man communing with divinity.

He was enchanted by the idea of the opera, a story set to music and acted out before an audience. Mathilde described the instruments of the orchestra, the costumes, the elaborate sets, the transformation on the stage of day into night, forest into castle, sunlight into thunderous storms threatening a group of hunters gathered around a fire or startling a beautiful woman as she rushed along a moonlit shore to the arms of her waiting lover.

The opera that most particularly affected Nikos was Donizetti's *Lucia di Lammermoor.* Often he asked Mathilde to play

the music from the great sextet in the second act, when Lucia
is tricked into marriage and her lover, Edgardo, returns to find
himself betrayed. Nikos's voice was untrained, but he taught
himself to sing Edgardo's stunned accusations as Mathilde, taking Lucia's part, melodiously protested the cruelty of her fate.

One evening in the fall, Mathilde greeted her companion
with the news that a company traveling from Milan would offer
four performances of Donizetti's sublime music at the French
Opera House in New Orleans. Nikos declared that he would
risk all to see this spectacle. Mathilde considered the problem.
"I can hide you in my box before the audience comes in," she
said. "No one need be the wiser. You'll have to wear an evening
coat. And a cloak."

They laid their plans in Mathilde's drawing room, where
they met with the curtains drawn, the door bolted, and the servants forbidden to knock on the door. She stood on a chair and
measured her friend's chest, arms, and neck; she would use her
father's measurements for the unnecessary pants. "I can't very
well order half a suit," she explained. "We'll need a long cloak,
enormously long. I'll order two and sew them together."

They agreed to travel separately to the city; Nikos was to go
by night on the river road. He knew the route, as it was on this
road that he had escaped the terrors of the town, the bustling
wharves and the drunken sailors who, as he rushed past them,
swore that he was the apparition of the drink they had just had
or the one they needed. Mathilde would take her carriage and
one trusted servant and meet him at her townhouse, where she
would let him in at the courtyard gate. There he would dress for
his first public appearance. Then he would follow her at a little
distance so that she could make sure the way was clear. Her

generous financial support of the opera house gave her access to keys, back staircases, and the largest box, draped inside and out with velvet curtains which could be opened and closed at the discretion of the box holder. In the past Mathilde had appeared in the company of a suitor or a relative; there would be talk about the tall stranger who stood in the shadows behind her gilt-edged chair, but gossip about Mathilde Benoit was nothing new. When the opera was over, Nikos and Mathilde would stay in the box until the crowd was gone and then disappear into the night.

Their careful preparations were successful, and at the appointed hour Mathilde took her seat at the front of her box, where she was observed in conversation with an elegant stranger who stood in the shadows behind her. Was it her cousin Gaston? The several pairs of opera glasses trained and focused upon the heiress never satisfactorily answered that question. The orchestra struck up the overture, the bustle in the audience subsided, the lights dimmed, and the golden curtains opened upon a misty Scottish moor. Mathilde heard Nikos draw in his breath. A squadron of men dressed in cloaks, embroidered doublets, puffy velvet breeches, and tall boots invaded the scene, responding raucously to their leader, who adjured them to search the ruins near the tower. Mathilde gave in at once, absorbed by the familiar story though acutely conscious of her companion, who stood utterly still in the darkness behind her. He was silent through the lovers' tryst and the brother's vow, but toward the end of the sextet he muttered *ingrata* along with the tenor. When the act was over and the lights flared up amid the applause of the audience, Mathilde turned to Nikos. He was blotting his streaming eyes with his handkerchief, his lips trembling with suppressed emotion.

"So you like it?" Mathilde said.

"Like it!" he exclaimed. "It's magnificent. This is the most sublime experience of my life."

Mathilde laughed. The audience had begun to move about. She drew the curtain half across and motioned Nikos to back in behind it.

During the intermission Mathilde did not leave her box. She opened the door to the hall and ordered a bottle of champagne and two glasses from the boy stationed there. When the wine was handed in, she poured out a glass for Nikos, who quaffed it in one gulp. "Are you miserable in this close space?" she asked.

"No, no," he said. "The air is very bad, but I don't mind." He held out his glass. "I could drink a bucket of this."

"I'm afraid it only comes in bottles," she said, refilling his glass. The gaslights flickered, dimming one by one, and the audience filtered in below them, the women fanning themselves, exchanging pleasantries with their neighbors. Mathilde looked down upon the crowd; she had no wish to be among them and sent a grateful thought to her father, whose industry and financial acumen had set her apart, above the reach of wagging tongues and petty gossip. The orchestra tuned up plaintively; it was dark in the house.

"You can come out now," Mathilde said, and Nikos, appearing from behind the drape, took his place as before. Mathilde leaned back to speak to him, but as she did so there was a searing flash of light and a clap of thunder, followed by gasps and nervous laughter in the audience. Nikos was so startled he backed into the door, threw up his hands, and cried, "Oh, gods." The stage curtain parted upon a lavishly furnished tower room; a fierce storm lashed the windows with rain, lightning flashed, and thunder cracked. "Wonderful," Nikos murmured, and Mathilde turned back to the stage, where Edgardo was proclaiming that the weather was no more fearful than his destiny.

After Lucia's mad scene, after Edgardo's dramatic suicide, after the applause and the several curtain calls, the curtain closed and the lights came up. Mathilde sat quietly in the box waiting for the audience to exit. Their timing was precise: They would make their escape between the moment when the house was empty and the arrival of the ushers, who would come in to pick up the glasses, the wadded programs, the forgotten scarf or jeweled reticule. Nikos was ecstatic, his pale eyes still moist from emotion. "It was just as you promised," he whispered. "But I hadn't pictured how it would feel. I thought it would be very pretty, very charming, though the story is sad, but I didn't expect it to be so overpowering."

While he chattered on, Mathilde arranged the cape over his back. "The singing was very fine," she observed.

"The singing," he said, "yes, and the acting!"

"Pull the hood up," Mathilde instructed, and Nikos complied, drawing the heavy velvet cowl low over his forehead. Mathilde stepped back to take in the effect. "You look like a man pulling a piano on hooves," she said.

All she could see of his face was his toothy smile. "Very funny," he said.

Mathilde opened the door a crack and peered into the hall. Then she slipped out and made a quick foray to the staircase and back again. She pulled the door open wide and motioned to Nikos, who held the hood up over his eyes with both hands, nervous now and frowning. "Follow me," Mathilde said.

"Don't go too fast," he said. "That staircase will be worse going down than it was coming up." In truth it was a difficult descent. The wide marble stairs curved perilously, the rail was low. He had to feel his way, step by step, his upper body bent over his knees. Mathilde stood at the landing, watching his awkward progress. "You're almost there," she assured him. He swished his tail and, pushing off with his back legs, took the last few steps in a hop. Mathilde dashed out in front of him, leading him to the stage door. This was a heavy cypress plank that rolled on casters. Cautiously she pulled it aside and peered out into the dark alley. Two men stood beneath the streetlamp on the corner, their voices raised in animated conversation.

"What's going on?" Nikos asked, pressing close behind her. Mathilde glanced in the opposite direction; no one was in sight.

A shout of laughter issued from the stair landing, followed by the rap of leather soles on marble; the ushers were descending.

"We'll have to leave the door open and make a run for it," Mathilde said. She approached her companion, pulling the cloak back from his flank.

"What are you doing?" he asked.

"Bend down," she said. "I'll get on your back and guide you. Once we're outside, go left, to the cross street, and go quickly."

"I don't know," Nikos said. "I don't think this is a good idea." Mathilde slid the door along the track. The two men beneath the lamp were still talking volubly, interrupting each other, their voices rising with an edge of hysteria.

"Trust me," Mathilde said. "Bend down." Nikos obeyed and in a moment she was on his back, arranging her skirt and pulling the cape over her shoulders, wrapping her fingers in his mane. "Go," she said, unconsciously digging her evening slipper into his side. Nikos surged into the alley, startling a shout from the arguing men, but before they could even be sure what it was they saw—a man surely, riding a horse covered in a long cape—Nikos reached the corner, and at Mathilde's cry, "Go right," he was out of sight. This street was mercifully empty but lined with tall, deep-balconied houses lit by gas lamps. "Straight on," Mathilde ordered, bringing her lips close to her mount's shoulder, "two blocks, then left into the alley."

"Hold on," Nikos said, breaking into a gallop. The clatter of hooves against paving bricks startled a night watchman, who rushed out from a side street shouting a warning, for racing in the Carré was strictly forbidden. Nikos veered away, his cape streaming out from his shoulders like a flapping black wing, leaving his pursuer rubbing his eyes in wonder, uncertain exactly what he had seen. Nikos swerved into the narrow alley, which was dark and quiet, both sides lined with stucco walls covered in vines. "Slow down," Mathilde said. "No one will see us here." He slowed to a trot, looking back anxiously over his shoulder. "Is he following us?" he asked.

"No," Mathilde said. "Walk now so you don't make so much noise." He slowed, bringing each hoof down carefully. His breath was labored and harsh, and beneath her knees Mathilde could feel the nervous quivering of his muscles. "We can go four blocks here, then we'll have to cross Rue Royale, and then it's just one more block to my house."

"I'd rather run," Nikos said.

"We'll be there soon," Mathilde assured him. She patted his back and found the evening coat soaked through with sweat. "Calm down," she said.

They had one more fright at the end of the alley, a lamplighter on a ladder replacing a globe, but he was so absorbed in his task that Nikos slipped by unseen on the opposite sidewalk. At Mathilde's house, she alighted from his back and opened the gate. Nikos, glancing about as if he expected to be apprehended at any moment, bolted to safety. He had his tie and coat off before Mathilde had closed the bar. "What a night," he murmured, "what a night." He followed her, shedding his sodden shirt, across the courtyard and in at the wide French doors. A servant had left a fire and a chilled bottle of champagne for the mistress's return, then gone off to bed.

Nikos made straight for the refreshment, skillfully popping the cork and filling two glasses. Mathilde was occupied with drawing the drapes. They didn't speak for several moments, during which snatches of romantic melodies and dramatic encounters lingered in Mathilde's imagination. When she turned to her companion, who held out a glass to her, his eyes golden in the lamplight, she had the sensation that she was on a stage; that an audience, poised between engagement and disbelief, hung upon her words. "An enchanting evening," she said.

"Nothing like it in my memory," Nikos agreed. "So many new sensations." He set his glass down upon the tray. "I'm trembling from the excitement and the strangeness of it all." Tears stood in his eyes; he sniffed, lifting his chin and running his palm across his cheek, down his throat. "No one has ever been on my back before," he said. He took up a napkin, dabbed at his nose, then shuddered and burst into sobs. "It was so unexpected," he moaned. "So wonderful and strange. I felt we were one."

Mathilde sipped her wine, at a loss for words. It hadn't occurred to her that no one would ever have ridden Nikos; he was, after all . . . Now he drew in his breath, swabbing his eyes with the napkin as he maneuvered between a chaise and a plant stand on which an enormous fern trembled in the humid air. "Mathilde," he said, holding his hand out to her. She took a step back. "These feelings are new to me," he explained. Then, clumsily, bending over his front legs as he folded them beneath him on the carpet, he came down upon his knees. "Mathilde," he said again. "May the gods forgive me. I am completely yours."

A VISIT FROM THE PRIEST

In the spring Mathilde received a card from Monsieur Delery, her favorite importer, who kept a shop on Rue Royale. He wrote to announce the arrival of a new shipment from Paris: fine brocade, carpets, tapestries, furniture, paintings, and statuary. She wanted an étagère for her dining room in the townhouse and an armoire for the farmhouse. On her next visit to town she made a point of stopping in at Monsieur Delery's emporium. As she browsed among the luxurious displays, the importer pointed out those items he thought might particularly attract her interest: a painting of the racetrack at Deauville, a carpet with a design of red roses on a pale green ground, which he was certain would look well in her dining room, a bolt of lavender voile embroidered with a gold thread that would make festive curtains for the summer season. At the back of the shop she paused to examine a grouping of statuary: a marble woman carrying a vessel on one shoulder, the folds of her gown disarrayed to reveal a taut white nipple on a veined white breast; a bronze greyhound, life-size, his legs gathered for a burst of speed; a marble bust of a garlanded emperor gazing stupidly across the table at an ebony panther with eyes of glittering green stone, crouched to pounce upon him. Mathilde was turning away when she spied, beyond the emperor's nose, partially obscured by the raised arm of a porcelain girl leaning on an arbor, the shapely legs of a horse. She leaned across the table for a closer look. Monsieur Delery feared she had grazed her hip against the table edge, for she let out a startled "Oh!"

Angling past the porcelain girl, Mathilde cast the proprietor the confident smile of a gratified customer. The statue, bronze on a black marble base, was not large. It was designed to grace a mantel or an entry table. "Where did you get this?" she asked as he came up behind her, worriedly stroking his chin. "Ah," he said, "that's old Chiron. A fanciful thing. It was in a box with Saint Jude and the Archangel Michael, inappropriately enough. I think it was the dealer's idea of a joke, but it's a fine piece of work."

"I'll take it," Mathilde announced.

Monsieur Delery gave her an anxious smile. "I wouldn't think this quite a suitable piece for the home of a single lady. I'd rather expect to find it in a gentlemen's club, if you don't mind my saying."

"I do mind," Mathilde replied. "I'll take this, and the carpet and the armoire with the rosewood inlay. Ship them all to the farm."

"As you wish," the doubtful proprietor acquiesced. There was no point in quarreling with a customer over a matter of taste, especially one so strong-minded as Mathilde Benoit. But oh, he thought as she turned her attention to a glass-fronted étagère, how this purchase would have horrified her father.

Once the statue was installed in the foyer, replacing a marble bust of Napoleon that had glowered at visitors for thirty years, Mathilde brought Nikos through the dark hall to view it. "It's Chiron," he said.

"Yes," she said. "Monsieur Delery told me. Did you know him?"

Nikos snorted. "He was before my time. Why would you buy such a thing?"

"I had to buy it," she said solemnly. "When I saw it, I knew it had been sent to me."

"By whom?"

"By the Fates."

"And are you tempting the Fates, Mathilde, displaying it here where anyone who visits you will see it?"

She smiled. "Why should I care what people say?"

"You should care what they think."

"I don't care," she insisted.

But she should have cared. The town was already outraged by Mathilde's indifference to the local swains and her preference for a man she had met who knew where, a man who, according to the servants, visited her only at night, a man so enchanted with his horse that he brought it into the drawing room. So rumor flew from house to house, flapping its feathered wings and wagging its countless tongues, and it wasn't long before Father Desmond heard the din and made up his mind to pay a pastoral visit on his wayward parishioner.

Nikos was in the drawing room finishing his favorite meal, a bowl of oat porridge and a glass of red wine, while Mathilde, seated at the piano, played to him from a new score. He claimed that oat porridge satisfied both his man and his beast. Chewing grass, hay, and grain was the opposite of pleasure in dining, but his stomach wasn't designed for much else. The standing order for a large bowl of porridge was one of the many mysteries that created a buzz in Mathilde's kitchen, despite her assurance that the doctor had recommended it for her health. As Father Desmond gripped the cord and slapped the clapper inside the bell, Nikos clanged his spoon into the empty bowl, refilled his wineglass, and lifted it to his lips. "Visitors?" he said.

Mathilde pushed aside a curtain that gave her a view of the drive. In the moonlight she recognized the prelate's old white gelding tied at the post, rubbing his long face against the fence rail. "It's Father Desmond," she whispered.

Nikos swallowed his wine. *"Chi mi frena in tal momento?"* he sang softly.

"Stay here," she said. "Don't make a sound."

He poured out another glass, frowning at her tone of command. "A priest in this house," he said.

"And stop drinking," she added, inflaming him further.

They heard the door open, the servant's greeting, her footstep in the hall. Mathilde glanced back anxiously. "Behave," she said as she opened the door and slipped out to ward off the servant.

Nikos narrowed his eyes. "Why should I?" he said.

Mathilde glided toward her confessor, her hand outstretched, a welcoming smile on her lips. "Dear Father," she said, ushering him into the parlor with practiced ease. "How long since you've paid me a visit."

"And how long since you've been to Mass," the priest replied.

"May I offer you a glass of sherry?" she said. "Or something stronger, after your ride? A brandy, or perhaps a liqueur?"

"Plain sherry will do," he said. "Strong spirits are not for me."

"I suppose you are always in the company of strong spirits," Mathilde mused, uncorking the cut-glass decanter on the tray.

"I don't know what you mean by that," the dull fellow replied. Mathilde measured out a thimbleful, tamping her temper as she pushed the cork back into the bottle neck. "Strong spirits?" she said. "The saints, the angels, the hosts of heaven."

"There's a great deal of scandalous talk about you in the town. Are you aware of it?"

She handed him the glass, her lips pursed, her eyes modestly lowered. "I've the feeling I'm about to be."

That was when they heard the first loud knock from the drawing room. "Good heavens," the priest exclaimed. "What was that?"

"The carpenters," Mathilde replied. "I'm having some shelves put in."

There was another knock, so hard it caused the lamp to flicker overhead. The priest was frankly incredulous. "At night?" he said.

"They're so busy—it's hard to get them to come. I have to pay them more, but it's worth it." Two more knocks, a crash, followed by a clatter as of metal objects settling on a brick floor. She could see him charging about the room, directing his hooves at the walls, taking up the tea tray and pitching it at the hearth. His drinking was a problem.

"What's going on in there?" the priest demanded, setting his empty glass on the sideboard as he moved for the door.

"I'm very sorry, Father," Mathilde said, following him into the hall. "I can't allow you to go in there."

"They say your visitor brings his horse into the house. Is that what's in there?"

"Father, you are a guest in my house. I forbid you to enter that room."

"Something more than a guest, Mathilde," he insisted. "I am your spiritual adviser. Your soul is in my care."

"Don't worry about my soul," she replied.

"It is your soul I fear for," he said. He moved toward the drawing room, and she didn't try to stop him. Instead she leaned against the hall table, and as he turned upon her a cold glare of remonstrance, his eyes fell upon the statue. "Holy Mary, Mother of God!" he exclaimed.

Mathilde bowed her head at the sacred name, a smile flickering at the corners of her mouth.

"But this is an obscenity," he whispered. Two sharp cracks rattled the panels in the drawing room door. The priest stepped back, bringing his hands to his lips. Behind the door a high male voice began singing in a language he didn't recognize. Mathilde, collapsed in giggles, clung to the edge of the table. "You have given yourself over to Satan," the priest concluded. He swept past her to the entry, where he took up his wide-brimmed hat from the stand and charged out into the night.

Mathilde waited until she heard the soft *clopping* of his horse moving away down the drive. Then she went to the drawing room, threw open the door, and announced with fake solemnity, "I have abandoned my God for you."

THE DEATH OF NIKOS

Upon painful and sober reflection the following morning, Mathilde had the statue moved to her dressing room, and Napoleon returned to scowl at those visitors, few in number, who called upon the wayward excommunicant. Father Desmond's letter, a copy of which went to the bishop, cited her worship of a heathen idol he had seen in her home, an image so appalling he refused to describe it, as the cause for her expulsion from the communion of Christ. It was rumored that he had seen something else, but there was as much talk of the *loup-garou*, a wolf-headed bandit who preyed on travelers foolhardy enough to venture out when a bad moon was on the rise. Sagacious citizens, who knew the night was the province of wicked men and fearsome creatures, stayed inside. Nikos was cautious; he wore a shirt when he ventured forth and chose his route with an eye to screening, though some nights, after too much wine, his spirits were so high he tempted fate by running full out on the levee.

Summer blazed into the bayou and with summer came the daily rains, the customary plagues of mosquitoes, fevers, agues, prostrations, and death. Nikos slept poorly, waking some days every hour with the conviction that a man carrying a rifle was moving stealthily closer in the blinding light outside his shelter. Mathilde too was worn down by the heat, the need for secrecy, and the upheaval in her own diurnal clock. She rarely rose from her bed before noon, she who had once greeted her groom on his dawn arrival at the stable door. Now she neglected everything: her horses, her social obligations, even her bills, which went unpaid and were submitted to a collector. She hired an accountant and had everything sent to him. "I can't be bothered," she told him. "I'm not well."

So word went out that she was ill and her neighbors took pity on her. Dishes were sent round and homely remedies, and prayers were offered up for the unfortunate outcast who, all agreed, would not recover her health until she made peace with her creator.

One night, as she stood in her open windows watching Nikos make his way across the soggy lawn, she noticed that he was moving lethargically, that his shoulders drooped, and that his linen shirt was unbuttoned, hanging limply from his shoulders. It was the same shirt he had worn that first day when she had seen him across the fence, a farmer's shirt which he admitted he had taken from a clothesline during his escape from the city. As he came into the drawing room, he pulled it off and dropped it on the carpet. "It's too hot," he said. "I'm good for nothing in this weather. And the flies!"

"I could rub you down with geranium oil," she suggested.

He coughed. "I don't feel well at all."

Mathilde looked up at his face, which was flushed and damp; the whites of his eyes were, she thought, tinged with yellow. "Let me feel your forehead," she said.

He lowered his head and she pressed her palm across his brow. "You're burning with fever."

"I just want to lie down," he said. "My hooves are killing me."

Mathilde pulled aside a low table and a stuffed hassock to

make room for him as he came ponderously down upon his haunches. "I'm going to get some ice," she said. "Rest here."

He groaned as he rolled onto his side, his torso propped on one elbow.

In the kitchen Mathilde chipped shards from the ice block, dumped them in a basin, and pulled a clean towel from the rack, and then she hurried back down the dark hall to her companion. She was conscious of a tightening, like a vise closing on something hard in her chest. She found Nikos lying flat on his side. He coughed again, a wrenching cough that shook his shoulders and drew his eyebrows down with pain. Mathilde took up the water pitcher and, kneeling beside him, filled the basin. She dipped the towel into the quickly chilling water. "When did you start feeling poorly?" she asked.

"This morning," he said. "I thought the day would never end."

She wrung out the cloth and laid it across his forehead. "How does that feel?"

"Heavenly," he said.

"Let me look at your feet." Mathilde kneeled beside him and set the lamp on the carpet next to his front hooves. "This light is so poor," she said. She pressed her thumb against the sole of one hoof. "Does that hurt?"

"Not much."

She pressed again at the apex of the frog. The hoof jerked and banged her thigh. "Ouch," they cried simultaneously.

"Sorry," Nikos said.

She recaptured the hoof and pressed around the edge of the sole. "It's hot," she said.

He coughed. "I'd like some water."

"Water!" she exclaimed. "You must be sick."

"How bad is it?" he asked. "Can you tell?"

"We'll try a poultice," she said. "It will be easy with you. The horses always tear them off."

All night Mathilde nursed Nikos with cold compresses and hot poultices. He slept a few hours and woke streaming with sweat. Toward dawn he announced that he felt some improvement and with no more than the usual difficulty got to his feet. "A little sore," he said. "But much improved. What a woman you are."

Mathilde smiled, pretending a confidence she didn't feel. "Can you get back to the barn?" she asked.

He paddled his front hooves, testing his weight upon them. "I'll just go slowly," he said. "A good rest and I'll be fine."

They stood together at the open doors looking out at the fading moon. The early light reanimated the dark bushes crouched along the path. Nikos rested his hand on her shoulder, and she leaned her head against his chest. "I'll be fine," he repeated.

"I'll come to you in a few hours," she promised.

"Get some sleep," he said.

She slept fitfully. At last the sun burned off the morning mist and the servant came in with the coffee tray. She dressed, pulling on a canvas apron with deep pockets over a light summer dress. She stopped in her father's office and took down the medicine cabinet. There were lancets for humans and fleams for animals, a scarificator with a powerful spring, purchased when her mother was ill because she couldn't bear the drawing of the blade. From which part should Nikos be bled, nearer the feet or the heart? Horses were bled from the jugular, but that would be too risky on a human. She settled on a lancet kit, a wad of wool for a compress, a roll of cotton bandage; these went into her pockets. Last she took up the pewter bleeding bowl with the volume marked off by lines. She knew how to open a vein inside the elbow; she'd seen the process often enough at school when a classmate fell ill or exhibited excessive agitation. She would start with that.

As she approached the barn she was relieved to see Nikos's torso through the window, but inside she found his face ashen and his pupils dilated. His stance, forelegs stretched stiffly out, his weight thrown back on his hind legs, confirmed her worst fears.

"Did you sleep at all?"

"I'm afraid to lie down. I won't be able to get up."

"We'll try the poultice again. And I'm going to bleed you."

He nodded, bringing one hand to his forehead and gripping his temples. "The cough is better," he said.

Mathilde dropped to her knees, running her hand down over the fetlock to the hoof. "Can you lift this foot?" she asked.

"I can't. I'll fall."

"What if you hold on to the stall and take your weight in your arms?"

"I'll try it," he said. It was a matter of two steps, each accompanied by a groan of pain. He rested his elbows on the crossbar and gripped his hands together, pressing down to take his weight into his shoulders. Mathilde was quick, pulling the hoof up and making a hurried examination. There was a spot of blood at the apex of the frog and a pinkish bulge inside the white line all the way around the sole.

"I can't hold it long," Nikos said.

Mathilde got to her feet. "Set it down," she said. "You're bursting with blood. We've got to get some of it out of you." She looked about for something to stand on and found a wooden bucket in a stall. This she set next to Nikos, who was speechless from pain. She stepped up on the bucket, drawing out the lancet case.

"How is this done?" he asked softly.

"I'm going to make a cut inside your elbow."

"You won't mind if I don't look," he said.

"Don't look," she said. "And don't faint either." She opened the case and took out the largest of the three lancets. "Hold this," she said, handing him the tortoiseshell box. Having thus distracted him, she took in a breath and drew the blade quick and hard across his arm.

The blood spurted out so forcefully it splashed across her neck as she bent down for the bowl. Nikos was silent, stretching his head up high on his neck as if trying to get out of his body. Mathilde watched the blood rising in the bowl; how much was enough? They'd taken two pints from her friend Juliette in school, every day for a week before she recovered. For a man, two times that? For a horse? She'd seen the farrier take a bucketful in a case such as this, in the end to no avail. The blood made a soft whishing sound, swirling down the side of the bowl. The air was still and hot; a sparrow flew in one window and out another. Nikos began to sag, his back legs bearing more and more weight until his rump approached the floor. Mathilde, concentrating on her task, stepped down from the bucket, following the blood with the bowl. "That's it," she said. She set the bowl on a bale of hay, holding his forearm up with her free hand. "Mathilde," he said weakly, and she looked up at his white face, his fluttering eyes. His front legs gave out and he shifted, rolling down on one side. Mathilde leaned over him, holding his arm, stanching the wound with the compress.

"My heart," he said. "It's racing so."

"Be calm," she said. She drew the roll of bandage from her apron pocket and wrapped it round and round the arm. Then she bent her ear to his chest and closed her eyes. The sound was a wild ride on a dark night. "Don't be afraid," she said. "You'll get up again. You need to rest."

"It feels good to lie down," he said, sighing, and then he yawned. Mathilde stayed with him until his heart had slowed and his eyelids were drooping with sleep. "I'll be back soon," she said. And she went out to find the farrier.

She found him banging out iron shoes amid a fountain of sparks at the forge he had set up outside his cottage. She greeted him and drew him into a conversation about his trade, about the special demands of the racing horses they both admired. Tactfully she brought him round to the subject of founder. A neighbor's horse had nearly died the year before, and the owner claimed that this farrier, who knew more about horses' feet than anyone in the parish, had saved the beast in a desperate hour. That, the farrier explained, was a difficult case. It was a mare and she'd gone in all four feet. He bled her for three days and gave her nothing but water, no food at all; that was essential to the treatment. Her fever went down but the feet were still swollen. For two days she couldn't stand, and the owner made up his mind to end her suffering, but the farrier had heard of a case cured by opening the sole, and that is what he did. A deal of blood and pus issued from the incisions; he bound them up and left her overnight. In the morning she was on her feet. But he knew of another case that hadn't responded to this treatment. The feet didn't heal and the bone protruded right through the sole. The poor animal was writhing in agony. When the vet finally arrived, he took one look and called for a pistol. "No one knows what causes it," the farrier concluded. "But for my money, it's overfeeding. Bad bedding will bring it on as well."

Mathilde went back to the barn praying for a miracle, but though her prayers pressed against the wall of her skull, they would not rise, and she remembered that this avenue of assistance was now officially closed to her. She resolved to call on the gods of Nikos, whoever they were, to guide her, to save him. At the barn she found him standing. He was weak, but the fever had subsided, and he could put a little weight on his front feet if he held on to the rail of the stall. "I slept a little, and when I woke up I knew I was better. I knew because I'm so hungry."

"No food," Mathilde cautioned him. "Only water, and I have to bleed you again, and if that doesn't work I'll have to open your feet."

He frowned, opening and closing his mouth as if to taste this bitter sentence, but he didn't protest. Mathilde took up the bucket and went out to fill it at the well.

o

For four more days and nights, Nikos suffered. Bleeding relieved him for a few hours, then the fever shot up again and he couldn't stand. Mathilde finally resorted to cutting his soles, and just as the farrier had described, a stream of pus, blood, and gas erupted from the wounds. She wrapped the feet with gauze soaked in vinegar, and the next day he got up again, though he was so weak from hunger and loss of blood he had to hang his arms over the stall gate to keep from sinking down.

It's never easy to watch an animal in pain, but if half of that animal is a man and he puts his trust entirely in your hands and you love him, well, what must that do to you? It wore Mathilde down to a hard nub of despair. The fever returned; the horn of the hooves cracked at the toe; on one foot the bone protruded through the sole. Nikos lay on the floor sweating and moaning. He said that he could see his island; that he would take her there. He called out names she didn't recognize, spoke in a language she didn't understand. His pulse was slow, his lips dry and swollen; tears leaked noiselessly from his eyes. The last night she sat on the floor with her back to the wall and his head in her lap, moistening his lips and forehead with water from the bucket; it was all she could do. He slept a little and so did she, her head dropped forward on her chest.

When she woke he was gazing up at her, his eyes spectral and distant. "Do you have a pistol?" he asked.

"Yes," she said. "I have my father's."

"Do you know how to use it?"

"I do," she said.

"Go and fetch it, dear heart," he said. "I'll never get up again."

○

Joseph Petrie, Mathilde's trusted groom, walking along the path to the barn, saw through the heavy morning mist a wraith of a figure—he thought it was a ghost—stalking through the knee-high grass between the house and the old storage barn. Her head was bowed, her hair a wild tangle falling over her shoulders. The wet grass parted before her as she advanced. She seemed to float across the field like a skiff in a marsh. He crossed himself and hurried along, not looking back until he was at the barn door. She was gone. He went inside, greeted his equine charges, and began his morning chores. He was forking a net of hay into the pony's trough when he heard the sharp pop of a shot fired at some distance. Joseph thought little of it; doubtless it was an early hunter out to bring down a duck for his dinner. The pony shoved him aside, eager for his breakfast, and the groom laughed softly, patting his thick neck. He was an old fellow, his mistress's first mount. Joseph took up a pitchfork and began mucking out the stall. He heard the *coo-coo* of a dove. A flush of sparrows rose up from the azalea bush outside the window and then he heard footsteps, unhurried and light, along the path. He didn't think it could be his mistress. She had been too ill to come out for over a week, and even if she had recovered, she wouldn't come from that direction. Then he recalled the ghost he'd seen in the meadow. His scalp prickled. He stepped into the aisle and propped his fork against the wall, squinting at the bright empty space beyond the open door. The footsteps stopped. He blinked, touched his eyes and looked again.

A woman stepped into the light. He would say later that she simply appeared out of the air. She was dressed in a summer gown covered by an apron so saturated with blood a butcher would have declined to wear it. Her head was lowered, her arms hung limp at her sides, her left hand gripped a pistol. It was the pistol Joseph recognized, his dead master's pistol, and then the woman lifted her eyes and he saw that it was not a ghost but a real woman, and that it was Mathilde. "I need your help," she said.

"What's happened?" he cried, bustling toward her with the certainty, he would later vow, that she had come back from some other world, and as it turned out, he was right.

"A poor, sick monster has dragged himself into the feed barn," she said. "I've put him out of his misery. I want you to help me bury him."

Joseph Petrie was well paid and sworn to secrecy, but he told his wife what he buried that day, and she told a friend, and soon the story, embroidered with colorful variations, was general knowledge. A few incredulous locals wanted to sneak in from an adjoining farm, dig up the grave, and see with their own eyes what was in it, but Father Desmond got wind of the scheme and threatened anyone who took part in such an unholy business with eternal damnation. So Nikos was left to rest in whatever peace he could find. Mathilde withdrew from the world, at first because she was too heartbroken, and then because she was too ill. By Christmas she was dead. Before she died she gave a great deal of money away, all to the benefit of local charities and schools. She endowed a library, a music series, and a racetrack. Her passing was an occasion of sadness to her community, and her wishes regarding her own remains, which were detailed in a codicil to her will, were respected. She asked to be buried without ceremony next to the unmarked grave near the pine woods. Joseph Petrie knew where this grave was and should be consulted on the matter. She bequeathed him a prime piece of land, all her horses, and her thanks for keeping the promise he had once made to her. For her own grave she requested a plain stone with her name and dates engraved upon it, no more. For the unmarked grave she ordered a second stone to bear the name Nikos and a peculiar epitaph: "His soul goes whinnying down the wind."

Over time much has changed on the bayou. A hurricane blew down the ruins of Mathilde Benoit's house a few years ago, and the rising water washed out the last bridges and the few remaining houses in the town. Most of these were owned by fishermen and trappers, who survived the storm by jumping out their windows into their boats. The rice fields turned brackish long ago, and the only thing that flourishes in the mud is crayfish. In the spring the heavy rains flood the former streets and fields, right up to the edge of the pine forest, but when the waters recede, the two gravestones are still in place. If you go to Acadiana in the dry season, you will find them there.

Valerie Martin is the author of ten novels, including *The Ghost of the Mary Celeste*, *Trespass*, *Mary Reilly*, and the 2003 Orange Prize–winning *Property*, as well as three collections of short fiction and a biography of Saint Francis of Assisi titled *Salvation*.

A Note About the Type

The text of this book was set in Garamond No. 3. It is not a true copy of any of the designs of Claude Garamond (ca. 1480–1561), but an adaptation that probably owes as much to the designs of Jean Jannon, a Protestant printer in Sedan in the early seventeenth century, who had worked with Garamond's romans earlier in Paris. This particular version is based on an adaptation by Morris Fuller Benton.